ALIVE!

Books by Loren D. Estleman

AMOS WALKER MYSTERIES
Motor City Blue
Angel Eyes
The Midnight Man
The Glass Highway
Sugartown
Every Brilliant Eye
Lady Yesterday
Downriver
Silent Thunder
Sweet Women Lie
Never Street
The Witchfinder
The Hours of the Virgin
A Smile on the Face of the Tiger
Sinister Heights
Poison Blonde*
Retro*
Nicotine Kiss*
American Detective*
The Left-Handed Dollar*
Infernal Angels*
Burning Midnight*

VALENTINO, FILM DETECTIVE
Frames*
Alone*
Alive!*

DETROIT CRIME
Whiskey River
Motown
King of the Corner
Edsel
Stress
Jitterbug*
Thunder City*

PETER MACKLIN
Kill Zone
Roses Are Dead
Any Man's Death
Something Borrowed, Something
    Black*
Little Black Dress*

OTHER FICTION
The Oklahoma Punk
Sherlock Holmes vs. Dracula
Dr. Jekyll and Mr. Holmes
Peeper
Gas City*
Journey of the Dead*
The Rocky Mountain Moving
    Picture Association*
Roy & Lillie: A Love Story*
The Confessions of Al Capone*
    (June 2013)

PAGE MURDOCK SERIES
The High Rocks*
Stamping Ground*
Murdock's Law*
The Stranglers
City of Widows*
White Desert*
Port Hazard*
The Book of Murdock*

WESTERNS
The Hider
Aces & Eights*
The Wolfer
Mister St. John
This Old Bill
Gun Man
Bloody Season
Sudden Country
Billy Gashade*
The Master Executioner*
Black Powder, White Smoke*
The Undertaker's Wife*
The Adventures of Johnny
    Vermillion*
The Branch and the Scaffold*

NONFICTION
The Wister Trace
Writing the Popular Novel

*Published by Tom Doherty Associates

LOREN D. ESTLEMAN

ALIVE!

A VALENTINO MYSTERY

A TOM DOHERTY ASSOCIATES BOOK

NEW YORK

S

ALIVE!

Edited by James Frenkel

A Forge Book
Published by Tom Doherty Associates, LLC
175 Fifth Avenue
New York, NY 10010

www.tor-forge.com

Forge® is a registered trademark of Tom Doherty Associates, LLC.

Library of Congress Cataloging-in-Publication Data

Estleman, Loren D.
 Alive! / Loren D. Estleman.
  p. cm.
 "A Tom Doherty Associates book."
 ISBN 978-0-7653-3331-5 (hardcover)
 ISBN 978-1-4668-0064-9 (e-book)
 1. Archivists—Fiction. 2. Motion picture film—Preservation—
Fiction. 3. Hollywood (Los Angeles, Calif.)—Fiction. I. Title.
PS3555.S84A75 2013
813'.54—dc23

                                    2012042847

Forge books may be purchased for educational, business, or promotional use. For information on bulk purchases, please contact Macmillan Corporate and Premium Sales Department at 1-800-221-7945 extension 5442 or write specialmarkets@macmillan.com.

First Edition: April 2013

Printed in the United States of America

0 9 8 7 6 5 4 3 2 1

To Frank Wydra, who left us with a smile,
a glass of Jack, and twenty years of memories

My dear old Monster; I owe everything to him.
—Boris Karloff

I

THE FIEND MUST BE FOUND

1

VALENTINO WATCHED THE mover strap the refrigerator-size crate to his hand truck and tilt it back to engage the wheels. The sight brought a lump to his throat and a sudden panicky urge to call the whole thing off and take back possession.

"Heavy. What is it?" The mover was a florid sixty with a head the size of a basketball, covered by what must have been the only knitted woolen cap in Southern California outside a studio wardrobe department.

"Just one of my vital organs," Valentino said.

"Huh. Well, you're better off not lugging it around." He wheeled the crate up the ramp into the van and came back down to hand Valentino a receipt. Then he closed and padlocked the doors.

A minute later the diesel engine expectorated a ball of black exhaust and trundled out of the alley next to The Oracle Theater, bearing yet another piece of Hollywood history into the Bermuda Triangle of the collectors' market.

Valentino would not bother to monitor the sale at Sotheby's, where he'd bought the item five years earlier out of his first big commission for rescuing a lost classic film from the void of nearly a century. It was the glistening leather rocking chair that both Humphrey Bogart and Sidney Greenstreet had sat in on the set of Sam Spade's apartment in *The Maltese Falcon*. He'd swooped in and bought it right out from under the nose of Teddie Goodman, an employee of Supernova International. She'd been acting for the CEO and founder, Mark David Turkus—"the Turk," as he was known to his friends as well as his detractors—a fanatic collector of movie memorabilia as well as an investor in film preservation and marketing, who had been on the other end of her cell phone. It had dropped the call just as Valentino's bid edged out the maximum they'd prearranged. Teddie could not counterbid without permission, and so had lost the contest.

She had not taken the experience in the spirit of healthy competition. The relationship between her and Valentino since that moment had been one of tit-for-tat rivalry escalating to the proportion of a minor arms race, straining their unevenly matched budgets in their obsession to outbid their bitterest foe on some article of interest to the archives.

Kyle Broadhead, senior member of the Film Preservation Department at UCLA, calculated that that soundstage prop had cost their institution more than a hundred thousand dollars over the succeeding years. Teddie was that determined to trounce her colleague at every opportunity. "That's what, twice your salary?" Broadhead had asked.

"Twice yours, for whatever you do for this department," Valentino had said. "Just what *are* your responsibilities, may I ask?"

"You may not, but I'll answer you anyway, in respect for our long-standing awareness of each other's existence. I cram infants' skulls with the product of my education and experience and bring luster to this great citadel of learning."

"How? You never go to class and no one's seen so much as a paragraph of that magnum opus of the cinema you say you've been writing for eight months."

The rumpled gray scholar slapped the ancient Wang computer on his otherwise naked desk; it gave off a hollow metallic ring reminiscent of its name. "It's all here, every word, assuming I can track down a printer that will teleport the fruits of my wisdom onto the page. As for my laissez-faire approach to teaching, I wouldn't insult my T.A. by hovering over him at the blackboard."

"They replaced the blackboards with dry-erase boards ten years ago. Not that you'd know."

"You are young, and place adolescent faith in the nobility of hard labor. It's no wonder Teddie Goodman is kicking your butt."

"Are you kidding? She makes me look like a lazy lout. Her idea of a vacation is to go deep-sea diving to rescue the lost reel of *Potemkin* from the bottom of the Black Sea."

"As is yours, could you but swim."

"I can, as a matter of fact. I've scubaed off Malibu."

"Not lately. You spend all your free time diving in Dumpsters after Art Deco bric-a-brac to rebuild that ruin of a picture house. But we digress. Teddie's your evil twin, you know. Her full name is Theodosia Burr Goodman. That was Theda Bara's before she changed it to become a silent-screen vamp."

"Teddie isn't Theodosia Goodman any more than Theda Bara was Theda Bara. She changed it herself so she could claim to be a direct descendant."

"Shrewd decision. I suspect it had a bit to do with why that starstruck Turk put her on his payroll. No sucker can compare with the self-made billionaire."

"At least I never pretended any blood relationship to Rudolph Valentino."

"My point precisely," Broadhead had said. "She suffers from no such inhibition, hence her superior track record."

"Right now I'd say it's neck-and-neck."

"An ephemeral condition at best. Supernova's pockets are ten times deeper than UCLA's."

In the alley now, recalling that conversation, Valentino was very aware of just how tight the money situation was, personally as well as professionally. He'd been forced to put the *Falcon* chair on the block in order to help pay for the never-ending renovations at The Oracle. He'd let his sentimental attitude toward the once-ornate, now-dilapidated movie palace suck him into the most expensive undertaking of any dozen careers. He was living in the projection booth. Few in L.A. could afford to rent an apartment and restore an architectural treasure at one and the same time.

He admitted to the petty consolation that Teddie Goodman would probably enter a bid on the chair on Turkus' behalf. The Turk would never allow it to go to another collector having missed out once, and would expect his pit viper to make good on her previous failure. She would know that in so doing she'd contribute to the finances of her despised opponent, and it would gall her no end.

It was unworthy reflection. When all was said and done he'd feel worse about the transaction than she. Broadhead, of course, would be amused, and say something about virtue being its own penalty. Valentino loved his mentor more than he had ever loved his own distant father, but the man could be a royal pain in the neck without even trying.

He walked around to the front of the building, where Leo Kalishnikov, his architect and designer, was staring at paint chips spread out on the folding card table he used to study blueprints. Today the flamboyant little Russian was dressed like a flamenco dancer, in a flat-brimmed black hat, tight pants, a bolero vest over a shirt with balloon sleeves, and suede pumps on his feet. An enormous canvas drop cloth covered the roof of the four-story building where cracked tiles and rotted boards had been removed, and the steel superstructure of the marquee under restoration thrust its gaunt skeleton skyward, a not-so-miniature Eiffel Tower. Depending on the mood of the owner, it all looked like progress or else the heart-sickening prospect of the point of no return.

"It is the bitch." It was one of those moments when Kalishnikov spoke like an immigrant straight off the boat. Other times he could be mistaken for a third-generation Midwesterner with a thorough command of the American vernacular. "Those scrapings could be turquoise or royal blue. There is fading to consider, and smut from this infernal air."

From the tiny Ziploc sandwich bag containing samples shaved from the exterior walls he drew his finger across the numbered chips in every shade of blue to the period picture postcard of the theater that Valentino had found in an antiques shop on Sepulveda. "It's hand-tinted. Can I trust the impulse of the artist not to place his peculiar stamp upon the work of another? As an artist myself I am dubious."

Valentino pointed at a chip that looked like robin's-egg blue but that had probably been dubbed something more exotic-sounding by a creative consultant at the paint company. "I like that one."

"But what is its provenance?"

"What's the difference? Who's to say it's wrong?"

"My inner self. It's what you hired me to provide, is it not?"

He stopped short of pointing out that Kalishnikov had made

him a present of his fee, agreeing to do the work at cost. The architect had made his name designing high-end home theaters for wealthy clients and had leapt at the opportunity to restore a genuine movie house to its former glory. That was part of the slippery slope that led to personal bankruptcy. Materials and long-distance calls cost money, and none of the carpenters, electricians, plasterers, plumbers, and skilled artisans who had signed on for the project had shared the Russian's altruism. On the university campus, The Oracle was known as Valentino's Folly—or as Broadhead put it, "the *Titanic* that never stops sinking."

"I'm fresh out of ideas," Valentino said.

"Fortunately, I am not. Somewhere there is someone who knows."

"What's it going to set me back to find him?"

"I have horse-trading skills. My great-grandfather was a Cossack. By the way, the glazier called this morning. Your check bounced."

Valentino groaned and went inside.

The tile man was laying the ceramic in the foyer, a time-consuming job as he had to keep referring to photographs to duplicate the original mosaic design; after nearly two weeks, only a third of the plywood sub-flooring was covered. In the auditorium, the linoleum that in the 1970s had been laid over the original teakwood boards made snapping sounds when Valentino lifted his feet from it, smeared as it was with old adhesive where the aisle runners had been scraped up and thrown away. Half the seats were stripped to their springs awaiting reupholstery. A sheet covered the three-manual Wurlitzer organ in the orchestra pit to keep sawdust and granulated plaster from entering the pipes. Valentino had wanted to postpone work on the instrument until the basic construction was completed, but the expert who had rebuilt it, the best in his field, was eighty-seven years old and time was of the essence. Practical order had no place where history was involved.

He opened the hidden panel in the wall and climbed the freshly sawn stairs to the projection booth. Eventually it, too, would be gutted and fireproof insulation installed to allow him to screen volatile silver-nitrate stock without violating the fire ordinances, but for the time being it was his sanctum. With the wall torn down that had separated it from the film storage area, it made a comfortable utility apartment.

Harriet Johansen hadn't called his cell phone. He checked his message machine in case she'd had trouble connecting, but she hadn't called the theater either. He supposed she was busy attending panels at the CSI convention in Seattle, but he missed her. He made a telephone transfer at his bank to cover the returned check, then left a message on the glazier's voice mail apologizing for the mistake and assuring him it had been corrected. Sometimes he was grateful for the technology that prevented people from making personal contact.

Harriet answered her cell on the fifth ring. Voices buzzed in the background. "Hi. I'm on my way to lunch and an autopsy. What's up?"

"Nothing out of the ordinary. I just wanted to hear your voice."

"That's sweet. Did I tell you about this fella I want you to meet? He's ex-FBI, has interest in the antiques business. You know, half detective, half geek. You'd like each other."

"Still dabbling in law enforcement, eh? Is he living on a pension?"

"I didn't say he retired. He's living in the family mansion, making more money buying Louis Quatorze chairs low and selling them high than he ever did chasing terrorists. He's kind of a hunk."

"Are you trying to make me jealous?"

"No, but I'm glad to know I still can. Gotta go. Call you later."

The line clicked. He held the handset a moment longer, then replaced it in the cradle. He *was* jealous. Had she ever called Valentino a hunk in front of others? He doubted it. He wasn't beefcake material, but evidently this former G-man was.

Someone was rattling up the steps, taking them two at a time. He braced himself for the gale. Jason Stickley, his intern, blew in after barely brushing the door with his knuckles. "Hey, Mr. V."

"Valentino, Jason. Mr. Valentino if you prefer. 'Mr. V.' belongs in a sitcom on Fox."

"Sorry, sir. It's just that I've seen that other Valentino on TV and you don't look anything like him."

He assumed the boy meant the fashion designer and not the silent-film star, whom he'd been told he did resemble slightly. The only reason Kyle Broadhead recommended these young scholars seemed to be to get them out of his class on the history of cinema. They were spoiling the curve.

Whom *Jason* resembled, he couldn't say. He looked like a toothpick sculpture and his daily uniform of black T-shirt and jeans only drew attention to his painful thinness. He had hollow cheeks, dark hair and dark, soulful eyes, a divot on his chin, and mystifying tattoos inside his arms, extending from under his short sleeves to his wrists, that appeared to represent piston rods joined by pins in the bends of the elbows. He hadn't explained them, although he must have been aware they were noticed, and Valentino himself was too private a person to ask. The effect was vaguely gothic, but only vaguely, and the lack of macabre makeup and piercings set the youth apart from the Goth crowd on campus.

If there still was such a crowd. The student union really ought to issue a program every semester to bring the uninitiated up to speed on all the cliques.

"Where's the fire?"

"Fire? Oh, you mean 'cause I was in a hurry."

And a fossil-to-student dictionary, while they're at it. But he merely rolled his eyes.

"This guy's been trying to reach you all day at the department. I guess he doesn't have your number here. Ruth sent me to tell you she's tired of taking the same call from the same guy. It must be important." He handed him a wad of pink office message slips torn off a pad.

Valentino shuffled through them, recognizing the secretary's spiky hand. Craig Hunter. He sighed. He'd called every hour on the hour since the office opened. "Did she say how he sounded?"

"'Stoned and drunk.' I'm just quoting her."

"I was afraid of that. There should be a law against operating redial under the influence." He tore up the messages and dropped the pieces into the fire bucket next to his chair.

"Not a friend, I guess," Jason said.

"The sad thing about it is he's just about the best I ever had."

2

"THE NAME CRAIG Hunter sounds familiar, kind of," Jason Stickley said. "Did he come to visit once?"

Valentino shook his head. "Not at the department. Condition he's usually in, the campus police might've picked him up on suspicion. You might have seen one of his movies when you were little, if you were accompanied by an adult or if you sneaked in. Action movies were his thing: plenty of explosions and lines some screenwriter thought were snappy."

"You mean like Nicolas Cage?"

"I'm old enough to remember when Cage made good art films. But Hunter was never in his league. He's the guy they went to after Bruce Willis, Steven Seagal, and Vin Diesel turned the part down. After a few of those, his pictures stopped opening, and in the end they went straight to video. It didn't help that he was arrested a couple of times for DUI and started showing up on the set four hours late. The last time I saw him on screen was in a bit as a nutso neighbor in a Seth Rogen comedy. I doubt he could get even that now, and that's why he's calling me, to hit me up for a loan."

"Bet you'd help him out if you weren't strapped." Jason's grin was meant to be friendly, but it made his face look even more skeletal.

"It would be the opposite of help. He'd just blow it on booze and meth. His wife was the most loyal and patient woman I ever knew, but even she gave up on him finally. She divorced him two years ago."

"No wonder you never gave him your number."

"Actually I did, back when it still seemed like there was hope for him. I'm sure he lost it, along with his career and his wife and his self-respect and every friend he ever had."

"Bummer."

Valentino smiled wearily. "I didn't know youngsters were still using that word."

"I like old-time things."

That put the finish on his brightening mood. "Don't you have a class to attend?"

Jason dragged a cell from a pocket, an odd design with an antique brass finish and protrusions that looked like exposed rivets, and checked the time. He belonged to the generation that never wore a wristwatch. "Metallurgy. Thanks, Mr. Vee—alentino," he corrected himself mid-stride. "I better fly."

Metallurgy, the archivist thought after he left. What was the boy majoring in, welding?

He spent the evening at the work table in the booth, cranking episodes of *Peter Gunn* back and forth on twin Moviolas, searching for matching frames. A&E had decided not to air the original films because of jarring jump-cuts where scenes had been deleted or damaged, and had donated them to the university for a tax deduction, but a number of previously uncollected *Gunn*s had shown up in the sale of an estate belonging to a retired ABC assistant director. If Valentino could restore the material from the additional reels, a "lost episode" DVD could contribute significantly to the department's treasury. More funds meant more purchases and better equipment to put them right.

It was tedious work, and hard on the eyes. After four hours he could barely distinguish Herschel Bernardi from Lola Albright, and his notes swam before his eyes. He'd hoped Harriet would call, but she didn't, and when he reached for the phone to call her he saw it was after midnight. Instead he cooked a frozen burrito in the little microwave to stop the growling in his stomach, unfolded the sofa bed, and went to sleep in his clothes.

The telephone had been purring for some time when he woke up enough to answer it. Ever the film editor, he'd managed to splice it into the dream he was having, a crazy thing about paint chips and burritos.

"Harriet?"

"Val?" A male voice, deep and thick with phlegm. He grunted something affirmative.

"It's Craig. Craig Hunter?"

He sounded unsure of it himself, a certain indicator he was calling from the bottom of a bottle. In spite of that condition he'd somehow managed to find Valentino's home number: the perfect end to a perfect day.

Valentino dragged himself into a sitting position and peered at the luminous dial of his alarm clock. He'd been asleep an hour.

"Craig, I'm not in the mood. I'm having a bad time of it lately."

A gurgling chuckle rang hollowly in his ear. "Brother, you're an amateur compared to me."

"Whose fault is that?" He wanted to end this conversation and get back to his nightmare.

"Listen—"

"Save the speech. I don't have any money. If I did, I'm through subsidizing half the distilleries and drug pushers in the U.S."

"Gimme a minute, okay? I'm in a bar in San Diego." It came out "Shandago." He had to have been pretty far gone to have forgotten his years of vocal training. He'd gotten as far as he had on his good looks and pleasing tone of voice rather than on his acting. The good looks had vanished, bloated and mottled with gin blossoms, and now he'd lost his only remaining asset.

"What did you do, drink up all the stock in L.A.?"

"Val, I need help. I'll make it worth your while."

"It would be worth my while if you'd stop pestering me for something you can only give yourself. Check into rehab."

"Hear me out. Don't—"

He banged down the receiver. When the purring started again he pulled the cord out of the standard and slid back down and back into unconsciousness.

His business cards identified Valentino as a "film detective," a romantic indulgence befitting a life on the outer edge of the motion picture industry. As a full-time consultant with the archives division of the Film Preservation Department, he kept irregular hours in a matchbox office in a building that had once supplied all the heat and electricity to the UCLA campus, a homely pile of architecture whose only point in its favor was the fact that no one in the university administration ever bothered to visit it. There, he, Professor Broadhead, and Ruth, the gargoyle in reception, went about the business of rescuing little pieces of time from erosion without interference on the part of authority—except when the moment came to ask for money to continue. Then the little men with calculators remembered they were there and wondered if the building might be razed to make room for another athletic training facility.

Fortunately, Valentino was usually absent at these times. Broadhead was a revered scholar in his field, showing his face on TCM and on extra discs issued with remastered DVDs, and knew his way around the wine-and-cheese circuit like the blind man in the labyrinth. He twisted this arm, pumped that hand, and shook loose dollars like jackpots from a slot machine. That freed his colleague to scour toxic landfills and crawlspaces teeming with spiders, tracking lost frames of ancient classics. At these times Valentino was more Sherlock Holmes than Joe Academic. It was this part of the job that had drawn him to it. His name, and the obvious associations it suggested, had made him a fanatic on the subject of old movies since early childhood. It also made him the butt of a million bad jokes, but on the other hand, it left an impression on people who knew celluloid history. They might misplace his card, but they seldom forgot his name.

Ruth pounced on him the moment he left the elevator. She rarely stirred from her station inside the doughnut-shaped desk where she served sentry, but she was a predatory old bird who swooped down with the power of her eyes. They were kohl-rimmed, as black as her hair, and equally inflexible. Age was her archenemy. She would attack every wrinkle and gray strand as soon as it surfaced, using all the weapons in her arsenal. Broadhead had speculated there were more poisons on her dressing table than in all the Japanese gardeners' sheds in Beverly Hills. "I'd be as disinclined to visit one as the other." But for all his shudders he was the only man on campus she couldn't intimidate.

"You had a call."

Valentino never knew from the burnished-steel tone of her voice if she thought he was at fault for not being there when a call came in or for the call having been made at all. Ruth was efficient and well-nigh indispensable, but she was one of those in favor of demolishing the building and eliminating the film program altogether as a frivolous waste of money and young minds. She tore a pink sheet off her pad and thrust it at him.

He glanced at it, saw the name Hunter, and stuck it in his pocket. "Thanks. Dr. Broadhead in?"

"Aren't you going to return the call?"

He shrank in on himself, a mouse in a hawk's line of sight. "Later." Lifting his brows, he cocked his head toward the door of Broadhead's office.

"He's working on his book. He doesn't want to be disturbed."

"When he wakes up from his nap, please tell him I'd like a moment of his time."

"You wouldn't be so cranky if you started your day with a healthy breakfast."

"What do you consider healthy?" He knew he'd regret asking. Prolonging a conversation with Ruth was definitely not the way to start one's day.

"Bacon sandwich, three-cheese omelet, and a strawberry milkshake. *Whole* milk. I wouldn't wash my feet in that one-percent swill."

"Is that what you eat?"

"Every day for the last forty years, except Sunday. Then I lay out a feast." She turned her head from side to side, like a spy in a Bob Hope movie, and leaned forward, lowering her voice to a foghorn whisper. "*She's* in there."

She made the pronoun sound like a vile epithet. He had no doubt who *she* was. Ever since Fanta had breezed into their lives, Ruth had behaved like the old herd leader, determined to resist challenge from a younger rival. The fact that Ruth had no romantic designs on Broadhead didn't enter into it. In her world, women typed letters and answered telephones and ran things from behind the camouflage of indentured servitude. The presence of any other female in the old power plant was a threat to her authority.

Valentino was just beginning to wrap his mind around the prospect of a morning romantic interlude—and trying even harder to avoid the image—when Fanta swept out of Broadhead's office with a chirrupy "'Bye, now, you old grump." She tugged the door shut behind her and grinned brilliantly when she saw Valentino. "Well, hello. You look like Georgie Jessel the night *The Jazz Singer* broke all the records. He turned down the lead, you know."

"I know. I'm surprised *you* do. You only audited Kyle's class for fun when you were studying law."

"Being engaged to him is like attending film school twenty-four-seven. Seriously, the bags under your eyes have bags."

Fanta had none. She was a fresh twenty-one, with straight hair in bangs and falling to the shoulders of an unstructured autumn-orange blazer. Beneath it she wore a black pants suit and black boots with two-inch heels that shot her up to six-foot-two. It was a far cry from the off-the-shoulder tops and torn jeans of her undergraduate years, which were only months behind her. The Halloween-candy color scheme was in keeping with the season, but the effect was spoiled slightly by the glossy white satin cover of the enormous book she held under one arm. It was the size of a Gutenberg Bible and looked like a photo album belonging to the Baldwin family, exes and all.

"I didn't get much sleep last night, but I won't burden you with the dreary details. How are the wedding plans?"

"Sleep," she said, "what's that? I'm postponing my bar exam until after the honeymoon. I can't bone up on *De Havilland versus Warner Brothers* and pick out the centerpieces for the reception at the same time."

"So you drafted your fiancé to help decide on invitations?"

She patted the massive volume. "His own fault. *I* wanted to hire a calligrapher to do them from scratch, but he said if we started going down that road we'd have to spend the wedding night in Fresno instead of Stockholm."

"I can't see you and Kyle in Niagara Falls, but why Sweden?"

"There's an old guy there who says he has Bergman's production notes for *The Seventh Seal,* but he won't let go of them without cash up front and Kyle won't pay him until he gets a look at them."

"He's really writing his book?"

"Of course. He made his reputation on *Persistence of Vision,* but this one will blow it right out of the water."

"You've *read* it?"

"What he's written. He wants to be sure some aging script girl doesn't sue him for libel."

Valentino was jealous. He'd known Broadhead far longer than she had, and he had never so much as discussed the book with him in any detail. He got away from that subject before he betrayed himself. "So he's working during your honeymoon."

"Hey, I'm just happy we're getting out of California. You think I just pulled Fresno out of my—?"

"Take it out to the back fence," Ruth said. "This is a place of business."

Fanta beamed at her. "Good-bye, old dear. You're getting an invitation, you know."

"Something old?" Her eyes were even fiercer than usual.

"That would be the bridegroom. What are nuptials without a guest who gives the couple six months at the outside?"

"I never said that."

"Really? My mistake. I misread your body language."

"Just don't include me in the wedding party. I've had more fun being a pallbearer."

Fanta bent down, gave Ruth's laminated cheek a pat, and whirled on out. The elevator doors opened at her touch. Valentino stared at the secretary, fascinated despite his horror. But Ruth's expression was as unreadable as a bisque-headed doll's. He fled to sanctuary, hoping Broadhead wouldn't ignore his knocking as he sometimes did. Fortune smiled. The professor's voice beckoned from the other side.

The office was nearly sterile, the bare polar opposite of Valentino's, which was cluttered with posters framed and rolled, kitschy knick-knacks, and piles of shooting scripts. The only exception—and it was new—was a slightly out-of-focus photo in a frame of Fanta on some gray, blustery beach, looking over her shoulder at the camera and laughing. She wore a leather windbreaker with the collar turned up.

Broadhead saw where he was looking. "It's bewitched. No matter where I stand in the room, it's me she's laughing at."

"It's always like that when they look directly into the lens."

"See for yourself."

Valentino walked to the far rear corner of the room, watching the photo. He crossed to the opposite corner, then to the next. It was true. She was staring at Broadhead and splitting her sides at the ridiculous sight.

"I'm not sure such a thing is possible, but you're right."

"She's part gypsy, you know. She cast a spell on me the first day she walked into my classroom."

"Try telling that to the review board. Good thing she waited until she was no longer your student before she made her move."

"What makes you think the first move wasn't mine?"

"You might stick your neck out on a point of film theory, but not in matters of romance."

Broadhead unscrewed his pipe and screwed it back together, a habit he'd acquired after the university banned smoking on campus. He claimed to have carved it by hand during the three years he was incarcerated in Yugoslavia on suspicion of espionage. "I'm to choose *this* sentiment on *that* paper stock in a third color. I'd suggest elopement, but I'm afraid of ladders."

"Isn't picking out invitations something a bride does with her mother?"

"She's in Luxembourg."

"Why Luxembourg?"

"Because she isn't U.S. ambassador to anywhere else."

"Fanta's mother is an ambassador?"

"Needless to say, she isn't available to discuss champagne fountains."

"Why do we even have an ambassador there?"

"I haven't the foggiest, but she seems to be earning her keep. We haven't been at war with the place in my memory." He stopped playing with the pipe and put it in a drawer. "When you didn't show up here yesterday, I'd hoped you were in Argentina, assembling a blooper reel for *Triumph of the Will*: Hitler falling on his prat in Nuremberg. But you have the look of an exasperated home remodeler. How normal. I mourn."

"It's worse than that. Craig Hunter's been calling me."

"*There's* a name from the past. I thought he'd have mixed up a cemetery cocktail by now."

"Not that he hasn't tried, based on how he sounded late last night. I wasn't diplomatic. I thought you might talk me out of feeling guilty."

"As emotions go, it's as useful as boxing gloves on a Buddhist. Being polite is no way to get rid of a pest."

"He tried again this morning, here at work."

Broadhead's telephone rang. "Let me show you a trick I learned in the Far East. No charge for this wisdom." He lifted the receiver and let it fall back down. "Needy drunks are like amateur housebreakers. When a lock won't pick they give up and try next door. You wouldn't have done him any favors by stringing him along."

Ruth opened the door without knocking and leaned in. "I just put through a call. Why'd you hang up?"

"Why'd you put it through? I said not to disturb me."

"It was for Valentino. That woman's still trying to reach him."

Valentino said, "What woman?"

"I gave you the message."

He fished out the pink crumple. He'd put it away without noting the first name. It was Lorna, Craig Hunter's ex-wife. She never called on her own behalf. The last time, Craig had been in jail in Mexico, charged with smuggling fighting roosters across the border in return for Colombian cocaine.

3

HE RETURNED LORNA'S call from his own office, surrounded by press-agent ephemera and props from movies so obscure their entire casts might have been in witness protection: Broadhead had compared the effect to "a Sunset Strip souvenir shop after the Big One." Valentino himself considered the Laurel and Hardy salt-and-pepper shakers, mountains of moldering *Photoplays* and *Silver Screens*, and the papier-mâché sarcophagus from *The Mummy's Brain* his personal totems, among which he found the peace that used to await him at home in the days before he'd sacrificed his private life on the altar of The Oracle.

"Val, it's so good to hear your voice."

"Yours, too."

He wasn't just being polite. Craig Hunter's ex-wife—who had put up with him long after everyone else had given him up as a lost cause, maintaining contact even beyond their divorce—spoke in the warm contralto she used all the time now. Its ironic undertone had typecast her as the leading lady's wisecracking best friend in several romantic comedies until her manager had hired a coach to raise it a full octave. That had led to sitcom stardom at ABC. When after three successful seasons she'd quit, announcing her plans to devote all her time to making one man happy instead of twenty million fans, she'd shaken the network to its foundation. Two years after the marriage broke up, she was still not returning agents' calls.

"I'm sorry I didn't call back right away," Valentino said, stopping short of adding *I thought it was Craig.*

"That's all right. We sort of lost touch. These things are a little like cancer. Old friends stop coming around." Candor like hers had kept the couple away from Hollywood parties. "I was wondering if you'd heard from Craig lately."

"He called me last night from San Diego."

"Did he say where in San Diego?"

He hesitated only briefly. There were no secrets between the divorced. "A bar. He didn't say which one."

"He must have used a pay phone. His cell carrier dropped him when he stopped paying his bills. Did the number come up?"

"I didn't check. He woke me up. If it was a pay phone, it probably came up 'out of area.'"

"Oh. What did he want?"

"He said he needed my help, but Lorna—"

"I know, Val. You don't have to say it. I reached the end of my own rope last week. He showed up here late, drunk or high or both, acting like the house was still his—me, too. I had to threaten to call the police to get him to leave."

"Did he threaten *you?*" Craig had always been sloppy and maudlin under the influence, never violent.

"No, nothing like that. He just wouldn't leave. But when I mentioned the police, he seemed to sober up right away. He mumbled something about being ungrateful and slunk on out.

I offered to call him a cab—he was in no condition to drive—but he acted as if he didn't hear me. I heard his car start up and leave. I've been worried sick ever since. I kept thinking he'd gone off Mulholland or something and was in a ravine some-where. You don't know how relieved I am he called you."

"Why do you think he was so worried about your calling the police? Forgive me, but it wouldn't be the first night he spent in jail."

"I have no idea. You don't suppose he's mixed up with the Mexicans and Colombians again?"

"I don't know. It's a short hop from San Diego to Tijuana."

"But what kind of help could you have given him?"

"I don't know. I wish I'd asked, but it was late and—" *he'd been calling me all day*; again he'd stopped short. In the light of this conversation, so persistent an appeal for help made Valen-tino look as bad as he felt for ignoring it. "You said he acted like the house was still his. What did he say that gave you that im-pression?"

"Oh, he was just being possessive. Should I call Missing Persons?"

"They'll probably just tell you to wait forty-eight hours, and I heard from him just last night." The abrupt change of subject, and the evasiveness of her answer to his question, made him curious. Far from keeping secrets from each other, he won-dered if the Hunters were sharing one.

"Will you call me if you hear from him again?" she asked.

"You don't have to ask, Lorna."

"I know, Val. Thank you." The connection broke.

He was compelled to call Harriet. Part of the resentment he felt toward Craig Hunter had had nothing to do with Craig's wasted life. Some small part of him had always wished he'd met Lorna first, and he felt guilty as well as impatient with himself for clinging to that ghost when he was so contented with what he had.

Harriet didn't answer. She was probably attending a panel and had her cell turned off. When her voice mail kicked in, he hung up without leaving a message. He'd managed to shift his burden to her for not being available, and wondered if she was sitting with her hunky ex-FBI agent.

The telephone rang while his hand was still on it. It was Harriet.

"Did you just try to call?" she asked.

"Yes. I figured you were busy."

"Are you angry about something?"

He felt a fresh flush of guilt. She had a better right to be jealous of him. He'd never mentioned Lorna to her. "I'm just a little tired." He told her about yesterday, leaving out Craig Hunter. That route led to questions, lies, and other evasions, and he was a stranger in such country.

"Oh, Val, you loved that chair."

"It's just a piece of furniture," he said. "It's been recovered a couple of times since Bogie and Greenstreet sat in it. I was the custodian for a while. It's time to let someone else take the responsibility."

"Someone like Teddie Goodman?"

"I'd rather not think about that. If the chair performs up to expectations, I can electrify the marquee and replace the plumbing with PVC pipe."

"I thought you said copper was best."

"It is, but the joints have to be soldered, and the State of California in its desire to protect its citizens has outlawed all products containing lead."

"And you said having a movie star in office would be a good thing."

"Well, they didn't let him bring along his special effects. How's the convention?"

"Dull today. The blowhard from Scotland Yard's debating the know-it-all from NYPD about whose electron microscope is bigger. Jeff and I are going to play hooky and brunch on top of the Space Needle."

"Jeff?"

"Jeff *Talbot,* the antiques fed. Didn't I mention his name?"

"Oh, him." He wondered if they were staying at the same hotel.

He'd forgotten she was a detective as well as a scientist. "He's a happily married man, Val. When he's not going on about Depression glass he's talking about his wife, whom I'm sure trusts him."

"I trust you. I just miss you."

"I miss you, too, but I've only been gone a couple of days. It isn't like I shipped out with the marines." Elevators dinged in the background. She must have been waiting in the lobby. "There he is. Call you later."

The conversation ended before he could point out she'd said that before and hadn't called before he called her. Which was just as well. They seldom quarreled in person, but long distance was always a challenge.

He took last night's *Peter Gunn* reels from his briefcase, marked as they were with bright yellow tabs where rediscovered material could be substituted for jump cuts, and placed them with his notes and instructions in a cardboard interoffice envelope. Then he called Jason Stickley's cell. A sepulchral voice that might have been the intern's, electronically enhanced, asked him to leave a message. Behind it, for some reason, clanged "The Anvil Chorus." The boy's resistance to categorization vexed the born archivist in Valentino. He asked Jason to come to his office when he had a chance.

When he arrived, breathless as usual and carrying a dry cleaner's garment bag covering something on a hanger over his shoulder, he wore a collapsible silk top hat with his usual jeans and T-shirt. The tall-crowned headgear underscored his attenuated anatomy, putting Valentino in mind of an undertaker in a black-and-white western.

Valentino, more curious than ever, but more determined than ever not to waste so important a professional tool as curiosity on something other than work, indicated the cardboard envelope balanced atop a stack of DVDs on the corner of his desk. "I need you to take that to the lab. The film editors are expecting it."

"Yes, sir." Reluctance or embarrassment clouded the thin face. "Would it be okay if I left this in your office until tonight?" He lifted and resettled the garment bag on his shoulder. Something metallic jingled inside. "I'm going straight to a party from my last class and won't have time to go home and change."

"What, and clutter up the place?"

Jason cast his gaze down. Underclassmen were humor-challenged.

"I'm kidding. No objections. Isn't it a little early for a costume party? Halloween isn't for two weeks."

"It isn't a costume party. Well, it is, but that isn't the point. Thanks, Mr. Valentino. I'd have asked Ruth to stash it under her desk, but I'm afraid she'd throw it out. She already thinks I'm a satanist or something."

"She thinks everyone's something or something else." He took the intern's statement to mean that he could rule out devil-worshipper from the list of possibilities. "Are you going to leave the hat, or is that what freshmen are wearing this semester?"

Jason had hung the garment bag on a set of wall-mounted

moose antlers from *North West Mounted Police* (and later the set of *Sergeant Preston of the Yukon*) and turned to pick up the envelope, still wearing the top hat. He said, "Whoops," and hung it next to the bag. "That reminds me: I have to go to the junk-yard over lunch."

Valentino wasn't aware that young men frequented junk-yards anymore. The intern didn't look like the hot-rod type. More to the point, he couldn't understand how a high silk hat would remind anyone of auto salvage. There were times, at age thirty-three, when he felt as out of touch as a man of ninety.

He had work to do, but when he was alone his attention kept wandering toward the transparent plastic bag, beyond which was solid black. Snooping was an invasion of privacy. After several attempts to focus on business, however, profes-sional inquisitiveness got the better of good manners. He stood and lifted the hem of the bag.

Inside was a frock coat made of black broadcloth with black satin lapels, and under it gray flannel trousers with pinstripes. Over these hung a white linen shirt with ruffles and a starched wing collar attached to it with studs. The material was rich, not at all the thin shoddy that one found in costume rental shops. It belonged in a Merchant Ivory film set in Victorian London.

Except for the chain.

This was not designed to secure a pocket watch. The links were case steel, each about an inch and a half long, and as thick as his little finger, a cargo chain forged to support heavy loads, incongruously coiled around the hook of a clothes hanger and joined at the ends by a brass lock the size of the palm of his hand, ornately embossed with an ivy design. He could insert his thumb in the top of the keyhole.

If Jason hadn't sworn it wasn't a costume party, Valentino

would have decided he was going as Harry Houdini, and laid his curiosity to rest. Now it burned brighter than ever. And why a junkyard?

The intercom buzzed. He jumped, letting the plastic drop into place, and took two deep breaths to slow his heart rate before answering.

Ruth used the instrument rarely, and usually only when he had visitors. Lately she'd begun putting telephone calls through without asking permission or identifying the callers. Every month, it seemed, she came up with a new imperious way to demonstrate to her superiors that they were temporary annoyances at best. In the beginning was Ruth, and she would be there at end of days.

"The cops are here," she said. *And it's about time,* her tone implied.

"Which one, Sergeant Clifford or Lieutenant Padilla?" The weary question reminded him that his was not the life of the ordinary university consultant. The last two times police had invaded his department had involved homicide investigations.

"This one's a Sergeant Fish. I didn't get his partner's name." Which meant she hadn't bothered to listen. She flipped the switch on her end before he could respond.

He rose as two men entered. The first had short sandy hair and clean-shaven cheeks with a suggestion of baby fat. He appeared to be not much older than Valentino's intern, but his eyes were not boyish. The other man, older, had the bold nose and flat cheeks of an American Indian. He wouldn't have looked out of place in plaited hair and feathers, chasing the cast of *Stagecoach* across the floor of Monument Valley.

"Sergeant Fish?" He automatically held his hand out for the older man to take.

The younger man took it. "Gill. Ernest Gill. This is my partner,

Detective John Yellowfern." He broke off the handshake to show a gold-and-enamel badge pinned to a leather folder. Yellowfern flashed his for a tenth of a second, then snapped shut the folder and returned it to his pocket with a flourish like a gunslinger twirling his weapon into its holster.

"I'm sorry my secretary is bad with names."

"Isn't that kind of what a secretary's supposed to be good at?" the Indian said.

"Settle down, John. Mr. Valentino, we're with the San Diego Police."

San Diego went off in his head like a late-night telephone bell. "Is this about Craig Hunter?"

Yellowfern said, "Heard from him recently, did you?" He made it sound like he'd broken the case, if there was a case. Valentino didn't think he and the detective were going to get along.

"He called me last night from a bar there. He was drunk. If I'd thought he was driving—"

"He wasn't in an accident," Gill said. "His body was found in the men's room of a place called the Grotto at one fifty-five this morning. The medical examiner says he was beaten to death."

4

BEATEN TO DEATH. He'd heard the phrase in movies and on television hundreds of times, but it had never carried the grisly picture that flashed into his mind when it was applied to a friend. Friend? Some friend Valentino was.

Numbly, he cleared piles of bound scripts and publicity stills from a pair of scoop chairs and sank into his own behind the desk. While Gill sat, Yellowfern wandered the room, looking at the posters on the walls and lifting carved and molded figures and turning them upside-down as if searching for marks identifying their rightful owners.

Gill opened a small memorandum book with a pebbled cover. "Phone company says Hunter placed a long-distance call to your home from the Grotto at one sixteen. What did you talk about?"

"He said he needed help."

"What kind of help?"

"I don't know."

Yellowfern turned from a framed invitation to the premiere

of *Ben-Hur* in 1925. "He asked you for help and didn't say what it was?"

"I didn't give him the chance. I hung up on him and unplugged the phone."

"That how you treat all your friends in trouble?"

"John," Gill said warningly.

Valentino wasn't fooled. He'd had experience with police and seen enough crime dramas to know when he was being double-teamed. "I assumed he was putting the arm on me, as usual. He'd obviously been drinking or worse. It wouldn't have been the first time he hit me up for a loan, but this time I didn't have any cash to spare. In his condition, he'd just use it to put more poison in his system. I told him if it was help he needed, he should get the professional kind."

"He say anything else?" Gill asked.

"He said he'd make it worth my while."

"What do you think he meant by that?"

"I have no idea. At the time, I thought he was stalling to keep me on the line until he got me to change my mind. Did you catch the person responsible?"

"Sure," Yellowfern snarled. "We drove all the way up here from San Diego in rush-hour traffic just to tell you we caught the guy. While we're here we'll pay a call on everybody who knew Hunter and let 'em know they can sleep nights."

Gill said, "We're working on it. We know robbery wasn't the motive. He still had his wristwatch and sixty dollars in his wallet. If it was money Hunter was after, it was more than he needed just to settle his bar tab."

"Maybe the robber panicked and ran."

Yellowfern put his hands in his pockets and rocked back and forth on his heels. "His arms were broken just above the elbows. It's a local signature. Grundage muscle does it all the time."

"*Mike* Grundage?"

"You know the name?" Sergeant Gill leaned forward.

"I watch television and read the papers. A grand jury's investigating organized crime in the motion picture industry and he's the star witness. What would Craig Hunter have to do with a thug like Grundage?"

Gill said, "We were hoping you could tell us. *That's* why we drove clear up here in rush-hour traffic."

"I wish I could help. The picture business is brutal enough without gangsters getting involved."

"Tough break, seeing as how you're so good at helping."

"That's enough, Detective." Gill put away his notebook. "If Hunter wasn't bluffing about making it worth your while, he may have been double-crossing Grundage in some deal. That would be motive enough to kill him and put his stamp on the job to make sure nobody else got any bright ideas. What do you know about any ties Hunter had to the mob?"

"Not a thing."

"We've seen his record. He shook hands with the Colombians and scored crack and meth all over town. So far as we know, Grundage steered clear of drugs, but there's less than six degrees of separation anytime you tap into any racket this side of Sacramento. He happened to be having breakfast with his lawyer when we dropped in on him this morning, so we never got him downtown. Either he pulled the string on Hunter or he's got a first-class psychic on the payroll."

"We could use one ourself. Our go-to swami's a whiz at telling us how right he was, *after* we dig up enough to go to court." Yellowfern had discovered Jason Stickley's costume and raised the plastic. Valentino hoped there were no Baggies in any of the pockets.

"Maybe Grundage has breakfast with his lawyer every day," he suggested.

"His mouthpiece is Horace Lysander. You don't retain him with Rice Krispies and coffee." The sergeant rose and held out a business card. "Thanks for your time. It's possible we'll need a statement from you later. You may have been the last person to talk to the victim."

Valentino stood to take the card, which bore the San Diego city seal on cream-colored stock. "Have you talked to his ex-wife?"

"We just came from her place. She hasn't heard from him in weeks."

Yellowfern fingered the heavy chain, tried to pull open the massive padlock, and gave up. Letting the plastic drop back down over the costume, he lifted the top hat off the antlers and tried it on. It perched comically atop his large head, and for an instant Valentino pictured how it would look with a turkey feather stuck in the band. (Was that racist, or the inevitable product of long exposure to horse operas?) The Indian hung the hat back up and turned away. "You in show business?"

"Not really. By the time I come along, the show's over."

"Kind of like with your pal Hunter."

Gill sighed but said nothing as he led the way out. Valentino wondered if their good-cop-bad-cop was more than just an act.

He didn't waste much time pondering the matter. He was more curious about why Lorna Hunter had lied to the police.

He wanted to discuss it with Kyle Broadhead, whose advice, cloaked in irony though it always was, was invariably sound, whether his friend took it or not. But he was staggered for the second time that morning when Ruth informed him that Broadhead was busy teaching his class in film theory.

"Did he ask you for directions to the building?"

"He might have been motivated by a call from Snapple. I think she wanted him to sit in on a meeting with her wedding planner." Ruth seemed never to run out of new and creative ways not to refer to Fanta by her proper name.

"You think, or you listened in?"

"Mister, I knew Rock Hudson was gay when he stepped on the set of *Giant*. I don't need to eavesdrop to know everything that goes on in this town."

"I'm going out," he said. "I may not be back today."

"Thank you so much for honoring us with your presence."

Once, acting on the vaguest of tips, Valentino had found twenty-six feet of the long-missing courtship sequence from the 1954 version of *A Star Is Born* being used to demonstrate a home movie projector in a camera store in Boise, Idaho. Restoring the missing pieces to the puzzle of Craig Hunter's murder seemed simple by comparison. *Why* was simpler still. He'd turned his back on an old friend, and the friend had died. He would not bail on him when it came to avenging his death.

Lorna Hunter lived in the house the divorce court had awarded her in Tarzana, named by its founder, writer Edgar Rice Burroughs, in the first flush of his success in selling his most famous character to Hollywood. Now, more than ninety years after Elmo Lincoln had first swung from vines in *Tarzan of the Apes*, the man whose prose had inspired it would scarcely recognize his sylvan retreat. A pedestrian took his life in his hands crossing its congested streets, and no tree-dweller would survive the haze of auto exhaust that rested on the roofs of block after block of tract housing.

Craig Hunter, in the first flush of his success, had bought two houses on adjoining lots, bulldozed them, and put up a five-thousand-square-foot crazy quilt of Georgian and Moorish design at the end of a street that twisted like a creek. It appeared to be in good repair, but Valentino noticed that the planed hedges and beds of exotic flowers of brighter days had been removed, leaving a patch of lawn, well-tended but ordinary, which would not require a platoon of forty-dollar-an-hour gardeners to maintain. Craig, had he stayed, would have tried to support them, but Lorna was too practical a person to waste her life just to keep up appearances. Offers still came her way, but she hated the Hollywood fishbowl and the long hours on a soundstage that didn't end with the shooting day, but continued through the round of high-profile parties, charity balls, and one awards ceremony after another.

A satellite truck was parked in front of the house, where a faded wannabe-starlet-turned-"special correspondent" stood in front of a camera holding a microphone decorated with the logo of a popular nightly entertainment program. Valentino guessed what angle the story would take: footage of the no-doubt shabby bar where the victim had last been heard from, a brief interview with a police spokesman, and a recap of Hunter's brief career, dressed up as a cautionary tale. It would be made to appear that he'd beaten himself to death with his own bad choices.

He hadn't. He'd been beaten to death with something intended to beat a man to death with, by someone who'd intended to beat him to death.

Jaws clamped, Valentino swung into the driveway, spoiling the reporter's standup (he hoped), parked under the carport, and climbed the flagged steps to the front door. Had it really been only three years since his last visit? The way down was faster than the way up, and began with a single misstep: an ugly scandal refused to go away, a heavily publicized movie failed to open, an actor showed up on the set wasted and unable to remember his lines. All three had happened to Hunter. Valentino pressed an intercom button beside the door.

"Who is it?" Lorna Hunter's low voice came out of the speaker. The words were slurred.

"Valentino."

"Thank God. The surveillance camera's broken. I was afraid you were that skinny-legged vulture in the miniskirt. I told her if she came back I'd set the dogs on her." Moments later a bolt shot back, a catch turned, and the visitor found himself in an embrace that smelled pungently of expensive scent and cheap gin.

"Thanks for coming," Lorna said when they separated. "Craig didn't have many friends left."

"I wish I'd been a better friend."

"The better ones were the last to go."

He touched her shoulder and they moved inside. A tall blonde with a clean profile that was even more classical at thirty-one than it had been at twenty—a cinematographer who had worked with Grace Kelly and Ava Gardner had said she was the only actress he'd photographed who didn't have a bad side—Lorna was slim and fit in a cashmere top, tailored slacks, and sandals on her bare feet. The unfortunate actress who'd been hired to replace her on her old sitcom had been shredded by critics in comparison. She'd only found work later as a quasi-celebrity on a dreary reality show.

"Can I offer you a drink?" In the spacious sunken living room she refreshed her glass from a bottle on the polished granite bar. Valentino was surprised to note that a framed poster from one of Craig's films, *Dr. Detonation,* retained prominent place on one wall.

"It's a little early for me. Maybe a glass of water."

She took a plastic bottle out of the built-in refrigerator and handed it to him, nearly dropping it when she let go before he had a good grip on it. He'd never seen her drink before, aside from the occasional white wine. At 9:45 A.M. she appeared to have a head start on the day.

Tipply or not, she caught his reaction, curling up on the end of a big white-leather-upholstered sofa with her gin and very little tonic. "I never understood what Craig saw in the stuff. I'm beginning to, today."

"It has its benefits. I don't think anyone would blame you under the circumstances."

"You're sweet. You always were. When everyone else was telling Craig he was getting ahead of himself—the place in Palm Springs went back to the bank, did you know?—you said there was no crime in enjoying one's successes."

"I may have been guilty of enabling him. I was young and stupid. Now I have no excuse."

"He knew he was to blame for everything that happened to him. Whatever his faults, he never laid them off on anyone else. God, I'm already talking about him in past tense. I've only known for two hours."

He drank from his bottle. He wasn't thirsty; it was just something to do with his hands while he settled himself on the opposite end of the sofa. "Did you know Craig was in this kind of trouble?"

"His gambling bothered me. It used to be just recreation, but the last several times I saw him, all he could talk about was poker and the ponies and getting even. It was another addiction on top of all the others."

This was new information. "When did he start gambling?"

"He staked his up-front money on his first big contract on the Super Bowl. The Cowboys delivered on the spread. It was the worst thing that could have happened. If he'd lost his bankroll, I think the shock would've brought him into line. That's Monday-morning quarterbacking, I know. Maybe he was doomed from the start. Palm Springs went first, on Internet poker. He tried to win it back on a parlay when the gross points came through on *California Ninja*. He broke even. I wish he'd lost his shirt." She drank off half her glass.

"Is that when the substance abuse started?"

She shook her head. "Again, it was recreational at first: the celebrity slippery slope. There was a well-manicured pusher on the A-list at every party in Beverly Hills, some of them at the top of the credits every time a picture opened. You start out snorting lines off a Venetian marble table and wind up on crystal meth in a five-story walk-up in East L.A. The alcohol was just an attempt to find the level you had before you took your first sniff."

"Did he try to get help?"

"I begged him to, but you know Craig—knew him. My tenses are all fouled up. He thought he was like the heroes he played, the men who answered every challenge with action and a clever comeback. That's the curse of this town. They tell you not to fall for your own publicity, then push you to go out and prove you're the man in the trailers." She swirled her drink. "Here I am, laying it all on Hollywood. Craig failed himself. We all failed him, me most of all."

"You didn't fail him."

"I deserted him."

"You didn't do that, either. You got out before he dragged you down with him. That wouldn't have helped anyone. It would just make another victim."

"I—"

"Stop saying 'I.' It's narcissistic." He smiled at her startled expression. Then he stopped smiling. "You didn't kill him, Lorna."

"Didn't I?"

He put his water bottle on the coffee table, took the glass from her hands, set it down, and held her hands in his. "No. He was alive when he walked into that bar. Whoever killed him didn't care what he'd been or what he'd become. For some reason—unpaid gambling debts or whatever—his going on living became inconvenient for someone, and I'm going to do everything I can to help the police find out who it was and why, whether they want my help or not. I know it's late in the day, but I owe that much to you and Craig. He asked me for help and I turned my back on him. I'm offering it to you."

"But what can *you* do?" She looked up at him with little-girl eyes.

He squeezed her hands. "I can ask questions. Beginning with why you lied to Sergeant Gill and Detective Yellowfern about when you last heard from Craig."

5

"YOU'RE HURTING ME."

He let go of her hands, but he didn't sit back. "He's dead. Whatever you say can't hurt him. You can trust me not to tell anyone anything that can hurt *you*."

"But I didn't—"

"Don't lie to me, too. When I spoke to you this morning, you said he showed up here late one night last week. He was drunk or on dope, you said, and you had to threaten to call the police to get him to leave. But Sergeant Gill told me you told him and his partner you hadn't heard from Craig in weeks. What made you change your story?"

"Nothing. I was confused."

"When? When you were talking to me or when you were talking to them? You don't have to answer that; I think you were telling me the truth. I can't think of a reason why you'd make up a story like that."

"All right. I failed him again. If the police found out I'd seen him recently, they'd keep asking questions. I didn't want to get involved."

"You were already involved enough to call me when you were worried about him. When was he here?"

"Friday night. It was late. I'd gone to bed when he came banging on the door. I knew it was him then and that he was in bad shape. He always forgot to buzz me on the intercom when he was drinking or using."

"Why'd you let him in?"

"It was Craig. Did you forget how charming he could be when he was half in the bag? I opened the door on the chain and there he was with his hair down on his forehead and that lazy smile he was wearing the day he proposed. All the signs of self-abuse slid away when he was like that. You forgot how quickly it could change to something ugly."

"You said once he was inside he started acting like he still had a right to the house and you, too. What did you mean?"

"He tried to get familiar, to use a euphemism I learned from my mother. My mentioning the police was like throwing a bucket of cold water in his face. He was considerably less charming and boyish going out than coming in."

"Where were those dogs you threatened to turn loose on the reporter?"

"That was just a bluff. I adopted them out after the divorce. The alimony checks kept bouncing. I had to trim the budget."

"You should have reported him to the court when they bounced."

"Putting him in jail wouldn't pay the bills. But I wish I had. At least he'd be alive."

"What about his behaving like he still owned the house?"

"He wanted to use the phone. No, he said he was *going* to

use it, as if he were still paying the bill. He said he'd lost his cell—I knew his server had canceled his contract—and his call couldn't wait until he got to his apartment in Long Beach. Craig's dream was to start his own acting school; he was babbling something about having enough money soon to open a chain of schools across the country. I figured he had a hot tip and wanted to call his bookie. I let him make the call from his old office. It seemed to be the quickest way of getting rid of him. When he came out he was excited, and that's when he turned Lothario. A good movie deal or a celebrity endorsement offer always affected him that way in the old days."

"Why didn't you tell me all this earlier?"

"It wasn't important then. I was just relieved you'd heard from him and he hadn't been in an accident."

"But why didn't you tell the police about the visit?"

She said nothing, looking sullen.

"Lorna, the police suspect Mike Grundage because of the way Craig was killed. Do you know who he is?"

"Of course. A company of his was one of the sponsors of my TV show."

"What!"

"Don't look so shocked. It was legitimate, a regional fast-food franchise. Did you think we were advertising a brothel?"

"Did you ever meet?"

"No. That would've been a PR disaster. Ad flacks are supposed to rub elbows with low characters, but not the players."

"Was Craig borrowing money from Grundage's loan sharks?"

"I don't know."

"But you suspected something like that, didn't you? You thought that's what the phone call might have been about. You kept the information from the police because it was sordid."

"Well, wasn't it? Hasn't his name been dragged through the

muck enough already? I know public figures don't have the same rights to privacy as everyone else, but does that mean they can't have any dignity in death either?"

He shook his head. He was tired of discussing the burdens of fame. "You withheld evidence for no reason. If you're sure he was excited and not scared, the time line doesn't work. If they agreed to back his acting school just last week, they wouldn't expect repayment so soon, or get mad enough to hurt him when it didn't happen. Anyway, the sharks don't kill you for not paying up. They'd have roughed him around at most, and worked out a payment plan of some kind. A dead man is a dead loss."

"How do you know so much about gangsters?"

"I've seen every film Martin Scorsese ever made."

"Even *The Age of Innocence*?"

"Yes, but that's irrelevant to this conversation."

She laughed in spite of herself. That made him feel better. Already he was helping. "May I look in Craig's office?"

She smiled. "You mean for clues?"

"I've also seen all the Thin Man movies ten times."

She uncurled herself from the sofa. He got up to support her, but she was more steady on her feet now than before. He followed her into a small den containing a reproduction Regency desk and chair and a stereo system as complicated as a NASA control panel. There was a shrine to the films of Craig Hunter, all six of them: Posters in steel frames of blazing helicopters, exploding bridges, and men running through machine-gun fire with ammo belts flapping, centered around an incongruously tranquil full-length oil portrait of a stern and dignified Hunter in a blue business suit with the presidential seal on one lapel, a prop from *Commando-in-Chief*.

"I didn't change anything," Lorna said. "Despite all, I always hoped deep inside me he'd come back someday, the man he

was when I married him. Pathetic, now. I guess it always was."
Her voice cracked on the last part.

"Without hope, he wouldn't have lasted as long as he did."
He pointed at a cheap-looking suitcase standing in the knee-
hole of the desk. "That doesn't quite match the room."

"Craig brought it with him Friday. He said there wasn't
room in his apartment and asked if he could store it here."

"That's another thing you left out about that visit. How
much else is there?"

"Nothing. I didn't mention the suitcase because it couldn't
possibly be important. Go ahead and look inside; the police
did. It's just some books."

He hoisted it onto the desk and opened it. The books, bound
in torn paper and dingy cloth with tattered dust jackets, were
filmographies: *Heroes of the Horrors, The Films of Boris Karloff,*
The *Films of Bela Lugosi, Lugosi: The Man Behind the Cape,*
Dear Boris—a dozen others, all with photos and paintings of
actors in grotesque makeup on the covers. "Was Craig interested in horror films?"

"He hated them. His first part was a nonspeaking bit in
Bloodbath IV. He was beheaded in his only scene. He said it
was a junk genre."

Valentino riffled pages, picked up books and held them by
their covers and shook them, but nothing came loose. "Why
the sudden interest, I wonder? Did he say anything that might
make you think he'd been offered a horror-film role?"

"No. But then he might have been ashamed to admit he was
considering one. He used to say he had more respect for actors
who appeared in porn. He said it was better to leave an audience feeling horny than murderous."

"We argued about that once. I don't believe any movie ever

really incited anyone to violence. Classics like these never did. After all the *Halloween*s and *Elm Street*s and *Saw*s, they wouldn't even give a child nightmares. Just a good time. May I borrow the books?"

"You can keep them. I prefer screwball comedies myself. Do you think they're clues?" This time there was no irony in her expression.

"I don't know. That's the problem with real-life murder mysteries: Either everything's a clue or nothing is." He closed the suitcase. The console telephone on the desk caught his eye. "Has anyone used this phone since Craig?"

"No. I almost never come in here."

He lifted the receiver and punched the redial button. After two rings a cool feminine voice came on the line. "Horace Lysander's office."

He hung up and looked at Lorna. "Who represented Craig during your divorce?"

"Cooper and Clive. Craig retained them ever since that phony paternity suit five years ago."

"He never used Horace Lysander? Maybe for the trouble in Mexico?" He remembered Lysander was a criminal lawyer.

"Is that who answered? I never heard of him."

"You would if you had breakfast with Mike Grundage."

He drove away with the uneasy sensation that he knew less now than when he'd come. He did know more about one thing than the police did: Lorna's story that she hadn't had recent contact with Craig had kept them from doing the same thing Valentino had done, and from discovering yet another link with Grundage through his attorney. For the same reason, they wouldn't attach as much importance to the books in the suit-case as Valentino did; not that it had any importance at all, as far as he could tell.

And the knowledge itself left him feeling ignorant. Lysander was a top-drawer lawyer with an impeccable reputation, despite the notoriety of many of his clients. If Grundage was involved in whatever deal Craig had had going, it wouldn't be through his loan sharks. A smart gangster kept his shady operations separate from the man who represented him in matters legal. Lysander himself would insist upon it as an officer of the court with a license to preserve. The size of his retainers alone would save him from temptation.

Finally, Valentino was unsettled in his mind about Lorna. Spouses and ex-spouses were routinely listed among the suspects in murder cases, but he couldn't imagine her setting up such a grisly act, even if she had a discernible motive. The reason she'd given for lying to the police was credible, but thin. Her grief seemed genuine, but he could not put aside the knowledge that she was an accomplished actress. The *but*s kept mounting.

He went to The Oracle. The directory in the projection booth would have the number of Lysander's firm. He wanted to make an appointment in private, and he couldn't very well do that on Lorna's redial with her present.

Leo Kalishnikov greeted him in the foyer, got up all in monochrome: matching white Borsalino hat, alpaca cape, and double-breasted suit, with a white necktie on a black satin shirt and a black silk handkerchief exploding from his breast pocket. Valentino wondered if the theater designer deducted the cost of his outlandish outfits from his income taxes. He knew for a fact the man was widowed, with two grown sons, and was convinced he was heterosexual, but stereotypes were everything in Hollywood: The so-called tolerant artistic community preferred its mechanics German, its gardeners Asian, and its decorating consultants as gay as an inaugural ball. The straight world was secure in its belief that all homosexuals dressed the part.

"Your timing's dead on." Today appeared to be a day when the American idiom was appropriate. "We've arrived at a color scheme."

"Have we?"

"*We* meaning myself and Google. This is Stan Sinakis, a house painter of uncommon skill. It's in his genes."

He thought at first it was *jeans,* and his gaze went immediately to the baggy pair worn by the man who stood at Kalishnikov's side, a palimpsest of many painting sessions smeared and stiffened with many coagulated shades. Valentino had paid him little attention, assuming he was a member of the regular crew. He was in his sixties, stout and white-haired, with corduroy shirttails hanging out and a painter's cap as stained as his trousers jammed down over his forehead. His face was red, a map of broken blood vessels, and his baggy grin appeared to be as indelible as the paint caked under his nails. "How do." He touched the bill of his cap.

"Stan's father, Miklos Sinakis, now unfortunately deceased, was a painter's apprentice, assigned to The Oracle's original construction. My faintest of hopes, that he would remember what color was used on the exterior, were dashed when I learned of his demise, but a greater treasure yet awaited me in the shadows of Stan's garage." The Russian's speech invariably reverted to a good translation of Gogol when he was excited.

"Pop never threw nothing away." Sinakis raised the paint can he was carrying at his side, rusted and calcined with many spills and drips. Age and exposure had reduced them to an unidentifiable shade. A faded grease-pencil scrawl on the lid read 5/7/27; now Valentino was excited.

"You're not serious."

"But I am," Kalishnikov said. "When I called, Mr. Sinakis said his late lamented father had kept the dregs from every job he'd ever had in the family garage, which Sinakis *fils* inherited. He spent the better part of today excavating the sample you see from the hoard. He asks but fifty dollars for his time."

"No offense, but is it worth it? Eighty years is hard on everything."

"I am assured by the wizards at Home Depot that a shard pried loose from the petrified contents will, through the magic of computer matching, deliver unto us once again the genius of Max Fink."

Fink was the tragic visionary who had built The Oracle— just in time for talking pictures to force him into debt retrofitting the theater for sound equipment, a setback followed closely by the Great Depression. "I was okay with turquoise," Valentino said. "You save me from solvency in the name of historical authenticity." Kalishnikov's speech patterns were addictive.

"You pretend cynicism, my friend. We are fellow zealots, you and I: madmen in a world overpopulated by the sane and the mundane. Pay the man."

Valentino reached for his checkbook. "I never paid more than seven dollars for a can of paint in my life."

"You will pay many times more than that before that part of the job is done. I estimate twenty gallons." The designer worked the buttons of a BlackBerry.

Valentino gave Sinakis his check and left the company before it could cost him more money. He went upstairs lugging the twin burdens of Craig Hunter's suitcase full of books and his own personal debt.

6

INSIDE THE PROJECTION booth his roommate awaited him, swathed in cheesecloth and resembling the Elephant Man. This was the rebuilt 1952 Bell & Howell projector he'd bought on eBay, a beautiful piece of machinery that would enable Valentino to screen old 3-D films once he found another to match it: *Bwana Devil* and the original *House of Wax* required two separate prints superimposed upon each other to make their monsters and man-eating lions leap out into the audience. He inspected the cloth to make sure it was keeping out construction dust and opened the suitcase.

He laid the books side by side on the sofa bed and on the floor in front of it. His own extensive library on the history of film, most of which was in storage until the last of the workmen packed up his tools and left, contained several of the same titles. He'd read them all, but he thought staring at the covers in the privacy of his home might give him an idea of the shape of the puzzle, if not its actual solution.

Without exception the books were about horror and fantasy

films produced many years before he was born, most of them by Universal. That studio had pioneered the concept of the chiller with *The Phantom of the Opera*, starring the great Lon Chaney (and one of the first of his one thousand faces), in 1925, and completed the cycle some thirty years later with *Creature from the Black Lagoon* and its two sequels, *Revenge of the Creature* and *The Creature Walks Among Us*. In between, a veritable herd of misshapen half humans had lurched through dry-ice fog and up crumbling castle steps carrying swooning women (scantily clad in nightgowns or swimsuits) in their arms. The monsters were electrocuted, burned alive, staked through the heart, shot with silver bullets, and smothered in quicksand, only to be revived by some clever scenarist in the follow-up.

When you yearned for a musical extravaganza or a luscious period piece, you went to MGM. If gritty urban dramas and prison flicks were your thing, Warner Brothers was the studio for you. But if you ran home from the theater and dived under the covers to protect yourself from demons under your bed, chances were the culprit was Universal.

Standing there with arms folded contemplating hand-tinted images of suave vampires, hirsute werewolves, unspooled mummies, and flat-headed walking corpses with bolts in their necks, he recognized a finer pattern still. Most of the filmographies were devoted to classic horror in general, but the individual biographies and chronologies were evenly divided between two actors: Boris Karloff and Bela Lugosi.

In the wake of Lon Chaney's death in 1930, Lugosi had kick-started the monster cycle back into life with *Dracula*, based on Bram Stoker's novel of gothic dread and the first American film to present the supernatural as something other than a sly hoax. It had been produced over the stern objections of the in-

house censor, and its box office receipts had rescued Universal
from bankruptcy in the depth of the Depression. Lugosi, who
like Count Dracula was a native of Transylvania, had mesmer-
ized viewers with the intensity of his gaze and heavy Balkan
accent and convinced a generation of moviegoers that the dead
could walk again and prey upon the living. Eighty years later,
the most amateur impressionist had only to say, "I vant to drink
your blood" for his listeners to know he was pretending to be
Dracula, whether or not they'd ever seen the movie and regardless of the fact that Lugosi himself had never spoken the
line.

Karloff was a chip off a very different block, a proper English
gentleman plucked from obscurity (after fifty-odd motion picture appearances) to don the famous flattened headpiece and
stitches of the Monster in *Frankenstein*. The mute role, famously
scorned by Lugosi when it was offered to him, had assured the
actor's future for the next forty years. As it was with the *Dracula* star's signature accent, one had only to assume Karloff's
stiff-legged, groping-armed walk to tell people (even those who'd
never watched the film) whom he was imitating.

The players' stories, however, followed opposite trajectories.
Bela Lugosi never again came near the success he'd known
when *Dracula* was in its first release, descending to steadily
more demeaning roles and deeper into poverty, while Boris
Karloff's star continued to burn brightly, keeping him active
and in the public eye until his death by natural causes at age
eighty-one. His biography was inspirational, his colleague's
tragic.

Valentino wondered if Craig Hunter had selected the two
lives for study because his own so closely paralleled Lugosi's:
early promise followed by disappointment after disappointment,
leading to substance abuse (and, although Craig could not have

predicted his own end, death in squalid circumstances). It was as if he'd hoped to learn from his predecessor's mistakes and rebuild his fortunes on Karloff's example.

His friend picked up *The Films of Bela Lugosi* at random and found a page corner turned down in the biographical section. Had Craig marked it himself for his own edification? But with nothing else to narrow it down, that page and the one opposite covered too much ground to indicate what had drawn his interest. The passage began with Lugosi's sudden stardom at age forty-eight and ended with his complaints about having been stereotyped as a fiend after appearances in *White Zombie* and *Murders in the Rue Morgue*. It wasn't an exact comparison with Craig's plight, if that was what he was after. Typecasting had not hurt him, despite his constant association with summer action pictures. His addictive personality had succumbed to the L.A. demimonde of drug parties and bar-hopping; Lugosi's struggle with narcotics had not begun until his career was in freefall.

The other books beckoned, but Valentino hadn't time for abstract speculation when he had a lead who might be able to furnish direct answers to direct questions. In the "Attorneys" section of the massive area directory he found Horace Lysander's name and number in a tasteful single line among competitors' display advertisements both dignified and garish. When the same cool voice answered, he identified himself and asked if he could speak with Lysander.

"Are you currently a client?"

"No, I just—"

"If you wish to retain Mr. Lysander's services, you'll have to make an appointment."

"Has he an opening this week?"

"The first week of November is the earliest I'm showing."

"Please tell him it's about Craig Hunter."

"I'm sorry, but I don't know the name, and I handle all of Mr. Lysander's appointments."

"I don't know if he had one or not, but they spoke over the telephone shortly before he was murdered."

"I see." He might have been a plumber describing a slow leak in the basement for all her tone changed. "I'll give Mr. Lysander the message, Mr.—?"

"Valentino," he repeated. He gave her his home number and the number of his cell. As an afterthought—because his office hours were erratic—he added his number at the Film Preservation Department.

Later, he was sure that but for that last-minute addendum, he'd still be waiting to hear from the busy lawyer.

He was hungry suddenly, for food and human contact. It was well past lunchtime, but he knew Kyle Broadhead paid as little attention to scheduling meals as he did, fueling up only when the tank was empty and impossible to ignore. Valentino found him in, and arranged to meet him at their favorite new restaurant.

The Brass Gimbal catered to industry insiders. The photos on the walls were more likely to feature great cameramen than iconic movie stars. Broadhead waved Valentino over to the Billy Bitzer booth and they ordered beer on tap and burgers from a waitress wearing a necktie that looked like a film strip. Valentino chose the Smash Cut, a quarter pound of black Angus drenched in Technicolor Sauce (a rainbow of ketchup, mustard, and guacamole), Broadhead a vegetarian burger identified on the menu as the Green Screen. "I'm a little worried about the special effects," he said, "but Fanta wants me to start eating healthy."

Valentino wasn't in the mood for small talk. He told him about Hunter.

Broadhead nodded. "Ruth filled me in on the police visit. She made it sound like a raid. I'm sorry, but the way he was going, this end seems almost merciful."

"What's merciful about a bludgeoning?"

"You haven't had the advantage of thirty-six months buried alive in a Communist prison, without clean linen or hope."

"So many of our conversations come back to that. Do I have to wait until your book is published to find out the details?"

"You won't find them in this one. I've decided not to write it as autobiography after all. I'd hate to invest so much angst in a project the CIA will never allow to see print."

Valentino had heard him drop hints before about his jailing in Yugoslavia on a trumped-up charge of espionage. *Was it trumped up?* This aging curmudgeon with unruly gray hair and a slept-in face was the least political person he knew; but wasn't that part of the criteria? The archivist could focus on only one mystery at a time. "Explain that suitcase full of books."

"It may be significant or not. Maybe he got them cheap and hoped to lay them off somewhere and score dope with the profit."

"You don't think there's anything to my theory?"

"Theories are based on fact, not guesses. Lugosi's travails are a lesson in the danger of hubris—he turned down *Frankenstein,* for pity's sake—but it's certainly not unique in show business."

Something Broadhead had said resounded deep in Valentino's subconscious. He tried to bring it to the surface, but lost it in the murk. His brain was a spare room crammed to the ceiling with running times, release dates, cast lists, and Hollywood lore, arranged in no particular order. At times it might have been empty for all it was of any use. "What about Karloff?"

"We measure failures against successes. He started out the lowest of the low, you know."

"He drove a truck and performed menial jobs in between pictures when he was starting out. Nothing unique there either."

"William Henry Pratt"—Broadhead used the actor's birth name—"was the son of a British civil servant and an East Indian woman: a half-caste. In Victorian society, that was the bottom rung of the ladder, with no hope of ascending ever. Then there were seven older brothers to bully him, mentally and physically. The abuse continued into adulthood, driving him into exile in Canada, then to the U.S. in search of work. He left at least three marriages in the dust before he was forty-five. Does any of this strike you as familiar?"

"It's the plot of *Frankenstein*—the Monster's part, anyway, roughly. It's no wonder he identified so well with a cobbled-up creature, alone and despised." Valentino had noted the swarthiness of the gaunt actor's features, which became more pronounced as his hair whitened. He'd assumed it was because of the California sun, shining down on him beside his swimming pool; stories had circulated of his eccentricity, basking beside it in a swimsuit and top hat, of all things. "How do you know this?"

"How does a popular-culture historian know anything? I got it from the horse's mouth."

"You knew Karloff?"

"I made my first dollar in this town—and precious little

more—working as a studio messenger. I delivered pages of Bogdonavich's screenplay to him when he was filming *Targets,* the last year of his life. Age confides in youth, as I am doing now. He knew the end was near. He was confined to a wheelchair, except when he gathered the strength and courage to stand before the camera. Crippling arthritis was the culprit, abetted not a little by three unsuccessful spinal surgeries to correct the miseries brought on by that sadist James Whale. Did you know he forced Karloff to carry Colin Clive up the hill to that windmill in *Frankenstein* dozens of times? That experience made him an early activist on behalf of the Screen Actors Guild. A man will tell things to a complete stranger he would never share with his own flesh and blood."

Their meals came. Valentino took one look at his burger, an obscene lump of cooked flesh covered with blood-red sauce, and knew he would never bring himself to take a bite. He couldn't erase the picture of Craig Hunter beaten to a pulp. He found the bitter taste of the beer more palatable. Was this how alcoholics were born? He couldn't ask Craig.

Broadhead, the healed-over cynic, poured ketchup on his sandwich and helped himself to it with apparent gusto. "All this is public knowledge now. Oscar Wilde said the posthumous biography brings a new horror to death. You've been preoccupied with your experiment in resurrectionist architecture, or you'd be aware of more recent discoveries in the history of our quaint industry. The ghouls who call themselves scholars would send George Romero screaming into the night."

"I first saw *Frankenstein* on my family's old black-and-white TV set, in my bedroom after they replaced it with a color television in the living room. I was sitting up in my bed with Pepi, my Chihuahua-terrier, curled up in my lap. Every time I've seen it since, I've felt that same cuddly warmth. I'll miss that next time, thanks to you."

"Don't. Karloff wouldn't appreciate your tears, nor would he feel he deserved them. His last marriage was a long and happy one, and it produced a well-adjusted daughter, who supplements her income talking about her father on DVD extras."

"What was he like?"

Broadhead put down his burger and wiped his mouth with his napkin. "I keep forgetting you're a sprockethead first and a scholar second. He was extremely gracious, in an Old World way you don't find anymore, even in polite Europeans. His conversation grew tedious when he talked about his American family, which he did often; but he had that wonderful warm baritone and that marvelous lisp.

"His famous gentle sense of humor was solidly based on irony," he went on. "Lugosi, and for that matter your friend Hunter, might have been able to keep things in perspective had they possessed such a thing."

"You're forgetting that Karloff was looking back from a position of triumph. Peering out from the depths of misery is a different thing altogether."

"True, although the aphorism rings false coming from one of your tender years. You have yet to experience true misery."

"Don't give up hope. I just spent fifty bucks on a can of paint older than you are."

"If you've come to me for sympathy, you wasted a trip. I've advised you from the beginning to let that *Hindenburg* go down in its own flames before they consume you."

"Noted. None of this has helped me figure out why Craig was murdered."

Broadhead raised his bushy brows. "I'm an academic, and by

definition useless in all things practical. Please tell me you haven't decided to play detective yet again."

"I don't have any choice. I still have two hundred cards that say I'm a film detective, and I can't afford to throw them out."

"That, too, is a decision I warned you against. Either I'm a singularly inept mentor or you're the worst protégé who ever lived. You realize the police are fully equipped to investigate homicide, even in a wilderness like San Diego."

"Granted, but with them it's just routine. You can devote only so much time to one case in an eight-hour tour of duty. My involvement is personal."

"Yes. Emotional baggage is so much more portable than the professional kind." Broadhead sipped his beer, made a face, and set down the mug. "Since counsel from me is so easily ignored, I offer more, knowing it will bring no repercussions. You should have a talk with that young man of yours. Find out whether he's a threat to himself and others or just odd."

"My young man? You mean Jason? He does what I ask and doesn't talk back. He isn't exactly a conformist, but the university doesn't offer credits for that. Did you forget you sent him to me in the first place?"

"That was when I thought he was just another campus goofball. On my way here I saw him coming out of your office, dressed like an undertaker and wearing what looked like the cross-section of a submarine on his head."

"A submarine?" He remembered the high silk hat. "He said something about stopping by a junkyard. I guess he found something to modify his outfit and used my office for a workshop. It's okay, as long as I didn't need it."

"He was wearing a chain and padlock. When he said he was on his way to a party, I asked if he was going as a hardware store. He said it wasn't a costume party."

"He told me the same thing."

"Well, he's your intern, and your property, so to speak. But I'm locking my office from now on. Assuming he isn't wearing a jockstrap made of skeleton keys."

Valentino was spared the labor of fashioning a rejoinder by his cell phone: the two-note theme of *Jaws*, which he'd downloaded for the Halloween season. He answered.

He recognized the cool voice immediately. "Mr. Valentino, I'm calling on behalf of Mr. Horace Lysander. Are you free to meet with him in his office at four o'clock this afternoon?"

7

NO SHADY MOB mouthpiece out of Central Casting, Horace Lysander was senior partner in a firm that took up two floors of a sparkling glass tower in Century City. The reception room outside the office was paneled in tiger maple, with ambient lighting that illuminated every square inch from behind soffits. The buff-colored leather upholstery gripped Valentino's hips and buttocks like a giant and gentle toothless dog.

He waited less than five minutes until the receptionist, a lacquered-looking redhead with the cool voice he'd heard over the phone, said, "Yes, sir," into her headset and told him he could go in. He got up and had his hand out to work the knob of the inner door before he realized it didn't have one. Something clicked and it drifted inward, then back into the frame when he was on the other side.

The office was fifteen times the size of his own, with an enormous Turkish carpet that predated California's founding and a glass wall looking out on the city, which appeared less smoggy from that point of view, as if that was the spot where the photographers who made picture postcards for the chamber of commerce set up their tripods. Built-in bookshelves held rows of legal volumes bound in cream-colored leather—superfluous in the Digital Age, but reassuring to clients—and German Expressionist paintings hung on the remaining two walls, their exaggerated perspectives and jagged lines reminding Valentino of cels from the original *Cabinet of Dr. Caligari*. There was about the place a sense of monolithic stability, with the cars looping freeway cloverleafs many stories below representing a world in a constant state of flux outside.

Lysander himself was more animated than the interior, a large, soft, smiling pink bald man in a beautiful gray suit who popped up from behind his desk and strode around it to shake Valentino's hand. The desk was a great oblong sheet of polished obsidian resting on a pedestal, heavy enough to require a reinforced floor to sustain its weight; an eternity in construction purgatory had made Valentino an informal expert on zoning restrictions in Los Angeles County.

"Are you working with the police?" Lysander's smile remained in place and his eyes on his visitor's, who was nevertheless acutely aware that his daily uniform of sweatshirt and jeans was out of place.

"No, they're not so desperate they've taken to hiring film archivists to assist in their investigations. I'm looking into Craig Hunter's death as a friend."

"Please accept my sympathy. At my age I've grown accustomed to burying friends, but it must be traumatic for one so young."

"Thank you. I'm older than I look, but I hope I never get so old I'll take murder in stride."

"As do I. As a criminal attorney I've seen more than my share of crime-scene photos and autopsy reports. I despair sometimes for the future of the race. Two detectives interviewed

Mr. Grundage in my presence this morning. We both assured them that we never had any contact with Hunter."

Valentino knew this for a lie, but it was too early to spring the trap. He wanted to know more about the man he was dealing with. "Craig was beaten to death and his arms were broken ritually above the elbows. Detective Yellowfern said Grundage practically has a patent on the method."

"If he'd said that here, in front of a third party, I'd seek damages for slander and defamation of character. Mr. Grundage has never been charged with a crime, much less indicted or convicted."

"That's a sterling claim for an upstanding citizen to post on his website."

If he expected the lawyer to bridle at that, he was disappointed. Many hundreds of hours in court had sealed his emotions inside layers of hard shell. "His father, Anthony Grundage—Big Tony—worked his way up from a common longshoreman in San Diego to become an influential labor leader during the Depression. The competition developed its tactics with crowbar in hand, not from behind a desk. His son would be the first to concede that he responded in kind. The Kefauver Committee indicted Anthony on six counts of extortion in interstate commerce in 1951, then dropped all charges for lack of evidence. However, his exposure on national television during his testimony branded him a notorious character until his death. Whatever improprieties the father may or may not have committed, it's irresponsible and actionable to apply them to the son."

"He's being investigated by Congress, just as his father was," Valentino said. "But you know that, having sat beside him during his appearances. Our senators and representatives don't take that step for their own amusement."

"I agree. Are you a native Californian?"

"No. I was born and raised in Indiana."

"I am. The first firm I interned with had a department that specialized in contract law and represented people in the entertainment industry. In your time here you can't have failed to note that publicity is the coin of the realm. Washington is no different. Face time means as much to a politician as it does to an actor. When it comes to headlines, the name Grundage is magic. Now, if there's nothing else you wanted to see me about, I have important calls to place."

It was a scene-ending line if ever there was one, but rather than turn away in dismissal, Lysander held his ground. Clearly he was expecting his visitor to make the next move. In that moment, Valentino realized the attorney had consented to the interview as much to gain information as to impart it. It was time for the archivist to play his card.

"There is something else. You denied ever hearing from Craig Hunter, but he called you in this office last Friday night."

Lysander didn't blink. "Who said that?"

"No one. Your number was on his redial."

"Anyone is free to dial my number. It's listed. Perhaps he misdialed."

"Angering you enough to tell your client, who had him killed using his modus operandi. That's no sillier than to call it coincidence."

"Be careful, young man. The line between hypothesis and false accusation is very thin."

"I have a witness who says he was in conversation for some time with whoever answered. It was the last call he made from that phone before he was murdered."

"And the name of your witness?"

Valentino shook his head.

"Young man, I've faced many an ambitious prosecutor. I know when I'm being bluffed."

"I told you I'm older than I look. Telephone company records will show whether a call was placed to your number and for how long."

For the first time he saw an authentic-looking reaction on the lawyer's face, a slight deepening of the pink on his cheek. "I need to confer with a client before I continue this conversation," he said. "Would you step outside for a few minutes?"

"Mike Grundage?"

"Please step outside."

Valentino did so, strolling the reception room and reading certificates of public service preserved in clear Lucite as the woman behind the desk whispered her fingers over her computer keyboard. She stopped typing, listening over her headset. She gave the visitor a chilly smile and pushed the button that unlocked and opened the door to the private office.

This time Lysander remained sitting. Valentino consigned himself to more butter-soft leather in front of the great mass of obsidian.

"What you and I discuss can never leave this office." The lawyer's hands were clasped on the glistening surface separating host from guest. Valentino kept his own hands off it, knowing he'd leave a wet mark. "I made that promise in return for permission to breach attorney-client privilege. I can go no further until you agree to that."

"If it's a criminal matter, I'm bound to report it. I have no such privilege."

"So far as my client and I are aware, it involves nothing illegal."

"If that's the case, I agree."

An index finger detached itself from the others and pointed

toward the ceiling. "If word of the conversation gets out, I face disbarment. That's nothing compared with the firestorm of litigation you will face from my partners. It will follow you for years, drain all your resources, and plunge you so deep in debt your heirs will never be able to repay it."

"I'm already there, Mr. Lysander. I'm rebuilding a theater."

"You'll lose it and everything you've invested in it. In the end you'll wish you and Hunter had never met."

He was used to that feeling; but he nodded.

The finger rejoined its mates. "Hunter's business was with Elizabeth Grundage, not Mike."

"His wife?"

"His stepmother. Tony, her late husband, controlled the stagehands' and projectionists' unions in Hollywood during the so-called Golden Age of the 1930s. They worked on the sets of *All Quiet on the Western Front, The Wizard of Oz, Frankenstein—*"

"*Frankenstein?*" He thought of that suitcase full of books.

"Yes. Of course, that was long before I was born, but my firm represented the family when Tony was too old and ill in mind and body to look after his financial interests, and counseled Elizabeth when his will was in probate."

"She must be ninety."

"Far from it. Tony remarried late in life, after Mike's mother died. The family has continued to retain me all these years."

"What business could Craig have had with a gangster's widow?"

"Quite apart from the slur on Tony's memory, I resent your characterizing Elizabeth in that way. She's a grand lady, not a cheap gun moll."

For the second time in the meeting, upset showed on the smooth face of the officer of the court. It could be artifice; Valentino gave him the benefit of the doubt. "I'm sorry."

Lysander nodded, apparently mollified. "I was bound by the seal of my profession to divulge none of this to the police, even when it involved Hunter."

"You admit he called you?"

"I state it, in strictest confidence, and only because Mrs. Grundage gave me leave to do so. He approached her last week with a transaction. When he found out later I'd advised Elizabeth not to become involved, he called me to complain. He became abusive, threatening. He was drunk. I hung up on him."

"This was Friday night?"

"Yes."

"What was the transaction?"

"I can't discuss details. She refused to allow me to, and as her attorney I agree with the decision. She's suffered enough at the hands of authority and the media through no fault of her own. These latest troubles involving Mike have tried her sorely. She's entitled to her privacy."

"Any transaction with the victim of a homicide is evidence that's being withheld from the police."

"But there was no transaction. She turned him down."

"All the more reason to come forward with the details. She can't possibly be held accountable—unless she told her son and he reacted in gangsterish fashion."

"Have you had any training in law?"

"Not unless you count helping restore three Perry Mason movies starring Warren William."

"Even if Mr. Grundage confessed to me that he had conspired to commit a murder—which I assure you he has not—I could not pass the information along without his permission." Lysander glanced at a platinum Rolex strapped to the underside of his wrist. "I can give you no more time. If you were consulting me professionally, I would send you a bill for two hundred dollars for the amount I've given you already."

Valentino kept his seat. "Why did you agree to see me at all?"

"I'm beginning to wonder."

"That doesn't answer my question."

"I must ask you to leave."

The archivist stood. "Craig Hunter developed a sudden interest in Universal horror films shortly before his death, *Frankenstein* among them. You told me his father had a direct connection with that production. All that, together with how Craig died, convinces me Mike Grundage is involved. He's a pretty slick character, from what I've heard and read. I think if he's as determined as you are to protect his stepmother from harassment, he wouldn't be dumb enough to break Craig's arms and point suspicion directly at himself. I think you may be thinking the same thing, and that's why you hoped I might be able to help."

"And what makes you think I'd look for it from an amateur like you?"

"In law, yes; but I'm an expert in what you called 'the so-called Golden Age of the 1930s.' I'm pretty sure now you offered to meet with me because of what I do for a living, but you're too tied up in legal red tape to come out and ask for my advice. Maybe after you've conferred with both Elizabeth and Mike, you'll be in a position to come clean with me. If you're convinced your client is innocent, and if you can convince me far enough to establish reasonable doubt, please call."

"It's worse than that, I'm afraid."

He'd turned to leave, but the defeat in Lysander's tone made him turn back. The attorney looked less plump and pink, like a neon bulb that had sprung a leak, losing precious gas.

"There's a third connection," he said, "one the police aren't aware of yet, but they'll find out once they finish tracing Mike's financial interests."

"You mean the legitimate ones." He could kick himself for alienating his source this close to an agreement; but the lawyer was preoccupied.

"He owns the Grotto, the bar where Hunter's body was found. Thank you, Mr. Valentino. I very much hope we can meet again—without the legal red tape, as you put it."

8

HE DIDN'T FEEL like going home—or rather, to The Oracle; his concept of *home* didn't include carpenters and plasterers and mad Russians drifting in and out at will. He went back to the office, where there was always work to be found, a new lead on *London After Midnight* to be followed up or a crisis in the lab to attend to that would distract him from an unsatisfactory day of sleuthing. Before, he was vexed by how much he didn't know; after his session with Horace Lysander, what he thought he'd known he didn't know now. The case against Mike Grundage had appeared to be open and shut, with only the *why* left unanswered. Now he seemed an unlikely suspect at best.

And what did *Frankenstein*, a sensational novel written in 1816 and adapted even more sensationally to the screen in 1931, have to do with a murder committed in the twenty-first century?

Ruth was on the phone, assuring someone that he had indeed called the university power plant, but that it wasn't a power plant now (and more's the pity, was her attitude). Valentino swept past her station, grateful to be spared another soul-destroying exchange, and opened his office door to find a woman seated behind his desk.

Their gazes locked for less than a second before he drew the door shut and confronted Ruth, who was putting down the receiver. "What's Teddie Goodman doing in my office?"

"She said she was a friend. I told her you might not be back, but she said she'd wait awhile. I told her to go on in."

"You let in a complete stranger?"

"I had to. There's no place to sit out here, and I can't work with people skulking about."

He wasn't even sure what work that was. He hadn't dictated a letter in weeks and Kyle Broadhead was entirely self-contained inside his monk's cell with his pre-Columbian computer. "What if she turned out to be a thief?"

"Thieves don't dress that well. They wear striped convict shirts and little black masks."

He turned back to his door to trade one headache for another.

"That was rude even for you," Teddie Goodman said when he was inside. "The social graces are lost on you ivy league types. I'm glad I dropped out."

He'd never quite been able to place her accent. At times she sounded like a bad imitation of Bette Davis in *Jezebel*, at others like Yosemite Sam. At the moment it was Bette, but neither dialect matched her insistence that she was a close relative of Theda Bara's, the Ohio beauty queen-*cum*-mysterious woman from the Middle East, here to snatch men's souls on the silent screen. She did bear a passing resemblance to the old-time vamp, a razor-thin mannequin with black-black hair swept back from her sharp features and bladelike nails, today painted deep red to match her lipstick and swath of scarlet spiraling up diago-

nally from the hip of her black sheath dress and over the opposite shoulder. Her salary as Mark David Turkus' personal
hatchetwoman at Supernova International allowed her to wear
the latest fashions from Beverly Hills and Paris, and to wear
them only once before turning them over to some less fortu-
nate wealthy woman. At the moment she was using Valentino's
desk as a vanity table, touching up her jet-trail eyebrows with
the aid of a black pencil and a compact mirror with a mother-
of-pearl case.

"Your inferiority complex is showing, Teddie. You can go
back and finish your education any time you want. Even your
so-called great-great-grandmother got her diploma before she
went into pictures."

"I never said she was my great-great-grandmother. An aunt,
maybe, or a cousin. That was the family talk. I never took the
trouble to look it up."

"Of course not. If you did and the Turk found out you're a
fraud, he might not like you anymore."

"I'm just not interested in the past. I'm no moldy fig like you
and that old crotch across the hall. Gary Cooper or Tom Ar-
nold, they're all the same to me, as long as I can make a buck."
She snapped shut the case and returned it and the pencil to a
red alligator clutch bag. He could picture her catching the ga-
tor with her bare hands and dyeing the hide with its blood.

He took the seat he'd cleared off for Sergeant Gill and
crossed his ankles on a pile of press clippings on the desk. "To
what do I owe this invasion of my privacy?"

"The *Maltese Falcon* chair showed up on Sotheby's online
catalogue this morning. What's up your sleeve?"

"Not a thing. Did you think I'd try to ring in anything but
the real McCoy on the appraisers?"

"Oh, I'm satisfied it's genuine. Boy Scouts don't run scams.

Movie nerd that you are, you'd never part with that chair unless you needed to finance something better. What is it, foreign or American? Silent or talkie? We can strike a deal if you come clean, split the theatrical and distribution rights. I'll find out what it is anyway, but if I have to go to that trouble I'll cut you off at the ankles."

He laughed in relief. Teddie Goodman always operated on the principle that she knew more than you did, whoever you were. He'd been afraid she'd come to gloat over having sniped him out of some acquisition he'd been working on for months or years. To reveal ignorance was a desperate sign. Maybe his shot in the dark had hit something after all, and her honeymoon with Turkus was over.

"Go ahead and bray, you hyena. I don't make threats just to hear myself talk."

He stopped laughing, but not because she'd ceased to amuse him. "Someday, Teddie, you'll snarl yourself in your own web. Not everyone's as devious as you. I've got bills to pay. I'm sure your spies have kept you posted on what's going on in West Hollywood."

"That white elephant? Why don't you just sell your blood?"

"I only had five quarts to spare."

"On the level?" She fixed him with eyes the color of teak, only without the warmth.

"I swear it on your great-great-grandmother's grave. Or your cousin's. Whatever. It's the truth. Not that it's your business."

"I don't believe you."

He was exhausted suddenly. The exchange had made him forget for a moment his friend's murder, but it all came rushing back into the void that existed between him and the creature seated behind his desk.

They really were polar opposites: He saw money only as a

means to the end of preserving film culture, while she rescued lost films only to finance her extravagant lifestyle. If he started condemning people for that, he wouldn't have forged the professional relationships he needed to continue his crusade. She suspected such altruism and held it in contempt. But she was very good at what she did, maybe the best in the business. Theodosia Burr Goodman was the *bizarro* Valentino.

"Believe what you want, Teddie. Can I call you a cab, or did you park your broom in the garage?"

"That's sexist, and lame besides." She stood, holding her bag. She wasn't as tall as she looked. He'd heard she'd come to town looking for work as a model at the height of the heroin chic craze, but had lacked two inches of the fashion industry standard. If only she'd had those two inches, Valentino thought; if only Major League Baseball had signed Fidel Castro to a pitching staff when he'd tried out. He told her he hoped the Turk enjoyed his chair.

"He doesn't enjoy anything, once he has it. We've got a lot in common." At the door she paused, then looked back at him with the expression of the malicious screen vamp she tried so hard to resemble. "Will you be seeing Lorna Hunter soon, or should I give her your regards?"

His reaction cheered her visibly on the way out.

For a horrible moment he thought (and chastised himself for sinking to Teddie's suspicious level) that he'd been betrayed. But he'd confided his mission only to Broadhead, and Kyle was Fort Knox when it came to keeping a secret under lock and key. He looked at his telephone. He couldn't remember if he'd used it after he'd called Lorna to ask if he could come by that morning.

He settled the question by pressing the redial button.

"This is Lorna Hunter. I can't come to the phone, but I'm

sure you know what to do." The recording sounded heartbreakingly chipper.

"Lorna, it's Valentino."

She picked up. "Val?" Her tone was alert, not fogged with alcohol now. He wasn't as relieved as he'd have been under other circumstances. He should have known his evil twin would think to do the same thing he had in search of answers.

He asked Lorna if someone had tried to call her recently.

"The phone's been ringing all day: reporters, calling about Craig. I don't have caller ID, so I've been letting the machine do all the work. Someone called a little while ago and hung up without leaving a message. Do you know who it was?"

He told her about Teddie. "She can't be trusted. She thinks I'm working on some kind of deal, and no one's better at wheedling out information. The police might consider what I'm doing interfering in their investigation. She'd use it as leverage against me. I don't care so much about that, but I don't want you involved."

"But what would she have to gain? There's no deal."

"She'd never believe that. She thinks everyone has an angle. It would be best if you avoided contact."

"I'm a past master at that, especially lately. But maybe you should let it drop. If you got in trouble over me, I'd never forgive myself."

"I'd be a worse friend than I've been if I let myself be scared off. If you hear my voice on the machine, pick up. I'll only call if I know something or to make sure you're all right."

"I hope you know what you're doing."

"I almost never know what I'm doing until I've done it. It's in my job description."

"You're a good friend, Val. Don't tell yourself any different."

He wished she hadn't said that. After they finished talking, he realized some of the anxiety he'd been feeling came very close to excitement. Under all the grief and regret he'd begun to feel the thrill of the chase. Damn her, Teddie was right. He was working on some kind of deal, and for some reason it involved *Frankenstein*.

The Oracle was all his, thanks to union regulations demanding time-and-a-half for overtime. He made sure all the outside doors were locked and entered the projection booth, only to be reminded that he wasn't alone at all. He was sharing quarters with werewolves, mad scientists, and the walking dead, sprawled across the sofa bed like unwelcome guests. Craig Hunter's portable library leered, hinted, nudged, and cajoled, but did not explain.

Wearily, Valentino gathered some of the books at one end into a stack to make room for himself, then rested them in his lap and selected one. He didn't know if he was looking for answers or just a diversion to settle his swarming thoughts and make him drowsy enough to sleep.

The book was *James Whale's Frankenstein*, part of the Film Classics Library line issued by Universe Books in 1974. The titles were aimed at the hard-core film buff who was accustomed to setting his alarm clock for some wee hour in order to catch a cherished classic on the *Late Late Show*, back when cable and satellite were in their infancy and round-the-clock movie channels a dream. The books featured frames from great vintage motion pictures blown up and presented in sequence, with the actors' lines captioned below in a photo-graphic novel effect, the next best thing to watching the films. Included in the line were *The Maltese Falcon, Ninotchka, Casablanca, Psycho,* and a host of other cinema legends, which had sold briskly for a few years until the first reasonably priced videocassette players appeared in stores. For the first time, amateur aficionados were free to screen any movie or TV show they wanted anytime. The Film Classics Library paled in comparison and was discontinued.

However, scholars like Valentino found it valuable for confirming a spoken line or a visible bit of business without having to fast-forward or backtrack through a tape or disc like a dog chasing an agile rabbit. But after turning a few pages, the movie lover in Valentino kicked in, whetting his appetite to see *Frankenstein* as it was intended to be seen, hearing the voices of the stage-trained cast and catching himself up in the illusion of the moving image. He closed the book, shifted the stack to the floor, and got up to rummage through the essentials of his DVD collection, spared from separate storage and arranged alphabetically by title on the built-in shelves that in The Oracle's glory days had supported big flat cans containing reels of silver-nitrate stock. Those same shelves had yielded a complete print of Erich von Stroheim's *Greed,* the multiple-hour silent masterpiece that had sucked Valentino into the vortex of property ownership and architectural restoration.

He came up with the 75th Anniversary Edition of *Frankenstein,* digitally remastered from the original negative, including scenes censored from 1931 showings and issued in 2006. After inspecting the disc for dust and scratches, he fed it into his DVR, which was connected to the DLP projector mounted on the ceiling and pointed through the aperture of the booth onto the poly screen he'd had installed at the front of the auditorium below. The time would come when in order to maintain the theater he would show real films via the big Bell & Howell to paying audiences, but he'd gone house-hunting to begin with to find a place to live *and* screen movies in all formats to aid him in research.

For the next seventy minutes, Valentino was a boy again, holed up in his bedroom in front of a grainy TV set with his dog resting comfortably in his lap. At times the production values were creaky, and now and then a hole appeared in the plot (How did the Monster find his way back to his creator on Frankenstein's wedding day? How did Ludwig know his daughter had been murdered and not drowned by accident? Why did Frankenstein lock his bride in her room, trapping her, with the Monster on the rampage?); but the buzz and crackle of weird electric gizmos in the brooding laboratory, the plummy vocal tones of theater actors projecting to the last row, and the dramatic, lumbering entrance of Karloff in full makeup and rig thundered over nit-picking details like a juggernaut hurtling downhill, obliterating everything in its path.

When the windmill containing the haunted, hunted creature collapsed in flames and the end credits came on, in a single shot under the heading A GOOD CAST IS WORTH REPEATING, he realized he'd watched the entire picture without once looking for an indication of Craig Hunter's sudden interest in it. And so he watched it again all the way through, this time with the commentary track turned on so he could hear what the experts had to say.

James Whale's direction held up, but at this remove it was obvious that none of the "name" players, the somewhat hammy Colin Clive, the stiff John Boles, and Mae Clarke as Clive's timid love interest, had contributed as much to the film's enduring legend as Jack Pierce's groundbreaking efforts with greasepaint, collodion, and aluminum struts to create a convincing creature assembled from corpses and brought to life, and Boris Karloff's ability, beneath all those layers of artifice and despite having no lines to speak, to move viewers with a deep sense of humanity and pathos. Edward Van Sloan, in a dynamic turn as Clive's mentor (who except for his lack of humor bore a certain resemblance to Kyle Broadhead), made a fine cerebral foil for the furious and bewildered artificial man, who eventually made him his victim, blind brute force destroying wisdom.

During production, after a female employee of Universal fainted at the sight of the actor in full makeup wandering the lot, Carl Laemmle, the head of the studio, had required Pierce to lead Karloff around between scenes with a heavy veil covering his features to avoid frightening any pregnant secretaries into having miscarriages. When the movie opened, ambulances were parked outside theaters in case of heart attacks among the patrons. Such stories smacked of the publicity stunt, but there was no doubt that Depression audiences were shaken by a new kind of talking feature in a landscape of frothy musicals and romantic weepies. Decades of familiarity and an ever-rising bar of cinema shock had sapped the film of much of its power to scare, but it still managed to fascinate on a first viewing, and to satisfy on a tenth. That was the definition of a classic.

But it brought no answers. What was in it for Craig? And if, from what Horace Lysander had said, *Frankenstein* was key, what were biographies and filmographies of Bela Lugosi doing in the suitcase he'd left with his ex-wife? Lugosi had turned down *Frankenstein*, after—

Valentino sat up straight, galvanized by the spark of an idea that had glowed dully much earlier in the day, then gone out. From among the books spread around him he excavated *The Man Behind the Cape,* a Lugosi biography. And found, a quarter of the way through, a long passage underlined in (he had no doubt) Craig's unsteady hand.

I I

WHEN THE HOUSE IS
FILLED WITH DREAD

9

"IT IS GOOD *to see you, Junior."*

The Havana cigar exits the sardonically curved lips just long enough for the Hungarian to finish the greeting, then resumes its place as he grasps the hand belonging to the nervous young man with the long-toothed grin. Those lips, that intense stare, and especially the suave, sinuous accent, have chilled and seduced millions.

"Good morning, Mr. Lugosi. I've been looking forward to this all week."

Carl Laemmle, Jr.—the most powerful man in the room, for all his youth and tiny stature—cannot help but behave like a starstruck fan. The tall Continental in the beautiful black suit towers over him by a foot, and although he is almost invariably cordial, his manner seems aloof, as though he's been a movie star for many years instead of just four months. Few who have met him suspect the truth, that his limited command of English is responsible for his distant manner. The man is shy and somewhat suspicious of being taken advantage of, with good reason: Dracula has saved the studio from bankruptcy, but Bela Lugosi was paid only five hundred dollars for playing the lead.

The young man turns away to welcome the two men who have entered the screening room behind the actor. Cameraman Paul Ivano, the only native-born American of the three, but who affects European ways, bows smartly; there is about the gesture a faint impression of heels clicking. Conversely, Robert Florey, a husky, six-foot-four Frenchman, stoops to pump Laemmle's hand like a bluff Midwesterner. He is one of Hollywood's legendary hosts, whose stock is high with every caterer, florist, and bootlegger in three counties. Both men address the twenty-three-year-old chief of production as Junior: His father, who founded the studio (and incidentally the West Coast motion picture industry), is "Uncle Carl" to everyone at Universal.

Last to arrive—with apologies—is Edward Van Sloan, minus the dignified hairpieces he usually wears on screen. In speech and carriage, the middle-aged actor is every bit the Broadway veteran, enunciating his consonants and accompanying them with broad but graceful gestures. He was in the first wave of talent imported from the eastern stage to lend voice to that frightening new innovation, the soundtrack. Many of the vamps, villains, and male and female leads who made the silent screen glitter cannot speak without demonstrating some accent or impediment inappropriate to their images; some cannot even act.

Junior pardons Van Sloan's tardiness with a shrug. "I expect to enjoy the show. Any test the Catholics tried so hard to stop is bound to be a sensation."

"Pious hypocrites, these special-interest thugs," replies the actor. "When Bela and I did Dracula at the Fulton Theater, we went through a gallon of pig's blood a week, and another pint when we added a second performance on Saturday. The Decency League said not a peep. We didn't spill a single drop in the film, and they came swarming out of the woodwork like—like—"

"Rats!" Lugosi finishes, in a respectable imitation of Dwight Frye's loony Renfield. Laughing, he seizes Van Sloan's hand. They know each other well from months on the road.

Junior's smile slips a notch. "Pious and powerful, don't forget. The pressure's even worse in England, where they have government censorship. Pop's ready to pull the plug on Frankenstein if we lose that market."

"Mary Wollstonecraft Shelley faced the same opposition when she published her book. That was one hundred years ago. Some things don't change. But we have to." Florey, who adapted the novel for his screenplay, taps a cigarette on the gold case it came from and fits it into a holder. "Tell Uncle Carl we can't go on telling stories about sheiks and bullfighters. Pictures talk now; thanks to you."

The round of laughter puzzles Lugosi. Ivano, the cameraman, fills him in, in his studied dialect.

"Junior would have made a splendid second-story man if he weren't born in show business. He circumvented Warner's Vitaphone patent by pilfering their sound equipment right off the lot."

"Under cover of midnight." Van Sloan's intonation is sepulchral.

Junior's grin returns. "Pop was proud as a peacock. He's a bit of a buccaneer himself. He came out here one step ahead of Thomas Edison's Pinkerton detectives. In those days, the Wizard of Menlo Park claimed sole ownership of the motion-picture-making process, and the courts backed him up."

"They told me in Budapest you were all gangsters over here." Lugosi draws thoughtfully on his cigar. "I can see now they were right."

The Hungarian always sounds solemn, even when he's joking. Junior, uncertain, changes the subject.

"How did you get along with the makeup?"

Florey, Ivano, and Van Sloan stiffen, anticipating an explosion. But Lugosi is merely peevish. "That barbarian Jack Pierce wanted to give me a square head. I am an artist, not a scarecrow." *He leans heavily on the makeup expert's name, ending it in a harsh sibilant:* Jock Peerrsss. *The Count would pronounce it just that way.*

"Bela did his own," *Ivano put in.* "It left his face free and took the lighting well."

Junior is a diplomat. "Pierce is an artist too. We don't want people confusing Frankenstein's creation with the boss vampire just because the same actor played both roles."

Florey gestures impatiently with his cigarette. "I'm still on record in opposition to Bela playing the brute. He's much better suited to Frankenstein himself."

"Fortunately, Robert has written me some lovely lines." *Bela blows a series of smoke rings.*

"You should thank Mary. The creature in the novel is quite articulate, and inclined to go on; I could've written sides. I don't suppose you could live with Percy without some of his epic poetry rubbing off on you."

"He goes on a bit as it is. But we'll discuss all that later." *Junior breezes through this dismissal. He's consulted with his father on Florey's script. Carl, Sr., doesn't know Percy Shelley from an act in vaudeville, but he agrees with his son that no one with ears would accept a Hungarian Frankenstein's Monster. They've decided the part will be mute.* "Well, let's see what you've all been up to this past week."

They take their places in plush tan mohair seats trimmed with glistening mahogany, an Art Deco theme introduced by Junior's interior designer, who redid the screening room immediately after Uncle Carl promoted his employer to his present position. The lights dim, the projectionist starts his machine whirring, and a beam of white shoots out and lands on the screen, with the smoke from Florey's cigarette and Lugosi's cigar curling in the shaft.

Director and studio chief watch the jumpy numerals counting down to the first frame with professional eyes, mentally adding editing and laboratory shellac to the rough-cut product to follow. Possibly a musical score; although that's a subject of controversy in this brave new world of the sound feature. Will the audience be distracted, looking around and wondering where the music is coming from? Such a simple invention—a common phonograph record, synchronized to the action onscreen—and so profound in its effect. It has changed everything about the way the business is run, from casting through promotion to distribution. How will Garbo's heavy Swedish accent and hoarse contralto play in Omaha? What will become of Fairbanks-style swashbucklers now that the camera is sealed in a soundproof cell and can no longer follow an actor swinging from a chandelier and bounding from the deck of one pirate ship to another? Can Ramon Novarro deliver a line without sounding like Blanche Sweet? Challenging times. It's no wonder the torch has passed to the Jazz Age Generation.

The screen test begins, on the gloomy Carfax Abbey set lately inhabited by the company of Dracula; if Junior likes what he sees, it will be transformed with painted canvas flats, clever lighting, and young Ken Strickfadden's whiz-bang electric pinball machines into Dr. Frankenstein's laboratory. The five men sit unspeaking throughout the moody creation scene building up to the entrance of the synthetic man: the money shot that will make or break the picture, for in the heart of everyone connected with it lurks the hope of duplicating the sensation of Lon Chaney's *unmasking in* The Phantom of the Opera. *That shot sent millions to bed with all the lights on, and kept Universal solvent throughout the horrendously expensive transition to sound.*

It starts off well. Ivano is a journeyman cinematographer and the scene is a setpiece that adapts comfortably to the camera's enforced incarceration in its bunkerlike enclosure, where the noise of its bearings and cooling fans cannot be recorded by the undiscriminating microphone. The lighting is basic, but serviceable, and the pace appropriate to suspense. Van Sloan is dependable as always. He reads his cynical lines in beautifully rounded tones to the contract player standing in for whoever will take his place in the lead. (Central Casting wants Leslie Howard, but Florey is holding out for someone equally British, but more dynamic. Is Ronald Colman available? Junior, who truly loves movies, wonders if he will ever again be able to watch one without being distracted by better alternatives.)

The tiny audience fidgets while the reels are being changed. Throats are cleared. Commentary of any kind is considered bad luck, in the grand tradition of the theater. Lugosi extinguishes the stub of his cigar with a contented sigh and applies himself to the art and science of igniting another so that it burns evenly. He seems sanguine; who knows what goes on inside the head of an Eastern European, and an actor at that? Dracula, for him, is a contemporary documentary. In the village where he grew up, people did not hang garlands of garlic on their front doors to welcome Father Christmas. Junior clears his throat. It's an ominous sign for Florey and Ivano, fellow Hollywood insiders that they are. Young Laemmle doesn't smoke and is not inclined toward excess phlegm.

The second reel commences to turn. All lean forward as Ivano's camera tracks in tightly on Lugosi in full makeup, the round peasant face framed by a Buster Brown wig blown up to Brob-

dingnagian proportions filling the screen, waxen and still but for the eyes, shifting from side to side with pin-lights reflecting off them, as they had in his signature film; an actor never abandons a trick that worked once. The shot resembles nothing that has ever been seen on film before.

The tense silence is shattered by a strident sound: Junior Laemmle's high-pitched laughter, innocent as a boy's.

An excruciating few seconds ensue: To the end of their lives, Florey, Ivano, and Van Sloan will swear that they seemed like five long minutes. Finally, the last foot of celluloid flutters through the gate like a fish frantically escaping an angler's net.

The lights come up indecently fast. Everyone blinks.

Silence.

Junior springs to his feet, youthful energy incarnate in a five-foot, ninety-pound frame. "I'll have my secretary arrange a conference. Thank you, gentlemen."

In comparison to the awful stillness following the end of the test, the round of handshaking seems lightning fast. Junior's size-six feet in hand-lasted leather actually pitter-patter toward the exit.

Florey, Ivano, and Van Sloan stand with hands in pockets, looking at one another and the blank screen, as if they hold it responsible for what has taken place on its surface.

"Ivano!"

Lugosi's loud baritone makes everyone else jump. He is beaming; no one has seen his face split so wide since the first review broke for Dracula *in* The Hollywood Reporter. *"My close-up was magnificent!"*

He thrusts a fistful of cigars into the cameraman's hand.

Van Sloan, at least, has the presence of mind to respond. "Bela, you were never better."

Lugosi slaps his back—the pair were never that close, throughout their Broadway run and the long trek during the road production, but there is something about Hollywood, the scent of the strange flora on the dry desert air, the bankrolls that seem to grow like coconuts from the palms in an impoverished world— and strides out, trailing dollar clouds of smoke.

"I never got the habit." Ivano offers the cigars to Florey.

The director keeps his hands in his pockets. "Keep the cigars. Burn the film."

10

THE SINGLE METALLIC beep fell so far outside the world of 1931 it snatched him from his dream, alert on the instant. He was sitting on the sofa, Bela Lugosi's biography lying open on his lap to the paragraphs Craig had underlined. The Oracle was dark but for the pool of light belonging to the lamp in the projection booth.

Valentino fumbled his cell phone out of his pocket and read the text message Harriet had left:

2 LATE 2 TALK NITE LUV U

He smiled and began to text her back, but then he saw it was almost 5:00 A.M. If that was late for her, not early, she must have been out all night. He harbored evil thoughts about antiques dealers and ex-FBI agents everywhere, and snapped shut the cell.

To stop thinking about Harriet, he thought about his dream. Harriet had told him he was the only person in the universe who didn't star in his own fantasies; in this case he hadn't even appeared, watching the action the way he watched movies. The lines Craig had marked in *The Man Behind the Cape* dealt with Lugosi's disastrous screen test for *Frankenstein*, but had not included details, apart from Junior Laemmle's laughter when the actor's made-up face appeared and Lugosi's gift of cigars to Paul Ivano over his delight regarding his close-up; the rest, including the conversation, had come from Valentino's own imagination.

Still, the episode must have gone something like what he'd dreamt. Robert Florey had mentioned it a number of times before his death, and Boris Karloff, who had not been present, had provided his own version. Karloff may or may not have seen the test, but he'd described Lugosi's makeup as "hairy, not at all like our dear Monster." Florey had compared it to the claylike features and massive wig worn by Paul Wegener in the German silent feature *Der Golem* in 1920. Whether or not Jack Pierce, the genius who'd created Karloff's iconic look as the Monster, had indeed tried to fit Lugosi with a similar "square head" was conjecture; James Whale, who replaced Florey as director, later insisted that the final product was the result of a collaboration between himself and Pierce. But it was true the star of *Dracula* had not gotten along with the makeup man and his arduous procedures, and that upon learning that he would have no lines to speak as the Monster, had left the production abruptly. He and Florey had then teamed on *The Murders in the Rue Morgue,* a box office bomb in which the star was upstaged by a gorilla. Universal dropped the men and kept the ape.

Robert Florey would have a moderately successful career as an in-house director with other studios, eventually moving to television; but for Bela Lugosi, rejecting the role that made

Karloff's fortune was the beginning of the long slide into Grade
Z pictures, drug addiction, unemployment, and a squalid death.
He was buried in 1956 in the opera cape he'd worn as Count
Dracula, forgotten by Hollywood, while Karloff was enjoying
a comfortable and active old age performing in movies and
on TV.

No one seemed to know what had happened to that two-reel
test. Florey was said to have ordered its destruction, but he
himself would not be drawn out when asked about it later. Valentino's predecessors had hoped it would turn up in the director's estate after his death in 1979, but it had not.

Now he felt that familiar drumroll of mounting excitement.
Had Craig somehow stumbled onto the reels, or guessed they
were in Elizabeth Grundage's possession and offered to cut a
deal with her on their sale? Horace Lysander had said her late
husband Tony had represented the stagehands' and projectionists' unions in Hollywood at the time *Frankenstein* was in production; had the nameless projectionist who screened the test
for Junior Laemmle and the others spirited it away and given it
to Tony in return for some favor that would further his career?

The theory (to flatter it with that term) was shaky even if
he'd had evidence to corroborate it. Why wouldn't Tony have
sold the reels immediately for whatever they were worth? And
if he hadn't and his widow had them, why would she need a
washed-up actor to help her sell them?

There was a possible answer to the second question, but
he'd be going out on a limb to secure it without more information.

He had a brainstorm. He flipped open his cell and had speed-
dialed Kyle Broadhead at his home before he realized Fanta
might be staying over. In the past, he'd been in the habit of calling the professor at all hours, knowing he was an insomniac

and likely to be available. But that was in Broadhead's widower days, before his courtship by a former student who was close to his equal in intelligence and more than his match in spirit. Valentino had his thumb on the END button when someone picked up. He hadn't heard it ring.

"You're no fisherman," Broadhead said in greeting, "so I have to assume you never went to bed. Are you trapped beneath rubble?"

"Rubble, no. Red ink, yes. Are you alone?"

"At this hour a gentleman would answer in the affirmative, regardless of the truth. However, I'm no gentleman. So— yes. My future intended is too busy orchestrating the romantic spectacle of the century to pursue romance. My cardiologist is celebrating."

Valentino told him his suspicions.

"Unlikely," said the other when he'd finished.

"But not impossible."

"I would have said impossible, B.F. But you may take it to mean the same thing now."

B.F.: Before Fanta. "What do you think those two reels are worth, ballpark?"

"The only pre-production poster known to exist hyping Bela Lugosi as the star of *Frankenstein* sold at Christie's a few years ago for a hundred thousand, a record in the escalating vintage-poster market. The possibility that a second might surface kept the bidding from going even higher. But there can't be *two* prints of a failed studio test on silver-nitrate. When you factor in inflation, ten times that figure would be conservative."

"A million dollars."

"Wizard figure, don't you agree? Even with tycoons trading in hundreds of billions and governments in trillions, it still casts a spell. A fanatic with Mark David Turkus' resources would be prepared to pay more."

"I wish you hadn't mentioned him. His pit bull was sniffing around my office yesterday, trying to find out what I'm up to. At the time I didn't know I was up to anything."

"Teddie's more of a ferret. Something in the weasel family, in any case. It isn't unusual for a creature of her type to suspect your motives before you have them."

"I can't fathom a million for thirty minutes of film. *Greed* ran eight hours, and went for a fraction of that. It barely covered The Oracle's new roof."

"*Greed* was straight drama. Adventure, horror, mystery, and science fiction have always been in greater demand. Give a first edition of Burroughs's *Tarzan* another ten years, and it will be worth as much as a Shakespeare First Folio, and *that* had a three-hundred-year head start. We're discussing capitalism, not artistic merit."

Tarzan made him think of Tarzana, and Lorna Hunter there mourning Craig. "I feel like I'm exploiting a friend's tragedy. I didn't go into this looking for buried treasure."

"Nothing says you can't do both. If those reels exist and you manage to get your hands on them, you could write your own ticket with the Turk."

"I'm bound by my position to offer them to UCLA first. But, Kyle, I have to maintain my focus. If it's a choice between finding that test and bringing Craig's murderer to justice—"

"You're not bound by your position to bring anyone to justice. But if you're hell-bent on meddling in things man should leave alone, no one is saying you can't do both. If that material has anything to do with why Hunter was killed, finding the one may include finding the other."

Valentino hesitated. "I can't tell if you're scolding me or giving me your blessing."

"I haven't the moral authority to do either, but if you're going to play Boston Blackie anyway, I want to be in on the game."

"But what will Fanta say?"

"I'm a grown man, and reasonably free of dementia. The question is irrelevant."

"That's funny. Seriously, what will she say?"

"She'll say, 'That's nice; have fun.' She's preoccupied with French lace and baby's breath, which is the most revolting name for a flower one could possibly imagine. Women have been plotting and planning these barbaric rites since Charlemagne was in short pants; you could unplug one bridegroom and plug another in his place without even slowing the machinery. I'm neglected and bored. Any change of pace is welcome."

"What about your book?"

"Undiverting. Méliés and Moliere are indistinguishable from each other at this point. My computer program almost crashed the other day, threatening to wipe out the work of months. It was the most entertainment I'd had since I started the book."

"Kyle, I wouldn't dream of risking death or imprisonment with anyone else."

"Thank you, Val." He sounded genuinely touched. "What will this be, the third police department whose rules we've flouted?"

"Yes, but there are so many in the area." He smiled into the phone. "You know, that speech about meddling in things man should leave alone isn't from *Frankenstein*. It's from *The Invisible Man*."

"I was aware of that. I selected it because it was a Whale project." Broadhead went on without pausing. "If Hunter hoped to enlist Elizabeth Grundage as his partner, he must have had something to bring to the table. A prospective buyer."

"I thought of that. Could it be Turkus?"

"Not if what you suspected about Teddie is right, and she's just nosing around. She'd have been in on the deal from the first and way ahead of you. Think of someone else with interest in the subject and the capital required."

Inspiration flashed. "Who bought that Lugosi *Frankenstein* poster at Christie's?"

"I was hoping you'd say that before I suggested it. Collectors are completists: One purchase in a specific area leads inevitably to others. It was J. Arthur Greenwood. I feel certain you know the name."

"I've known it practically all my life. Isn't he retired?"

"Giving him ample free time to let his collectors' mania run rampant. His place in Beverly Hills is a museum. Fortunately, you shouldn't have much trouble wangling an invitation. When these packrats aren't actually scrounging for more arcane bric-a-brac, they're hunting for a fresh pair of eyes to appreciate their plunder."

Valentino knew that feeling. He'd had it himself often, in the days before he began dismantling his collection to raise money to continue work on the theater. "I don't suppose you have his number."

"The man is listed, can you believe it? He *encourages* communication with readers who raised themselves on his magazine. I understand he made personal arrangements with the chamber of commerce to include his address on all the tour bus routes."

"Thanks, Kyle. I'll call him later this morning."

"When you do, remember to keep your eyes on the prize.

Once you film freaks get together, you talk about everything but what you came for."

He thanked him for the advice and said good-bye. Nobody knew more about film than Broadhead, but he parked his interest at the office. Striking up a conversation with him on the subject outside business hours was like trying to hitch a ride with a cab driver after his shift was over.

With a clear course of action ahead of him, Valentino felt drowsy enough to sleep without wrestling the linens. He cleared the rest of the books off the sofa, unfolded it into a bed, undressed, and spent the next two hours in a state of complete unconsciousness, without dreaming about dead actors and real-life episodes he had not witnessed. When he awoke, he remembered Harriet's text message and frowned. He texted her back:

4:30 2 EARLY 2 B LATE

But he didn't send it. He cleared the screen and wrote:

LUV U 2 GOT 2 RUN

This one he sent. He could talk to her about her night later. She probably had a good explanation, and if she didn't, he wasn't going to be one of those techno-poops who fought by e-mail.

J. Arthur Greenwood was listed, sure enough. The retired publisher had built his empire around *Horrorwood,* a fan magazine filled with fun facts and iconic stills connected with weird and fantastic movies beginning with the nickelodeon era and continuing through all the *Friday the 13th*s and *Texas Chainsaw Massacre*s, until the material got too gorily graphic for a man who revered the classics. Many years after he'd sold out to a bigger chain, he'd continued to add to his world-class collection of horror and science fiction film props, posters, and press kits, and corresponded with the children and grandchildren of the original baby boomers who'd discovered their frightening favorites through his publications.

In his eagerness to get to the bottom of the mystery, Valentino dialed the number before he remembered it was seven A.M., far too early to be calling a resident of Beverly Hills. But the voice that came on sounded alert. "Yes?"

"Is Mr. Greenwood available?"

"Speaking."

The voice was uncannily youthful for a man in his eighties. He proceeded cautiously, in case he'd connected with a son or grandson. "Sir, my name is Valentino."

"The fashion designer, or another? Certainly not *the* Valentino. The telephone rates from the Other Side are monstrous on weekdays."

The pleasant amused rumble convinced him he'd reached J. Arthur himself; his jokey sense of humor and reliance on puns had unnerved his early financial backers, who'd considered his target audience to be dead serious on their subject of interest, but he'd held out, and won the affection of tens of thousands of readers.

Valentino told him who he was. "At the moment, sir, I'm on the trail of a certain film property that you may know something about."

"That hardly narrows it down. What property?"

"I'd rather discuss it in person, if you don't mind."

"You're with UCLA, you said?"

"Yes, sir."

"I hadn't realized the competition in academics was so cutthroat. Is USC tapping your phone?"

"I'm afraid this has to do with a police case."

The pause on the other end lasted a nanosecond long enough for Valentino to wonder if he'd frightened Greenwood off. But when he responded, the voice that was so much younger than the man was even.

"If this has to do with Craig Hunter, I can see you here at eight o'clock."

11

J. ARTHUR GREENWOOD had turned his house into a museum; not that it hadn't been one for many years before he'd acquired it.

It was one of the few remaining mansions built by a generation of actors who'd earned four-figure salaries by the week and paid very little in income taxes. Most of the silent stars' homes had been dozed and replaced by housing developments, condos, and (as was the case in Beverly Hills) even larger and more opulent monstrosities sheltering highly successful producers, dot-com billionaires, and the occasional Arab sheikh, but Specs O'Neill's sprawling stucco-and-tile Spanish Modern mansion remained, owned and leased by a succession of later movie and television players, some of whom had remodeled the interior beyond all recognition. The ballroom where Nazimova had danced with Rod La Rocque had been partitioned off to make guest suites, the walls of the servants' quarters had been torn down to create an indoor spa, and the baronial dining hall where Oscar Levant had notoriously thrown a sloe gin fizz into the face of Miriam Hopkins had been retrofitted into a screening room; O'Neill's original screening room having been converted into several nurseries to stack a later star couple's litters of children adopted from Third World countries. Upon his retirement, the current owner had realigned everything to display the accumulated memorabilia of a lifetime, most of which had spent decades in storage.

The estate had once occupied twelve acres, most of which had been sold off to take advantage of skyrocketing local real-estate values. Finally, a sexagenarian British-invasion rock star had filled in the Olympic-size swimming pool with concrete and erected in its place an open-air recording studio, all the better to judge the sound quality of concerts in MacArthur Park. As Valentino passed it on the way from his car to the front door, he saw a bevy of laborers mixing cement and pounding the existing concrete with jackhammers, preparing yet another metamorphosis for some later tenant to veto and turn into something more ghastly yet.

Specs O'Neill, the original owner and builder, was a silent-screen comic once regarded as a contender for the throne of King of Comedy, on a par with Charlie Chaplin and Buster Keaton. His trademark Coke-bottle glasses and nearsighted "Mr. Magoo" shtick were no longer politically correct, but in their heyday had rolled audiences in the aisles. They'd failed to translate to talkies. He'd lost most of his fortune in the 1929 crash, and the Depression had reduced him to manual labor in order to keep up his alimony payments to three ex-wives. In his later years he'd supported himself sporadically as an expert consultant in comedy film productions, but the job was basically a bone thrown his way by film school directors motivated by nostalgia and pity, and by that time he was living in a trailer on Long Beach. He'd died in 1970 from a combination of old age, pneumonia, and complications of alcoholism. Valentino, who'd been instrumental in securing and restoring a dozen of his Mack Sennett comedy shorts, had found them hilarious and timeless; but the PC wheel would have to take another full turn before timid distributors allowed them to be released to DVD, or whatever jazzy new format took its place in the interim.

Specs was just one more of the pioneers who'd been exalted, then humbled, then ground up into compost by an ungrateful Hollywood. It hadn't been a new story when Billy Wilder exposed it in *Sunset Boulevard* in 1950, and it was far from over. Craig Hunter was its latest victim. *Entertainment Tonight* and its television-tabloid clones had already buried him and moved on to the next tragedy ripe for exploitation. That was good for Lorna's privacy, but bad when it came to summing up a man's life. Probably he wasn't even bankable enough to make the *In Memoriam* feature at the next Oscars.

The doorbell button was a tiny grinning skull exquisitely carved from ivory and set in bronze. When he pressed it, a recording of a virile organ playing Bach's "Toccata and Fugue in D minor" issued forth. Lon Chaney played it every Halloween when a revival theater screened *The Phantom of the Opera.* Valentino planted his thumb where Vincent Price had planted his, as well as Christopher Lee and Elvira, Mistress of the Dark.

After fifteen seconds the door opened, appropriately on creaking hinges. Valentino thought at first the figure standing inside the frame was a dummy, something one could procure at any of the pricier novelty shops that appeared every October on the Sunset Strip and vanished November 1, powered by batteries and howling prerecorded Halloween greetings. But this figure was flesh and blood, seven feet tall in a white houseboy's coat, tuxedo trousers with stripes on the sides, and white hair worn in bangs like Andy Warhol's famous plastic wig. His face was fully as pale, sunken-cheeked, with pink eyes rimmed by transparent lashes: a true albino, or whatever it was they preferred to be called these days. "*Genetic freak*" would not be it.

"Yes?" J. Arthur Greenwood's own greeting, delivered in a *basso profundo* that was intended to sound as if it had emerged from the crypt. Greenwood himself could not have approached it without his youthful tremolo betraying him.

"Valentino. I have an appointment."

The lofty white head bowed and the figure pivoted to make room in the doorway. "Enter freely, and of your own will."

The foyer, as cavernous as it had been during the O'Neill residency (Valentino had seen pictures in an ancient copy of *Photoplay*), was tiled in black-and-white checkerboard marble, with framed original artwork for covers of *Horrorwood* illuminated in recessed arches in the walls that had once displayed the Irish Catholic comic's plaster saints. They were expert renderings in oil of Lon Chaney, Jr.'s Wolf Man, Karloff's Mummy and Frankenstein Monster, Lugosi's Dracula, Gale Sondergaard's Spider Woman, and the whole menagerie of gorillas, dinosaurs, blobs, alien invaders, and giant bugs that had crawled, slithered, stomped, and swooped through the backlot of every studio, major and minor, since pictures began to move.

"This way, please."

The pallid giant led him past a grand staircase and down a corridor lined with first-issue movie posters mounted in archival frames, the images glowering and snarling at him across the decades. Valentino noticed two things apart from the décor: the presence at both ends of the hallway of surveillance cameras with angry red lights, and the fact that his guide wore shoes with built-up heels that elevated him beyond his already preternatural height. Whatever his eccentricities, the retired

publisher placed as much importance upon protecting his pos-
sessions from thieves as he did upon presenting them in the
most dramatic settings, both architectural and human.

The door at the end of the corridor, the visitor felt sure, had
not come with the house. It was made of dark oak planks pit-
ted with wormholes, with a brass ring the size of a man's head
serving as a knocker, heavily coated with verdigris. It looked
eerily familiar. He decided he'd seen it in many an A and B
thriller; selected, in the latter case, to match new footage shot
on the sets of catacombs and castles with stock bought from
productions with bigger budgets.

Greenwood, Valentino decided, had acquired much of his
collection from the same auctions and estate sales the archivist himself had attended, and yet the two had never met.
Probably the publisher had placed his bids by telephone through
intermediaries, to keep the figures manageable. Reserve bids
and fixed prices had a way of being artificially inflated once a
wealthy hobbyist's interest was known.

The knocker made a reverberating boom when the albino
used it, although nowhere near as resonant as after an experienced Foley artist got hold of the soundtrack in post-production.
The light, friendly voice the visitor had heard on the telephone
invited him to enter.

The man turned a handle forged from iron and coated with
rust; or some paint that aped the effect. Hinges creaked again
as he pushed the door inward. "Mr. Valentino, sir."

The room was surprisingly cheerful—Valentino had expected a dank dungeon—with French doors letting in plenty
of sunlight through sparkling panes and an impressive display
of tropical flowers flourishing in a garden outside. The walls
were painted a warm white, apparently so they wouldn't distract the visitor from the room's exhibits, arranged on built-in

glass shelves and spotted about among comfortable-looking chairs and sofas upholstered in what appeared to be watered silk. There were photos in stand-up frames of smiling movie stars, most of them now deceased and all of the pictures inscribed to Greenwood; ray guns; carved Tiki gods; wooden mallets and stakes for vampire hunting; a *Star Wars* Stormtrooper helmet; swords and daggers of every description; a splendid four-foot miniature of the tramp steamer that had brought the original King Kong to civilization, probably used for long shots in the movie; and hosts of exotic and sometimes unidentifiable properties even Valentino couldn't link to a particular film, and he flattered himself that he'd seen them all. A cluster of shrunken heads hung by their hair from the ceiling in a corner, like ornamental balls advertising a pawnbroker's shop. A ten-foot robotic sculpture stood silent sentinel in another corner: a stand-in for the fearsome Gort in the first *Day the Earth Stood Still*.

"Welcome to my depressurization tank. I come here to unwind whenever life in L.A. gets too bizarre even for me."

The young voice issued from an octogenarian dressed like old Hollywood, in a paisley dressing gown over flannel trousers and a foulard knotted loosely around his crepey neck, the ends tucked inside the collar of a salmon-colored silk shirt. Italian loafers gleamed softly on his rather small feet.

Greenwood was a large man in spite of them, and burly, with a fine head of hair slicked back and dyed—as was his pencil moustache—a disconcerting shade of black. It called attention to the lines and sagging flesh of his face; but inside the cobwebby wrinkles that surrounded them glittered the bright eyes of a happy child. He rose from his chair with the help of an ebony cane with a silver handle shaped like a wolf's head (was it the same weapon Claude Rains had used to kill his son the werewolf in *The Wolf Man*?), and took his visitor's hand in a firm grip.

"Thank you for seeing me, Mr. Greenwood."

"Thank *you*. I've bored everyone I know with my interests. A fresh victim is always welcome. That will be all, Ronald."

The tall albino inclined his head and backed through the doorway, pulling the door shut. Greenwood watched Valentino's gaze follow him out. He smiled, showing a set of teeth younger than anything in the room.

"I found Ronald waiting tables at Olive Garden. They put him on only when they were short-handed. His appearance frightened some customers out of their appetites. Do you think I'm exploiting his unique physical characteristics?"

"That's not for me to say, sir."

"Well, I am; but I suspect he's happier being employed because of them rather than in spite of them, and he doesn't have to survive on tips."

Valentino smiled politely but said nothing. His work had taken him to many a wealthy household, but he had very little in common with people who hired other people to answer their doorbells.

"Excuse me one moment." Greenwood circled behind his chair and raised the ferrule of his cane to press a button set flush to the wall beside one of the display cases. Something made a whirring noise and a heavy pair of drapes, as plain as the walls, closed over the French doors, leaving the room illuminated only by canister lamps in the ceiling. The publisher's smile narrowed a fraction. "I hope you're not easily spooked."

"Not by anything in this room."

"Well said, and honest. You'd be surprised how many people who claim to be fearless find pressing appointments elsewhere once they're shut up in here."

As a matter of fact, the enclosure with its grotesque *objets d'art* took on a far more macabre mien without the reassuring presence of sunlight, but the visitor found it not at all unpleasant. It reminded him of the pictures on the pages of *Horrorwood,* and of happy childhood hours spent lost in them.

"I'm paranoid about discussing the collecting business in front of an exposed window," Greenwood said. "There are spies everywhere. I've lost opportunities because of them."

Teddie Goodman came to mind. "There's nothing quite so lost as a lost opportunity."

"Exactly! It's odd, really: I sometimes forget just what I have, but I never forget the things I missed. They ache like amputated fingers."

His guest found himself grinning. This was an area of interest they shared in spades.

Greenwood conducted him on a tour of the room, beginning with his cane, which he said was one of three that Lon Chaney, Jr. carried in *The Wolf Man.* Chaney had broken one, misjudging his weight, and Claude Rains had shattered another in an early take when he missed Chaney's stunt double at the film's climax and struck a tree. Valentino touched the shrunken heads from *Jivaro,* relieved to learn that they were cast from rubber, although the hair was real, obtained from a horse's mane and tail. The weight of a gargoyle from *The Hunchback of Notre Dame* surprised him: It was papier-mâché filled with sand. There was, of course, a story for every piece, and the visitor was loath to interrupt him in order to get to the subject of his visit. He realized that for all his riches and bright spirits, the publisher was a lonely old man, starving for a fresh audience to show all his stuff. The seamed face fell, but only for a moment. Greenwood indicated the end of a sofa set at a right angle to his chair.

When they were seated, his eyes grew even brighter. He flushed deeply and leaned forward to grip Valentino's knee. "Tell me all you know about those test reels," he said. "I'd kill for them."

12

"YOU'RE EXAGGERATING, OF course," Valentino said.

"Am I?"

Greenwood's grasp was cutting off circulation in his leg. He took hold of the publisher's hand firmly and pried it loose. "If you are, it's inappropriate. If you're serious, you should be having this conversation with Sergeant Ernest Gill and Detective John Yellowfern of the San Diego Police. I think Craig Hunter *was* killed for those test reels."

The collector's madness faded from the eyes of his host, replaced by the gentility of old age. "Please forgive me. I'd heard about the murder on the news this morning, but I didn't realize you were close to the victim."

"Did you know him?"

"He was one of my last interviews for the magazine, on the set of *Bloodbath IV*. I didn't see him again until somebody brought him to one of my occasional poker parties. He was looking for a game, and he had cash. I should have turned him away."

"Why?"

"He wasn't the same pleasant young actor I'd met years ago. He was a bad loser, and griped about all the small talk during what was supposed to be a friendly game. He especially disparaged my collection. 'Kiddie rot,' he called horror films."

"Did you invite him back?"

"I'm uncomfortable with scenes, particularly in my own house. I had hoped he'd lose interest, but he showed up three more times. Also he was into me for a bundle. I consider myself a man of honor, and expect others to live up to their obligations as well. But he kept losing and giving me markers."

Valentino shifted gears. "What do you know about the *Frankenstein* test?"

"I'll wager I know more than you. Do you want to go into its history?"

"I'm more interested in where it is now. Mr. Greenwood, were you behind Hunter's offer to buy it from Elizabeth Grundage?"

"Was that who he was negotiating with? He never mentioned any names, only that he was sure who had the reels. I assume she's related to Mike Grundage. They said on the news he was being questioned."

"Craig approached you?"

"Yes. He owed me a lot of money, as I said, and he offered to front for me in return for tearing up his markers. Ever since I bought the *Frankenstein* poster, everyone assumes I'd pay any outlandish price for rare items. If it got out I was interested in this particular property, I'd be out a million, and lucky at that. Naturally, I agreed to his proposition."

"You took his word for it that he knew where the test could be obtained?"

"I told you I'm a poker player. I can see through most bluffs."

"Sir, I knew Craig better than you. Gambling was only one of his addictions. Addicts are practiced at lying to get what they want in order to maintain their habit. Also, he was an actor."

Greenwood twirled his cane, frowning. "You're calling my hand. Very well. I knew he was telling the truth, because he showed me a piece of the film."

"He *had* it?" Valentino's heart turned a somersault in his chest.

The publisher leaned his cane against the side of his chair and raised his hands, holding them roughly six inches apart. "Six frames, exposed onto safety stock from the original. I put on my best pair of reading glasses and held them up to the light. He chose Bela Lugosi's close-up. The wig was as outlandish as I'm sure you've heard—a throw-forward, if there's such a word, to an era of really cheesy visuals in horror films—but there was no mistaking those features, especially the eyes."

His lips pursed, poking out the ends of his moustache like a staple coming loose. "His face was all wrong for Count Dracula, you know, although of course he owned the role from 1927 on, from the time he first appeared onstage in the cape until they buried him in it. It was a round, peasant sort of face, not at all aristocratic. But the eyes were mesmerizing. They still manage to transfix every member of the audience as if he's looking at each alone. They didn't really need those pin-lights in *Dracula*. Do you remember him in *Frankenstein Meets the Wolf Man*?"

"Unfortunately, yes." A dozen years after Lugosi had haughtily turned down the role of the Monster, his deteriorating financial circumstances had forced him to step in as the third actor to wear the flat headpiece and spikes in his neck. Kind critics had assigned his disappointing performance to a change in the original script that had rendered it meaningless.

"I'm not referring to his tragic overall effort. There's a moment near the end, when he's on the operating table, and the dumb-cluck mad scientist of the piece is feeding him electricity through the electrodes in his neck. You see his eyelids flicker, and an evil spark comes to his eyes. No pin-lights this time; the special effect came from deep inside the soul of a hideously underrated artist. You remember the moment?"

"I do, sir. Yes, I do." It was one of the seminal moments of his life, experienced during one of the last afternoon movie broadcasts during the transition to cable; he'd run home from school to watch it. He hadn't known then it was a disappointing attenuation of a franchise that had started out with such bold promise, only that it was an entertaining circus of crackling electrical equipment, men turning into beasts, and castles with squat turrets that were like nothing to be seen in Fox Forage, Indiana. It was a moment best left to adolescent memory, like a beloved children's book that didn't hold up under the cold light of adulthood. Valentino had often wished that he could see it again as he had that first time, before he learned how to spot stunt doubles and Raggedy-Ann dummies being flung off steep cliffs.

Greenwood seemed to see what Valentino saw when he conjured up his mind's eye. "Well, that's what was on that brief strip of static film: Lugosi's incandescent soul, caught in a jar. No one on earth could replicate it. I'm as sure as I'm sitting here that that screen test exists, at least in part."

He almost didn't want to ask the question, because he was sure he knew the answer. "Did he leave the strip with you?"

"No, and I'm just as sorry about that as you are. He conducted business the same way he played cards, keeping everything close to his chest."

"One of my sources says Craig was very excited over a call

he made not long before he was killed. It was to someone close to the Grundage family. He said something about being set for life, or words to that effect. That doesn't sound like a man who was merely paying off a gambling debt."

"You seem to know a good deal more about the case than what was on the news."

Valentino realized he'd tipped his hand, to borrow Greenwood's poker language. He knew a showdown with the police over his amateur detective work was inevitable, but he wanted to put it off as long as possible. "The news isn't reporting everything the authorities know." That at least was probably not a lie.

"Are you suggesting Hunter was planning to hold me up for more money once he'd bought those reels on my behalf?"

"I hate to speak poorly of someone who was once my friend, but an addict is capable of just about anything."

"And here I was considering paying him a finder's fee for a job well done. Well, I've been a young fool and a middle-aged fool. I guess it was time I was an old fool."

"No fool ever built an empire from the ground up, as you did. Mr. Greenwood, I doubt very much you overlooked the possibility of a double cross."

The publisher had his cane in hand again. He studied the ornately cast silver wolf's head. "What you're saying is I beat him to death with this stick when the subject of extortion came up, and took the film off him."

"He wasn't so far gone he couldn't fight off a man more than twice his age, whatever sort of bludgeon you had."

"*Now* who's playing the fool? People in my tax bracket don't commit their own murders."

"Someone went to the trouble of breaking both his arms above the elbows to make it look like Mike Grundage was involved. I believed you when you said you didn't know who had the film. Craig wouldn't have told you, in case you decided to make an end run around him and buy it directly, and if you found out on your own, I believe that's just what you'd have done, regardless of the markup. You wouldn't take the chance of Craig offering it to someone else with a bigger bankroll: Mark David Turkus, for instance. Why pick Grundage to frame if you didn't know he was involved?"

Greenwood said, "For someone who spends all his time assembling pictures of dead people, you show a lot of knowledge about human nature."

"I often have to deal with the living in order to resuscitate the dead."

"If I didn't already know all the lines by heart, I'd swear you were quoting an old horror movie."

"It sounded a little purple when I said it, sir. It must be the surroundings."

The publisher smiled fleetingly. "You're right, of course, about just how far I trusted Hunter. He said the owner was reluctant to sell; that was just to boost the price. Having that strip meant he had the whole film, as no one hostile to the idea would bother to provide the go-between with proof it existed. You understand I had to string him along until I could figure out how to get him to part with it without my having to sell the farm."

"And the answer was . . . ?"

"I was still working on it when I heard he was dead. A true collector leads with his heart, not his head. Would you like to see where it led me most recently?"

Valentino nodded, not sure where the man was going. Greenwood levered himself up and approached one of the built-in cabinets loaded with eerie bric-a-brac. He manipulated a hidden

switch. Again something whirred, and the cabinet slid side-
ways, disappearing into a pocket in the wall. In the recess left
behind, a fluorescent light flickered on, setting aglow the
stone-lithograph image encased in Plexiglas within. A gigantic
man towering over a city's skyscrapers stood half-crouched in
the center of the poster, scooping up ordinary-size humans
with both hands and shooting what appeared to be laser shafts
from its eyes into the panicking crowd at his feet. The painting
seemed to anticipate both King Kong and Superman, and certainly bore no resemblance to anything in Mary Shelley's *Frankenstein*. Yet there was that electrifying name, splashed across
the top in bilious yellow letters, and beneath it and to one side,
in a color-matched box, the legend:

> "*. . . no man has ever*
> *seen his like . . . no*
> *woman ever felt his*
> *white-hot kiss . . .*"
> *Surpasses in THRILLS even*
> *DRACULA . . . world's*
> *greatest hold over picture*
> *for 1930 . . . with*
> > *BELA*
> > *LUGOSI*
> *Dracula himself . . . as the*
> *leading spine-chiller . . .*
> *as a story it has thrilled*
> *the world for years.*

The archivist had seen the poster reproduced many times,
the last time in a full-color catalogue issued by Christie's auction house, but that was nothing compared to standing before

the original. The inevitable closed tears and deterioration in the creases where it had been folded for shipping contributed to, rather than subtracted from, the effect; Valentino had learned to suspect items of this nature that seemed too pristine in the age of laser copying. The colors remained startlingly vibrant, and such reds and yellows were no longer seen outside vintage ephemera. The bases of the dyes had been found to be toxic or something and banned in most countries of the world. He had no doubt it was genuine.

It had been advertised as the only known poster announcing Lugosi as the star of *Frankenstein* before he left the project. As a preproduction component, it may have been the only one ever made. The original artwork had probably been destroyed, the printing plates washed and recycled for the next project: Few in 1931 had thought such things would ever be as valuable as storage space. Christie's had expected it would sell for between forty and sixty thousand dollars. Greenwood had bid a hundred thousand, securing ownership and establishing a record in the poster market, which had risen steadily ever since the pop-culture revolution of the 1960s.

"Atrocious, isn't it?" Greenwood said, gazing at it. "The artist obviously had never read the book. I doubt he even knew what it was about. The creature doesn't even look like Lugosi; more like John Hodiak, who was about fifteen at the time and couldn't have been the model. Of course, no one knew then whether Lugosi would be playing Dr. Frankenstein or the Monster, which gave the illustrator a blank slate, so to speak. I often wonder if the hacks who committed that Japanese atrocity *Frankenstein Conquers the World* in 1968 weren't influenced by this image. No one saw a sixty-foot Monster on film until then. It was Nick Adams' last picture. He killed himself not long after it wrapped."

"So many tragedies connected with the character."

"Isn't it the truth? James Whale drowned himself, Colin Clive drank himself to death, Dwight Frye wound up in the gutter, remembered only as Dracula's Renfield and Frankenstein's hunchback. Valerie Hobson married high, but through no fault of her own found herself in the center of a sex scandal that brought down the British government. Maria Ouspenskaya, the gypsy woman, died smoking in bed, and of course we all know what happened to Lugosi."

"And now Craig Hunter."

Greenwood operated the switch, sealing off the poster. "Hammer Films was right. There is a Curse of Frankenstein."

"I suppose any franchise that has continued so long is bound to have its share of sad ends."

"Happy ones, too." The publisher stroked the head of a fine alabaster bust of Boris Karloff *sans* makeup, as if for luck. "I saw the first one in a neighborhood theater when I was a boy. I identified with the Monster, who couldn't help what he was, but was persecuted by ignorant villagers because he was different. I was a fat kid with asthma, a bully magnet. I couldn't defend myself, but that poor clumsy brute with clodhopper feet could and did. I found justice there in the dark. Outside, I couldn't even smack a wasp. Still can't."

Valentino wanted to believe him, but he thought the man was working too hard to sell himself as an innocent. "Can you think of anyone who'd want that footage badly enough to kill for it?"

"Dozens, but they'd have to know Hunter had it."

"You might not have been the only customer he had lined up. Maybe he was running an auction of his own."

He left Beverly Hills thinking that at least he knew now what he'd only suspected before: Craig Hunter had had the *Frankenstein* test. But what good was that? Acting on evidence wasn't much better than playing a hunch. He wondered if he should go to Gill and Yellowfern with what he'd learned, take his medicine for interfering in an official investigation, and let them do the job they were trained for. The more questions he asked, the more convinced he was that Craig had engineered his own fate through greed, and once he'd found out how deep in the hole he was, had unreasonably called upon the last friend he had to dig him out. Even a lost cause like Craig wouldn't expect him to take things further than he had already. Lorna herself had offered to release him from his promise.

He took out his cell, hesitating before he called the operator to connect him with the San Diego Police Department. He'd gotten himself into serious trouble once for trying to keep a precious film property out of the corrosive atmosphere of an evidence room. Was he being inconsistent in the case of the *Frankenstein* test? Was consistency important?

He was still deliberating, driving with his thumb hovering over the 0, when the cell rang. The screen read UNKNOWN CALLER. He often ignored such calls, which were usually from sneaky telemarketers. This time he took it, for no other reason than to postpone his decision.

"Valentino?" A cold sort of voice, not mean or cruel, although he instinctively guessed it could be without effort.

"Who's calling, please?"

"I asked first."

"This is Valentino. Your turn." He had little patience with people who knew nothing of telephone etiquette.

"My name is Mike Grundage. The reason I'm just now getting around to calling you is I just came away from another visit with the police, second morning in a row. Before that, I didn't know you existed."

Valentino pulled into a loading zone in front of a restaurant. He couldn't drive and have a conversation with a notorious underworld character at the same time.

"I think you know what this is about," Grundage said.

"I only know someone I once knew is dead."

"There's a lot of that going around. When can you be in San Diego?"

"That's a two-and-a-half-hour drive."

"I didn't ask for travelers' information."

It was barely mid-morning, but he had to consult with someone. "I can be there tonight, but I need to know if it's worth the trip." He heard his own voice shaking. He hoped it sounded like a bad connection on the other end.

"You're with some college, right?"

"UCLA. Film Preservation Department."

"Colleges are always looking for money. I can swing some your way, strictly legit. No greasy bills tied with rubber bands." His voice didn't warm up when it chuckled. "It doesn't all have to go on the books, though, if you get my drift."

"I'm not interested in personal profit, Mr. Grundage. I want to know about Craig Hunter, and what happened to something he had in his possession."

"I want to know about Hunter myself. I shouldn't have to tell you the reason for that. About the other, well, you can clear up a lot just talking."

"Where do you want to meet?"

"Little place called the Grotto. It's on E Street. Miss it, you're in the bay. Eight o'clock."

Valentino's temperature dropped. "That's the bar where Hunter was killed."

"Tavern. They serve food too. His body wound up there, sure enough. Another pain in the hip pockets. Business is down, but it'll pick up."

"So you do own the Grotto."

"Come hungry. The Chicken Cordon Bleu's from an old family recipe. You'll be glad you had it."

13

BROADHEAD SAID, "I'M going with you."

Fanta said, "No, you're not. You won't fly, and you get carsick after twenty minutes."

Valentino had caught the pair together in Broadhead's office, rare event. Something that looked like a large-scale map of the Salisbury Plain, complete with Stonehenge, turned out to be a seating chart for the wedding reception, spread out on the desk and spilling off the edges. The professor sat back making gurgling noises in the stem of his pipe while Fanta stood with a finger still planted on some sketched feature, like a general studying a battle plan.

"My dear young lady," Broadhead said, "I hiked across Manchuria, assembling documentary footage of Mao's Long March. I don't even like chow mein."

"You were my age. And you said you liked my chow mein."

"I wasn't under oath. *Now* who's kvetching about the age difference?"

"*I* don't care, but you'd slow Val down having to stop and

puke every few miles. Who knows how a gangster will react if he's late for dinner?"

Valentino always enjoyed watching them bicker. "He might resent having to nuke the Chicken Cordon Bleu."

"That's another thing. Eighty years of mob movies says all they eat is linguini and lasagna. What's he say when he puts someone on the spot, *Au revoir*?"

Fanta ignored him. "What did Harriet say?"

"I can't reach her. She must be in a seminar."

"Text her."

"I doubt I can get it all on that tiny screen."

She took her finger from the seating chart and stabbed it at him. "Take dictation: WE NEED 2 TALK."

Broadhead said, "Only girls leave that message."

She moved so swiftly Valentino missed it. He heard a crack and she was pointing at him again, Broadhead rubbing at the pink print of her palm on the side of his face. "Send it. When she takes delivery on a fish wrapped in your sweatshirt, she'll want to know what part I had in it."

"You know, you could give an old man a stroke, hitting him like that."

"Shut up, Kyle." She glared at Valentino until he finished sending the text. "What about the police?"

"I almost called them. But if they get to those test reels first, you know what will happen to them."

"Déjà vu. *Greed*. It's how we met." She blew a gust of air and started folding up the chart. "Someone should go with you, but it isn't Kyle, and it isn't me. I've canceled two appointments already with the director of the chapel. If I miss tonight, there's just the Strikes 'n' Spares. It's a combination bowling alley and rib joint. The rate at which all the movie stars divorce, shuffle, and remarry, you can't find a venue this side of Encino."

"What's wrong with Encino?" Broadhead asked.

"Hell-o." She opened her mouth and jabbed her finger down her throat. "Every twenty minutes."

Valentino said, "I'd call Henry Anklemire in Information Services, but before I got halfway down the coast I'd aim the car at a telephone pole just to shut him up."

"Even if you got there, Grundage would whack you both the minute the little flack tried to sell him the Golden Gate Bridge. But none of these suggestions would intimidate a thug. He'd do you both in a heartbeat."

Fanta shook her head. "You're not thinking like a lawyer. This isn't Chicago 1929. One body's bad enough: Grundage wouldn't be so anxious to meet if Hunter weren't a serious inconvenience. A second body—or a mysterious disappearance—would turn up the heat, although maybe not enough to stop him from acting the way thugs act from instinct. A third might give him pause. It tips the odds more in Val's favor."

Broadhead unscrewed and reassembled his pipe, often a sign he'd found need to attempt a puzzle he couldn't handle comfortably. "But who? We're two academics and a lawyer. Not exactly Friend material on Facebook."

Someone tapped on the door. The professor barked an invitation.

Jason Stickley opened the door and poked his head inside. He wore his mysterious costume, complete with chain and padlock dangling outside his Victorian morning coat and top hat, with an assortment of gears and cogs attached to the crown and his eyes obscured behind a pair of black rubber goggles. The young intern peered from face to face, as if the scratched and discolored eyepieces made it difficult to distinguish one from another. At last he focused on Valentino.

"Ruth said you were in here," he said. "I've got another party, but there's time, if you need me for anything."

Fanta and Broadhead glanced at Valentino with significance.

He said, "How important is this party?"

"Awesome."

Valentino smiled to himself. He'd wondered if youngsters still used that word.

"I hope it's anything but. I'm counting on racketeers being more civilized these days. But Professor Broadhead and his fiancée insisted I don't go down there alone." He was driving, the young man seated beside him with his tricked-out top hat in his lap. The compact's low roof allowed no room for it on his head.

"That's an interesting couple, those two."

"Not as interesting as how they became a couple."

"I really want to hear it, but can you drop me off at the party for just a minute? I was supposed to bring— something, and they'll have to send someone else."

"Keg, or twenty-four pack?" Valentino grinned at the windshield.

"Um."

"Don't worry, I won't bust you. I'm grateful you agreed to come along. Where's the party?"

Jason directed him into a neighborhood he hadn't known was there, made up of rows of industrial-looking brick buildings sharing common walls, with panes missing from gridded windows set too high up to provide a view from inside. "People *live* here?"

"No. We all chipped in and rented a place for tonight. They made buzz-saw blades there in the olden days."

"I'll reimburse you for your part."

"You don't need to do that, Mr. Valentino. This is going to be way more interesting."

"Again, I hope not."

At length they drew up before a building that looked like all the rest. The year 1909 was chiseled in the yellowed cornerstone. With all the constant razing and rebuilding, it was astonishing to be in a part of L.A. that predated Hollywood.

"Be just a sec." Jason got out and put on his hat. Climbing the concrete steps to the door, frock coat draping his scarecrow figure, he looked like an undertaker in a Poe film.

The door opened, letting out light and loud, discordant music that Valentino decided had been composed by a Russian modern master to celebrate tractors. He wondered, with amusement that would scandalize his ultraconservative department head, if Jason Stickley and his friends were communists. Another young man dressed similarly, in a formal cutaway over a starched white shirtboard and a bowler hat crusted over with machine parts, threw his arms around the newcomer and they retreated inside. The door closed, shutting off the music.

Valentino's cell rang. It was Harriet.

"So what do we need to talk about?" she said sprightly.

"How's the conference?"

"Swell. Jeff's on a panel tonight, about the history of crime-scene equipment. He's brought some stuff from his own collection. I can't wait."

"They have panels at night?"

"All day, and practically all night. It's a big do. They have to run concurrently to fit everything in. We're lucky when we get to eat before midnight."

That would explain her being up until almost dawn that morning, but he wasn't sure if she was telling him the truth.

Cautiously he said, "I hope the LAPD is paying you over-time."

"You said you wanted to talk?"

"I'm at a party," he found himself saying. "I think it's going to get noisy. If you can't reach me later, it's because I won't hear the phone."

He hated lying, and he wasn't doing it because he didn't be-lieve what she'd said about the convention program. If he told her what he was up to, he knew she'd try to talk him out of it, and probably succeed. It didn't make him feel any less guilty.

"Since when do you go to noisy parties?"

"You know how much I love Halloween. Anyway, it gives me something to do besides miss you."

"That's sweet. Trying a little too hard, but sweet. What are you going as?"

At that moment, a young woman (he assumed it was a woman) came along the sidewalk wearing a Victorian wedding gown and a deep-sea diver's brass helmet. She hoisted a long train of ivory-colored lace over one arm and went up the steps to the party. "Madonna."

He'd always liked Harriet's laugh. It was a flat-out guffaw, lusty as a man's. "Which one, *Truth or Dare* or the mystic Jew?"

"Virgin."

"That's getting to be a long time ago. Do you think anyone will recognize it?"

"Well, if they don't, I'll be in disguise, so I won't embarrass myself." The door opened again and Jason came out. "My host is coming over. I'll call you later. Enjoy your thing."

"You, too. Just don't get carried away and start singing." They exchanged endearments and the conversation was over. Jason slid into his seat as Valentino was clapping shut the phone. "Miss Johansen?"

"Yes."

"What did she say about our adventure?"

"She told me to enjoy myself."

"Awesome. If I had a girl I bet she'd bust my chops over it."

"Bust your chops?"

The boy blushed and smiled. "I like saying old stuff like that. Old stuff's da bomb."

Valentino didn't know where he stood now in the matter of understanding Jason's generation. Was he talking to him in the language of his contemporaries, or parroting something that was utterly passé? The archivist pulled away from the obsolete factory, passing a group of young men and women in outrageous costumes, but all part of a theme he'd begun to recognize, if not identify. He knew where they were headed.

"It's none of my business, but my curiosity is burning a hole through me."

"The clothes?"

"You don't have to answer if I'm prying."

"No problem, sir. Sometimes it's just hard for people who aren't into it to understand." He rumpled his black hair. The hat was on his lap again, his black rubber goggles loose around his neck. "It's steampunk."

"Steampunk?"

"Yeah. I guess you'd call it kind of a backlash to the whole 'information superhighway' deal. What it is, it's Queen Victoria and steam engines."

"Uh-huh." Although he wasn't following, not at all.

"See, at the same time people were wearing high stiff collars and bustles, the Industrial Age was chugging along, eating coal and pouring out big clouds of steam and smoke and making a racket. What gives us steampunks a charge, I guess, is that—that—"

"Juxtaposition?"

"Yes!" He flashed Valentino a look of gratitude mixed with astonishment. "The contrast. So what we do, we dress and act like people did back then—society people—but we mix it up with cogs and chains and old-time factory stuff. These parties, they're not really costume things, not just. When the budget will stand it, we eat things like roast suckling pig with an apple in its mouth, using all the right forks and like that, but the centerpiece is a bouquet of pistons."

"But what do you get out of it?"

"Well, I can only answer for me, but I don't know how a computer works, do you?"

"I don't suppose anyone does outside technicians."

"I'm not so sure they do, either. Oh, they know how to operate them and fix them, and some even know how to build one from scratch, but I'm not sure they know how it actually *works*, how it does what it does. But you can look at a steam engine, see the flywheels spin and the belts turn and the drive rods move up and down and figure it out. That's, well, it's—"

"Reassuring?"

"Reassuring, that's it. The rest is just kid stuff, I guess." His voice trailed off on a slightly sullen note.

"I must be a kid, then. It makes perfect sense to me."

Jason turned to him, and his grin was so broad it threatened to split his narrow face straight across. "I sort of thought— I hoped you'd say something like that. I've got a hunch you're one of us."

"I wouldn't go that far. I don't think I'd be comfortable lugging all that on top of my head."

The boy examined his hat. The interlocking gears attached to the crown created the illusion, when he wore it, that they were the machinery that raised and lowered his pipecleaner limbs. "I lucked out at the junkyard. I paid them just over scrap price for the guts of a grandfather clock. You can go broke if you don't know how to shop. What I meant was, this *Frankenstein* deal, for instance. Everybody in that movie had an English accent and drank tea, all veddy veddy proper, and here's this guy stirring them all up with his flat head and bolts in his neck. And that laboratory, which is seriously cool, all those things spinning and spitting sparks and the operating table going up and down on pulleys."

"Steampunk."

"Yes, sir."

"I guess it's better than sprockethead." Valentino swept up the ramp and entered Interstate 5 heading south to San Diego.

14

THE GROTTO WASN'T as seedy as Valentino had expected. Located directly on San Diego Bay with a dock in back where boaters could put in to replenish their stock of refreshments, it had a faux stone façade, a bar and restaurant on the first level, a second story reserved (according to a sign) for private parties, and a rounded tunnel-like entrance with waterfalls on either side bathed in colored lights. *Tawdry* was the word that came to mind.

Before they went in, Jason Stickley asked Valentino if he should leave his top hat behind and remove the padlock and chain hanging around his neck. Valentino considered, then shook his head. "The more attention we attract going inside, the better chance we have of coming back out."

The boy's smile was sickly. Here in actual enemy territory, they both found it difficult to laugh their adventure off as melodrama.

"You can stay in the car if you like," Valentino said. "I wouldn't go in myself if it weren't for that damn film."

"I'm fine, sir. Just a little stage fright."

"We're both being silly. It's people who know too much who get hurt, and we know less than nothing."

Passing between the ever-cycling waterfalls, he wondered who was waiting at the other end: a mug from Central Casting with a blue chin and a lethal bulge under one arm? Even the most tattered cliché from the bottom half of a double bill made sense in those surroundings. Out under the last rusty glow of the sun, the Pacific rolled on and on over bones that had never been found, weighted down with cement, and those same waves lapped conveniently at the back door.

"Valentino." Not a question this time, uttered in the same cold flat tone he'd heard on the telephone.

Standing just outside the end of the tunnel, Big Tony Grundage's son was smaller than he appeared in photographs and on the TV news, a dark, compact presence with narrow, serious features, dressed in the West Coast business uniform of sportcoat, black T-shirt, casual slacks, and glistening loafers. He was clean-shaven, with splinters of gray in his two-hundred-dollar haircut. His eyes were wolflike, brown and slanting. He didn't offer to shake hands.

"Yes. This is Jason Stickley, my assistant."

Belatedly, Jason swept off his hat, holding it in front of him at waist level as if to deflect bullets. Mike Grundage didn't look at him. "You didn't say you'd bring company."

"You didn't say I couldn't. It's a long drive, and I have to go back tonight. He can spell me at the wheel." He'd had this explanation ready.

"If you trust him. You've met Horace."

Valentino was enormously relieved to recognize the attorney, whom he hadn't seen in the dim light until that moment.

Respectable lawyers made it a point not to be present when their clients committed transgressions such as homicide. Lysander, carefully dressed as ever, shook his hand without smiling.

"These days I don't say a word, public or private, without him in the room. Let's go upstairs."

Grundage led the way through a room crowded with customers dining and drinking, towing a banner of silence through the buzzing conversation. Everyone appeared to recognize him, and to be curious about who was with him. What was that line about gangsters in *Goodfellas*? "Movie stars with muscle."

At the top of a carpeted staircase flanked by underwater photography on the walls, the atmosphere changed. This was where the private parties took place, in a large quiet room with long cloth-covered tables and comfortable-looking chairs. Lysander, bringing up the rear, paused to snap a velvet rope into a ring, with a sign reading INVITED GUESTS ONLY across the landing. Valentino wondered what other menial tasks the officer of the court performed for his notorious client. His unease returned.

The big room was unoccupied. They passed through it and into a curtained alcove, sealed off by the attorney once again when he twitched loose two ties, allowing the curtains to fall together. The room was just large enough to contain a small covered table, laid out sumptuously for a meal, and three chairs. "Please, Horace." Grundage nodded toward a fourth chair in a corner, which Lysander dutifully moved to the table.

"I ordered," said Grundage when they sat down. "There's Chicken Cordon Bleu for all of us. I always make sure there's enough for seconds."

Valentino said, "Thank you. I'm not sure we're hungry."

"You don't break bread with thugs, that it?"

The vitriol of the response emboldened more than intimidated him. If this man was determined to behave according to type, there was little that would change his mind. The die was cast. "For someone who's so careful about what he says, you jump to conclusions easily. A friend of mine was found murdered on these premises. It doesn't do much for the appetite."

Most of the room's illumination came from an electric candle glimmering in a glass vessel on the table. It reflected off his host's eyes in lupine fashion. "The ocean's twenty feet from the kitchen, friend. If I wanted to ditch a stiff, I wouldn't do it in my own toilet."

"Mike." Lysander's sleek bald head moved infinitesimally from right to left. Grundage held up a hand, stopping him in mid-shake. All his attention was centered on Valentino, who said:

"I'm not accusing you. Frankly, I wouldn't need much persuasion to decide you're not responsible. That's for the police to prove, one way or the other. Tonight I'm chiefly interested in what happened to the *Frankenstein* test."

The wolfish eyes fixed him for all of twenty seconds, an eternity. "Well, we've got that much in common."

Just then, as waiters will, one arrived with their meals, which he propped on a folding tray and set out before them, guests first, host last. A warm, tantalizing aroma issued forth the moment the covers were removed, setting Valentino's stomach juices to riot. He realized he hadn't eaten in hours, and that Grundage was truthful about one thing at least, that the Chicken Cordon Bleu served in The Grotto was second only to the original, if indeed it didn't surpass it. Why did criminals and ruthless dictators dine better than the virtuous?

Grundage took the tall slender wine bottle from the waiter

the moment it was uncorked. "California Riesling's the best in the world; don't believe anything the krauts tell you." He tilted it toward Valentino's glass.

The archivist covered it with his hand. "None for me, thanks."

"Rummy?"

"I like to keep my wits about me. Jason's underage."

Jason, who had lifted his glass for pouring, colored and set it back down.

"Far be it from me to break the law." Smiling for the first time—a tight-lipped turning up at the corners that warmed his personality not a jot—Grundage filled his glass to within a half inch of the rim and then Lysander's. The attorney's hand shook a little as he retrieved it. Valentino wondered if he was a rummy, to use his host's term; worry increased.

"My old man was superstitious. I'm not. I don't toast." Grundage sipped from his glass and waved the waiter away. (Lysander, his guest noticed, took a healthier sample, replaced the glass on the table, and removed his fingers from the stem with what looked like reluctance.)

"My stepmother's a good woman. She spent a lot of time trying to keep me away from my father's business; but I'm his son, and that's that. I don't want her mixed up in this."

"I can't promise that." Valentino picked up his fork. "Not until I know what *this* is. What did you mean about you and I having something in common? Don't you know where the test is?"

"First, we eat. The old man told me you can't conduct good business on an empty stomach."

They dined virtually in silence, broken up only by the tink of silver on china and the strains of old standards performed by current artists on a sound system better than most restaurants'. The food was sumptuous to look at, cooked to a pleasing shade, the meat fork tender, the side dishes colorful, but the taste was lost on Valentino. Had he seen too many mob movies, or didn't gangsters fatten their victims before sacrificing them? Jason, he saw, ate with apparent pleasure; the student union couldn't compete with The Grotto's kitchen, and thin people in general out-trenchered the rest of society.

Grundage pushed away the remnants of his dessert and snatched his napkin from his collar: the only vestige Valentino had noted of his plebian ancestry. Their waiter materialized instantly to clear his side of the table. When he departed: "What's in it for you if you lay hands on this gizmo?"

His guest applied sparkling water to his dry mouth. "That was an excellent meal, Mr. Grundage. I can't imagine why I'd never heard of this place."

"I throw bums and food critics out of the joint. It's crowded enough. We chew, we swallow, we shove it out the back door, then we think about the next meal and how do we get our mitts on it. So how do you?"

He'd decided he couldn't do business with Mike Grundage by appealing to his interest in history. This was nothing new. He'd spent his share of time in the hot seat at budget meetings, making his case for the profit potential in film preservation apart from its historical responsibility. Gangsters and boards of directors responded only to the promise of a healthy bottom line.

"Laying hands on that screen test means we can market it through theatrical distribution followed by DVD rentals and sales. An investment of, say, a hundred thousand dollars could yield half again that amount retail. Universities are businesses, too." He watched the wolf-eyed face for some reaction. He'd severely undervalued the item under discussion in the interest of horse trading.

"Your friend Hunter offered my stepmother a quarter million."

Valentino smiled despite himself. "Craig would've been hard pressed to come up with a tenth of that."

"I'm just telling you what my stepmama done told me. You saying she's a liar?"

Jason burped and giggled. Valentino, knowing incipient hysteria when he heard it, pressed his knee against the young man's. The giggling stopped.

"I'm sure she's a woman of integrity. I'm just telling *you* what I know about Craig."

Grundage seemed mollified, on the subject of his stepmother. "What's this thing worth really?"

"Do you have it?"

"What's that got to do with what we're talking about?" The proprietor of The Grotto showed irritation for the first time. Valentino wondered suddenly if he had money troubles. The grand jury investigation, and his obligations to Lysander's legal firm, must have been a constant drain. The man was strapped for cash. That was something Valentino could relate to.

"Mr. Grundage, once I'm convinced you're in possession of the property we're discussing, we can move on to honest negotiation. Right now I can't understand why you would be. Your father could have obtained it easily enough from a projectionist in the union he represented, but it seems to me he'd have sold it many years go. Why hoard it?"

"Because that's what he did. My old man was a packrat. After he died I moved my stepmother out of that barn they lived in and set her up in a luxury condo. I threw out most of the crap he piled up and put the rest in storage. He probably forgot he even had the film."

This sounded plausible. J. Arthur Greenwood had said almost

the same thing about his own collection. "But how did Hunter find out about it?"

"This whole town's a chatterbox, just like L.A. I had all the stuff we kept in Elizabeth's name inventoried for insurance purposes. Somebody spilled his guts."

"May I ask why she turned down Hunter's offer?"

"Horace told her if a grifter was offering that much, she should hold out for a million."

Valentino glanced at the attorney, but continued to address himself to Grundage. "He told me he advised her not to sell it on any terms, and that's when Craig threatened him."

"I told him to tell you that. He called me, not Elizabeth, when you were in his office. I figured you'd lose interest if he said no way. I'm tired of people coming around asking questions. Hunter did call Horace and called him all kinds of an S.O.B. Why would he get so sore if he was fronting for somebody, unless he planned to double-cross him and hold him up for more?"

"He was fronting for a man named Greenwood, a private collector. I talked to him."

"So how high was this Greenwood prepared to go?"

"He hoped to get it for less than a million."

"Which means it's worth more."

"Not much more, if it is. Things are bad all over."

Grundage smiled his chilly smile. "This is starting to sound like a haggling session. Who you working for, Hunter's big fish or yourself?"

"Neither. I got into this on his ex-wife's behalf, to find out who killed him and why. When I learned the *Frankenstein* test was involved, I naturally became interested as a representative of the Film Preservation Department."

"You saying there's nothing in it for you?"

"A finder's fee. I've got expenses."

Lysander spoke up. "You have more than that, young man. That eyesore in West Hollywood is eating you alive."

"I set Horace on you," Grundage explained. "I like to know everything I can about a man before I set up a meet. What's your fee?"

"The amount depends on the profit UCLA realizes from DVD rentals and sales, less the cost of transferring the film from silver-nitrate to safety stock and restoring it as closely as possible to its original condition, which is likely to be substantial."

The racketeer made a yak-yak motion with one hand. "I didn't bring you down here to ask how your business is run. What's your offer?"

"Mike, we need to discuss this with Elizabeth before we commit to anything."

"Relax, Counselor. Everybody knows you got the hots for her."

"That's an ugly way to put it." Lysander's face flushed deeply.

Jason hadn't spoken since they'd entered the restaurant. Now he said, "You haven't mentioned whether you had the film."

Valentino glanced at him, surprised he'd broken his silence and by his own neglect in not pressing the question.

Grundage was still smiling. "Kid's got a head on his shoulders. You never can tell, can you? You might as well tell 'em, Horace. They don't have it."

The archivist's heart sank. "You mean *you* don't?"

The lawyer answered for him. "Three nights ago, someone broke into the storage unit. Those two reels were the only things missing."

15

JASON WAS A good driver, careful and in control. He kept steady speed with most of the other cars on the freeway and didn't lose his temper with southbound drivers who refused to dim their lights.

"You think Craig Hunter stole the film?" He kept his eyes on the road.

Valentino glared at the darkness outside his window on the passenger's side. "A few years ago I'd have said no. But by the end he was capable of anything. If Elizabeth Grundage wouldn't do business with him on Lysander's advice, he might just have done it out of desperation. Maybe he made up his mind that night he called Lysander to chew him out. It would explain why he was so excited. He'd found a way to cut out the middleman and keep all the profit for himself."

"Mike Grundage must have suspected he was the thief. Does that put him back on the list?"

"He was never really off. But if he did kill Craig, we know

he didn't get the film back. This trip was a fishing expedition
on his part to find out if Craig had slipped it to me."

"What do you think he did with it?"

"I've been racking my brain over that. If he had it in his
apartment in Long Beach, the police would have found it when
they searched the place for clues after he was killed. I hope he
picked a stable hiding spot."

"Stable?"

"That old silver-nitrate stock doesn't hold up well to adverse
conditions. If there was anything left of it after all those years
in the Grundages' possession—Lord knows how *they* treated it;
winding up in an ordinary storage unit isn't an encouraging
sign—it might be turning to vinegar in a damp crawlspace
somewhere."

"Maybe he put it in a bank safety deposit box."

"Not much better, but if he did, it will turn up when it's
examined by the authorities. That's standard procedure after
someone's death."

"Then you can start negotiating with Elizabeth Grundage."

"Provided the police find and convict Craig's murderer before nature takes its course in a muggy evidence room in San
Diego. I've been down this road before."

"Can I help?"

"Help me with what?"

"Solving the murder."

But it was late, and the sleep he'd been missing caught up
with him before he could answer. His last thought as he slipped
under was that everyone he spent time with, no matter how
casually, seemed to know him so well.

———

"Sound! Roll 'em! Action!"

The villagers, who have doused their cigarettes and put the occasional flask back on the occasional hip, respond with aching muscles to the commands issuing from the megaphone. They collect their torches, take the bloodhounds by their leashes from the trainers, and resume babbling nonsensical strings of vowels and consonants, tumbling over the brambles and uneven earth of the backlot and hoping this is the last take: It's getting on toward midnight, and there is no Screen Actors Guild to demand decent hours and extra pay for overtime. The hounds' baying echoes their own miseries.

But none of the extras is suffering as much as the man in the heavy boots, steel braces, dense padding, and two sets of union suits still clammy with perspiration from yesterday's shooting in a blazing Southern California summer. The man at his side has been drinking heavily between takes and gives him no help as he sags into his arms—all six feet and one hundred eighty pounds of him—and forces him to carry him on his shoulder up the steep hill to the gaunt windmill at the top for the seventeenth time since sundown. For some reason, the director has taken a dislike to the actor in the ponderous and painful makeup, and seems to draw sadistic delight from torturing him physically, wasting film in the process: But film costs only two cents a foot, and the actor himself is being paid less than the amount budgeted for that part of the production.

So once again he hauls his heavy and inebriated colleague a quarter-mile up a sixty-degree slope, his breath heaving and sawing in his throat, sweat making gullies in the greenish greasepaint on his face and dissolving the mortician's wax used to fashion his drooping eyelids into particles that burn his eyes like acid.

"And . . . cut!"

He lowers the other actor onto his unsteady feet and stands
panting with hands braced on his thighs, the backs of those hands
built up with thick artificial veins, waiting for his heartbeat to
slow. If the windmill's blades rotated at that same rate the entire
building would take to the air.

"You were a little slow on that one, Boris," drawls the man
with the megaphone in his meticulous (and entirely fabricated)
West End accent. "Remember, you're a superhuman creation.
You're not driving a truck. Let's go again, shall we? Places!"

He won't even be invited to the premiere.

"Mr. Valentino?"

Stirred from yet another dream in which he didn't appear,
he changed positions, wondering why his bed had so many
hard surfaces suddenly. When Jason shook him by the shoulder, he jumped, bumped his head against the window, and remembered he wasn't in The Oracle. A blinding light was shining
in his face. He shielded his eyes against the powerful flashlight, saw the pale oval of a face beneath the visor of a uniform
cap looking through the window on Jason's side, and beyond it
the blue-and-red strobes of a police car bouncing off the front
of the theater.

Taking Jason's and Valentino's driver's licenses, the officer
examined them with his flash, then returned them. "Come
with me, please, sir. Not you. You can leave."

The boy had reached for the door handle. He looked at Valentino.

"It's all right. You can drive the car to campus in the morning. I'll take the bus."

Jason opened his mouth to say something, but the officer

tapped his flashlight on the window frame and he started the engine. Valentino got out and accompanied the man in uniform inside as the car drove off.

All the lights in the foyer (those that had been replaced so far) were burning. He found the boyish sergeant with the eyes that were not boyish and the detective whose profile belonged on an Indian-head penny waiting there. Others in uniforms and plainclothes bustled about in the shadows.

Gill spoke first. "We're cooperating with LAPD on this one, since it involves our case. Would you mind telling us where you were this evening?"

"San Diego."

"Wish *I* was in San Diego," Yellowfern said. "Paying your respects to Mike Grundage?"

"As a matter of fact, I was."

Detectives were very difficult to surprise, even more so to get a reaction from when one succeeded. The pair exchanged a glance. Gill said, "I got the impression you weren't in each other's social circle."

"He invited me to the Grotto for dinner. I was going to tell you about it later."

"How *much* later?" Yellowfern snapped.

"Time enough for that," said his partner. "One of your neighbors called in a possible B-and-E. Someone was prowling around inside with a flashlight. They saw it through the windows."

"What's a breaking-and-entering in West Hollywood have to do with San Diego Homicide?" The reason for the crime was clear to him now. Grundage, suspecting Craig had given him the test reels for safekeeping, had lured him far enough out of town to give his people in L.A. time to search the theater. Gill and Yellowfern would have heard the report on their radio and investigated it on a hunch, based on the location.

The sergeant said, "I said that's how it was called in. It's a little more than that now." He made a beckoning gesture with his finger.

Valentino followed the pair into the auditorium, where the recently rewired crystal chandelier made a pond of light reaching the base of the staircase to the projection booth. The door to it was open and something lay at the foot.

The woman was sprawled in an impossible position. She was dressed exotically even by entertainment-capital standards, in brilliant red and midnight black, the waist cut narrow and the shoulders square. Her face was in the shadow of the stairwell, but Valentino could spot Teddie Goodman, his arch-rival, under any circumstances.

16

AS HE WAS staring, a foot twitched at the end of a shattered leg and a low, heartbreaking moan issued from the shadow of the stairwell. Valentino looked at the detectives, horror-stricken.

"Yeah," Yellowfern said. "We lucked out. In six months she'll be able to tell us who helped her down the stairs, if she doesn't croak first."

Gill was more human. "The ambulance is on its way. We can't move her till then." Just as he finished speaking, a siren gulped into the block.

"Can't you cover her with a blanket or something? I heard you do that for shock."

"Not till the EMS crew says. You never know with internal injuries. It's tough, but that's how it is. You know her?" Gill touched the arm of an LAPD officer, stopping him on his way past. "Let's have a light."

Valentino looked at the face in the glow of the officer's flash, just to be sure. It was turned to one side. A virulent purple bruise had blossomed up from her cheek, swelling and closing the eye. He clutched his stomach, sorry he'd eaten such a big meal.

"Her name is Theodosia Burr Goodman. She works for Mark David Turkus."

"The skillionaire?" Yellowfern said. "What's she do for him?"

"The same thing I do for UCLA, only for a lot more money. Where's that ambulance crew?"

Gill said, "Calm down, we haven't been here long. If she's making such big bucks, what's she doing breaking in places?"

A man and a woman wearing Emergency Medical Services uniforms came in carrying equipment and a stretcher. Valentino and the detectives moved out of their way. "Could we talk about this someplace else?"

Yellowfern said, "When the coast is clear, we can go up to your nice comfortable apartment, only there's no place to sit. Your girlfriend or somebody else trashed it good. Either that, or you're one rotten housekeeper."

His first fear was for the Bell & Howell projector. Then he felt shame for worrying about an inanimate thing while the attendants were examining Teddie's vital signs. By silent consent the three moved down the aisle until they found adjoining seats whose cotton batting generations of nest-building mice had not yet thoroughly plundered. Valentino, of course, sat in the center.

Gill had his notebook out. "The way it looks right now, someone came in on her while she was tossing the place and gave her a shove. That made you a suspect, but I can't remember the last time anyone named a gangster as his alibi."

"You can ask my intern, Jason Stickley. He was with me. One of your men sent him home."

"Not one of ours," snarled Yellowfern.

"We screw up, too. The order was to bring in Valentino." Gill pointed his pen at the archivist. "You can give us contact info on the intern later. Maybe Grundage'll back you up, although based on experience he wouldn't tell the pizza guy his address when he was ordering. We'll get to what you were doing with him. What was your girlfriend looking for?"

"She's not my girlfriend. She works for the competition. She thought I was on the trail of something Turkus would want. Maybe she thought I had it, or that she could find out what it was and where to look for it if she went through my things."

Yellowfern chuckled nastily and propped his feet on the back of the seat in front of him. "Sounds like true love to me."

"Shut up, John. What'd she think you had?"

He sighed and told them about the *Frankenstein* test; about everything connected with it, starting with June 1931 through Craig Hunter all the way to that evening. He'd already made up his mind to come clean. One person had died, another might yet. It wasn't worth it for thirty or forty minutes of film.

For once, Yellowfern was speechless. While Valentino was talking he placed his feet back on the floor and leaned forward and twisted in his seat to stare at him, knuckles whitening on the arm. It was Gill who spoke, with cold fury in his voice.

"I hope you get the same job in San Quentin. Those cons can use a break from *Horton Hears a Who!*. You're still a suspect in my book. You threw this Goodman woman down those stairs just the same as if you were here."

"It was all guesswork until tonight," Valentino said. "It didn't even count as evidence. I didn't really believe the film existed until Lysander told me it was stolen. I only had an old man's word he'd held that sample strip in his hand, and the word of a half-crazed collector at that."

Gill shook his head. "You've been running around grilling our witnesses, and one we didn't even know about. *Anyone* who had contact with Hunter just before he died is material. We'll start with interfering and work our way up to obstruction."

"Don't forget accessory after the fact." Yellowfern had found his tongue.

"Let's not get ahead of ourselves."

Valentino looked to Gill, the reasonable one, for mercy. But the sergeant had turned his head to summon an officer. When the man in uniform came, he said, "This man is under arrest. Truss him up and read him his rights."

Which was how Valentino found himself in jail for the first time in his life.

In holding, anyway. His cell in the West Hollywood station of the Los Angeles Police Department was small but clean, and the cot looked tempting, but he used his one call on Kyle Broadhead.

"Have you been arraigned?" Broadhead was always calm, always practical.

"No. I'm not even sure what the charge is. It seems there's a menu to choose from."

"I can't bail you out until bail is set. I'm afraid you're in for the night. Do you want me to call Harriet?"

"God, no."

"Didn't tell her what you were up to, did you?"

"She thinks I'm at a party."

"I bet Fanta breakfast in bed you wouldn't. She's the winner there, though. You've tasted my cooking."

"You know, your sense of humor doesn't always fix things."

"That's what Fanta says. I'll see what I can do, but you'll have to make the best of it till morning."

"I suppose I deserve this, with Teddie in intensive care or worse."

"You don't have a crystal ball. Also, you didn't invite her to burgle your home. She made that decision all by herself."

He lowered his voice. It was a busy precinct, with uniformed and plainclothes officers drifting back and forth past the bars. "Do you think it was Grundage's henchmen?"

"You need to brush up on your post–Hays Office vernacular. I seriously doubt anyone on his payroll writes *henchman* in the 'occupation' blank in Form 1040. Maybe she slipped."

"Gill and Yellowfern are pretty certain she was pushed."

"Don't believe in accidents; how Freudian. Don't fret over it. Teddie wouldn't, if the shoe were on the other foot."

"I'd never commit a crime just to lay hands on a film."

"Spoken by a man in the hoosegow for doing just that. I know some people. I'll make some calls."

"What do I do meanwhile?"

"Learn to play the harmonica."

He'd hoped for some glimpse of Sergeant Clifford, a West Hollywood criminal investigator who was not exactly a friend, but at least a familiar face, but either the tall runway-model type was off duty or had been reassigned, because all he saw were strangers.

He was gripping the bars. He'd always wondered why prisoners did that in movies, but now he knew it was to cling as closely as possible to freedom as the barriers permitted. When his fingers cramped, he rested his wrists on the cross bars with his hands dangling outside, palms down; his hands, at least, were at liberty. He fought exhaustion as long as he could, not wanting to surrender himself to the depths of his incarceration, but at last his body surrendered in protest. He retreated to the cot and gentle darkness swaddled him.

When he opened his eyes, daylight had softened the harsh white of the fluorescents in the ceiling and someone had drawn up a desk chair to sit facing his cell. The man was an aging adolescent type, wearing an argyle sweater vest over a pink shirt, khakis in need of pressing, and what must have been the last pair of PF Flyers gym shoes on the planet. His ginger-colored hair looked as if he cut it himself, with a cowlick sticking up from his crown, and his eyes were furtive behind tortoiseshell glasses, like those of a boy too shy to maintain eye contact.

He was one of the ten richest men in the world, and had recently celebrated his fiftieth birthday by paying for a seat on the space shuttle.

"Please don't be offended when I don't offer my hand," he said in a voice barely above a murmur. "That's how disease is spread."

Valentino swung his feet to the floor and brushed back his hair with both hands, as if sleeping on it would have made it any untidier than his visitor's. "How do you do, Mr. Turkus?"

Mark David Turkus' smile was tentative, oddly innocent. "I'm sorry, but I don't remember if we've met."

"We haven't, but your face isn't exactly unknown." It had appeared on the cover of *Forbes* when he'd sold all his Internet stock just before the dot-com bubble burst in 2000, and again when he'd bought the early film library of every major studio in Hollywood. He'd started Supernova International in his parents' basement at age twenty-six and now it had offices on five continents.

As Turkus seemed to search for an appropriate response, Valentino asked him about Teddie Goodman.

"She's critical but stable; the doctors at Cedars of Lebanon got her blood pressure to stop dropping and are draining blood from the abdominal cavity. She has many broken bones, of course, including her left cheek and eye orbit. I'm flying in specialists, but there will be months of therapy and cosmetic procedures. That was a steep flight of stairs."

"I'm very sorry."

"I'm the one who should apologize. I haven't been as curious as I should have been about how she gets results."

"The police are holding me responsible."

"They insist on assigning responsibility for everything. The world's more random than that."

"I'm not so sure they're wrong in this case. Teddie and I have had our differences, but I never wished her harm. She might not be where she is if I'd come forward."

"And if I'd been on the ball, *Citizen Kane* wouldn't have gone to Ted Turner. Regret is a useless emotion. You can't change the past, but you can affect the future."

Valentino said nothing, waiting. Turkus leaned back in his borrowed chair, bent one leg, and clasped his hands around it just below the knee, exposing a sagging white gym sock and three inches of pale ankle. "My attorney is at City Hall, waiting for a writ for your release. The police can hold you for forty-eight hours without charging you, but there's no reason you should sit here going stale while the *Frankenstein* test is floating around out there somewhere."

"What are you suggesting?" Although he could guess.

"Don't worry. Teddie's job is safe, and she'll have the best people working around the clock on her case. Her iron will, I'm confident, will do the rest. I'm offering you ten percent of the gross profits for exhibition, sales, and rentals of the property if you can deliver it for a million or less."

"I can't do that, sir. I'm a paid consultant for the UCLA Film Preservation Department. It would be a conflict of interest."

"They can't possibly match this offer."

"I'm afraid that's irrelevant."

"Would your conscience be clearer if I put it on a hiring basis? I'll need a replacement for Teddie until she's ready to return to work. After that you'll perform as a team. There are too many properties wandering around lost out there for one person to track down. It makes no sense that the two best scouts in the business are operating in competition, duplicating each other's efforts. That's bureaucratic thinking. You're leaving one position for another that pays much better, with more opportunity for advancement. That's not betrayal, just good capitalism."

"It still feels wrong. I began this search as a representative of the university."

"The job includes the company jet whenever I'm not using it, and a town car for your personal use. A medical plan U.S. senators can only dream about."

"I owe two more payments on my compact and I'm accustomed to flying economy. As for the medical plan, I guess I'll just have to take good care of myself."

"You realize what you're turning down."

"I'm trying not to think about that, Mr. Turkus."

He scowled. Then he unclasped his knee and lowered his foot to the floor. "Well, I'm not a vindictive man. I'll go through with that writ."

"That won't be necessary. I have friends who are looking out for me."

"Not all friends are equal; lawyers certainly aren't. I'm offering you a get-out-of-jail-free card."

"Thank you, but it isn't exactly free, is it?"

The tycoon's shy smile broke the surface. "You're wise in your generation."

Valentino felt himself returning the smile. "Ernest Thesiger. *Bride of Frankenstein.* Wrong film."

"They're all the same to me. Movies are an investment, not a passion."

"Thank you, sir."

"For what?" Turkus was standing now, a lanky six-foot-two despite his stoop. "You've refused all my favors."

"For making me feel better about it. With me, they *are* a passion."

"You may be right. I'd probably fire you in the end."

"It's more than probable."

The billionaire leaned forward. His smile now was wicked. "But what a severance package."

17

"AS IT TURNS out," Broadhead said, "most of the friends I thought I had in this town are dead. The others are good only for reminiscing. I hate reminiscing. This is the best I could do."

The best he could do was a criminal attorney who had secured the acquittals of more than half the celebrated felons in Hollywood, a sly-faced former NFL first-draft choice. He wore a chinchilla coat—in a Southern California autumn—over a suit spun from virgins' hair and showed diamond grillwork when he smiled, which was more or less constantly.

"Don't sign the receipt till you count the money in your wallet," he said. "I'm just saying." He winked at the officer behind the bulletproof glass, who shot him a poisonous look back and snatched the receipt from under the last stroke of the pen in Valentino's hand.

The former prisoner distributed his belongings among their various pockets. "I can't afford him. I'm sure you can't either, asset to the institution though you are."

"You'd be surprised: a nickel here, a nickel there. I haven't bought a suit since Nixon. But I wouldn't spend a penny on the best lawyer in America if I were up for high treason. As far as I'm concerned, the serpent slithered out of Eden right behind Adam and Eve and hung out his shingle. No offense, Counselor."

"None taken, I assure you. There are days I can't stand my own company." Diamonds twinkled.

"Then, who—?"

"Fanta," Broadhead said. "You can't overestimate the allowance an ambassador can offer her daughter when she counts her euros."

"Kyle, I can't accept."

"Sure you can. We'll write it off as the bridegroom's traditional gift to his best man. She never touches a penny. It goes into blue chip stock and keeps on growing obscenely, like an obese child playing *Grand Theft Auto*." Suddenly serious, he said, "I've been, don't forget. A holding cell in West Hollywood is a Hilton Garden Inn compared to a craphole in Zagreb, but it's all the same when you want to go out for air and they won't let you."

Valentino shook hands with the attorney, who said, "This is the end of it. Cops don't get the chance to scare the pants off square citizens often. When you call their bluff they generally go away and lean on some schnook with a rap sheet as long as Baja. Just in case they don't." He produced a card with a magician's flourish—Valentino swore he actually conjured it from inside his French cuff—and vanished in a cloud of glitter and chinchilla hair. The archivist wondered if he'd been there at all.

Broadhead seemed to understand. "He's just a special effect, animatronics and computer generation. He sleeps in a prop room, up on a hook. Let's away."

They left the station in Valentino's compact, Broadhead behind the wheel, punishing the gears and using the indicators
in the middle of lane changes to confirm for other drivers the
decision he'd already acted upon. Horns serenaded his every
move. Under normal circumstances his passenger would have
been perched on the edge of his seat, gripping the dash and
tromping on phantom pedals on his side of the car. But movement was freedom. He subsided into the cushions, watching
the scenery stutter past. "Any news on Teddie?"

"I called Cedars of Lebanon, but the Privacy Policy police
wouldn't tell me anything. I wouldn't worry about her. Some
people are just too nasty for the Other Side."

"I can't help feeling responsible."

"That's cop talk. It's their business to make everyone guilty.
You didn't tell her to burgle your home. If she'd asked, the
answer would've been no. Where to now, the office? Bury
yourself in work?"

"The theater. I've been in these clothes more than twenty-
four hours, and I need to assess the damage to the projection
booth."

"I drove past on the way to the hoosegow. The police tape is
gone. Somebody must've robbed a bank or else they turned on
the light at Krispy Kreme." Broadhead clicked off the turn indicator, which had been clicking for five minutes. "That's all
you're doing, I hope: changing clothes and sweeping up."

"Meaning what?"

"Meaning when what you're doing lands you in jail, it's either time to stop doing it or choose the criminal life. I wouldn't
recommend the latter in your case. So far you've been caught
every time."

"You can save the lecture. If Craig had that film, he hid it so

well I wouldn't know where to begin looking for it. Gill and
Yellowfern will have turned his apartment in Long Beach inside out by now."

"You can't get them all, Val."

"I'd like to get enough of them so that doesn't become the
department motto."

"If that's your 'I give up' speech, it needs work."

"Don't worry. I know when I'm licked."

"Better."

The Oracle looked more deserted than usual when they
pulled up in front; Valentino supposed the police had turned
the workers away during their investigation. He made a note to
call Leo Kalishnikov and get them back. He was starting to
think the place was cursed as surely as *Frankenstein*. Everyone
connected with it seemed to have come to a no-good end starting with Max Fink, who had gone broke building it and took
his own life.

He opened the door on the passenger's side. "You can take the
car on in. If it's as bad as they said, I won't be in to work today."

"Ruth will be disappointed. She's volunteered to act as your
parole officer." Broadhead waved good-bye and peeled away
from the curb without looking, forcing a city bus to whoosh its
air brakes and redistribute the passenger load from back to
front.

Valentino was reaching for the front door when it swung
open. A large man he'd never seen before stood in the doorway,
wearing a suit two sizes too small in the coat and a gap-toothed
grin. Before Valentino could react, something hard nudged his
right kidney from behind and the big man stepped aside. He
had no choice but to step across the threshold.

The man behind him followed noiselessly and pulled the
door shut against the constant murmur of L.A. traffic. Valentino

started to turn to get a look at him, but a blow to his solar plexus changed his mind. He emptied his lungs and groped for support at the big man's fist. His legs were swept from under him. As he fell, a knee connected with his chin, snapping his jaw shut and chipping a tooth. That was the last thing he saw for a while. But he could hear.

"Bust his arms?" A wheezy, broken-windpipe voice.

"Boss said no."

The second voice was flat and toneless.

Wheezy said, "Well, hell. If roughing up's all he wanted he coulda called a couple of locals and saved us the drive up the coast."

"You want to kind of shut up?"

"What for? This guy's out like the Macarena."

"You ever been cold-cocked?"

"I guess I cold-cocked my share."

"It ain't the same thing. Don't talk about stuff you don't know nothing about."

Now Valentino smelled stale cigarette breath, felt the heat of a face bent close to his. The owner of the flat voice said, "Forget *Frankenstein*, Rudolph. Or treat yourself to a plot in Forest Lawn."

"Rudolph, why Rudolph?" Wheeze asked. "His nose ain't so red."

"Not the reindeer, you dope. The old-time movie star. Don't you ever watch nothing but porn?"

The door opened on a hinge that needed oil and shut with a thump.

Valentino had thought they'd never leave. He allowed himself to slip into unconsciousness.

––––––

His cell phone woke him. Groaning, he rolled over, worked it out of its pocket, and clenched his jaw against a wave of nausea to answer.

"That must've been some party," Harriet said. "I've been trying to reach you for hours. I tried the theater, your office, and your cell I don't know how many times."

He'd been too preoccupied to check for missed calls when he got his phone back from the police. "I forgot it. I've been out running errands." He tested his chipped tooth between thumb and forefinger. At least it wasn't loose.

"You sound hungover. What kind of example is that for a nice boy like Jason?"

He'd nearly forgotten the excuse he'd given her to cover up his trip to San Diego and his meeting with Mike Grundage. "I wasn't drinking. I was just out late. I'm sorry I didn't call."

"I can nag you later, when it doesn't cost us both minutes. Listen, I'm—"

His phone beeped twice and went dead. No bars showed on the screen. It hadn't been charged since yesterday morning.

He was pulling himself up from the floor, using the wall for support, when the land line rang upstairs. It would be Harriet again. He knew he'd never reach it in time, and in point of fact he didn't want to. At least she couldn't know for sure he was in The Oracle. Whatever she had to tell him could wait until he'd put himself together enough to frame excuses.

The plumbing had been restored in the women's restroom off the foyer. He lurched inside, splashed his face with water, and let it drip as he entered the auditorium and climbed to the projection booth. He was beginning to feel a little less like the victim of a four-car pileup. Wheezy and his partner were professionals who knew how to deliver a beating that wouldn't cripple a man.

Which of course meant that they also knew how to deliver the other kind.

The warning about the *Frankenstein* test had been redundant. Their conversation about whether to break his arms and the drive up the coast (from San Diego, where else?) had made it clear whose orders they were following and therefore why.

The room where he kept his apartment looked even worse than it had when he'd first seen it, after many years of neglect and vermin in residence. Furniture was upended, Craig Hunter's horror-film books were scattered, and stuffing from the slashed cushions and mattress of the sofa lay in clumps. The Bell & Howell projector, he was relieved to learn, was unharmed, although the dust cover had been snatched off to confirm the take-up reel mounted on it contained no film.

He found the telephone on the floor, where likely an investigating officer had replaced the receiver in its cradle, and sat down amid the wreckage of the sofa with the standard in his lap to call the number on Sergeant Gill's business card. The San Diego detective answered on the first ring and listened to Valentino's account of his attack.

"You're just a trouble magnet," Gill said when he finished. "You're back on the street, what, twenty minutes, and you're someone's handball. Grundage must have a pipeline into the West Hollywood station. I doubt his hired boys came prepared to camp out indefinitely waiting for you to get sprung."

"You're sure they're from Grundage?"

"You mean apart from that gag about breaking your arms? The one you saw sounds like Pudge Pollard. He lost his teeth tending goal for Colorado before the NHL turned him out for gambling. He wasn't unemployed a month when Grundage recruited him. The one with the bad throat would be Dickey Wirtz. He drank a bottle of Clorox to get off the laundry detail in Folsom and threw it up before it could eat out his stomach. Dickey hangs with Pudge, who keeps him from falling down open manholes. I'll have headquarters fax Pollard's mug up here so you can ID him positively, but I'm sure it's them. At least now we know we're on the right track with Grundage. All we have to do is prove it."

"Do you think it was Pollard and Wirtz who pushed Teddie Goodman down the stairs?"

"Let's just say you're lucky you met them on the ground floor. You're sure you don't know where that film is? Evidence like that could help lock up Mike and his boys until they're tripping over their whiskers."

"I'm sure." As sure as he was that vintage film would never survive police custody.

"Because that legal talent you have made me wonder if you had a big-time buyer all lined up."

"That was a favor from an old friend."

"I should have such friends. What I've got is John Yellow-fern."

Valentino had no response for that.

Gill said, "My guess is these characters won't be back, but I'd change the locks. They're way too familiar with the ones you've got. When I say they won't be back, I'm assuming you're taking their advice and forgetting all about *Frankenstein.*"

"I came to that decision last night. Too many people had been hurt already."

"You've got a piece of that, Sherlock. It's why we locked you up." Gill broke the connection.

Valentino got out a big garbage bag, scooped all the debris into it, and straightened up what hadn't been destroyed. Evidently Pollard and Wirtz, or whoever had surprised Teddie in the act of ransacking the booth if not them, had decided he'd hide the film in his private apartment and not anywhere else in a building where stranger traffic was so heavy during construction. His brief acquaintance with Grundage's men convinced him they wouldn't have abandoned the search from panic over the implications of committing physical assault. Compared to this world, Frankenstein's was looking less and less terrifying.

Someone had been knocking on the front door for some time before he got down the stairs. He hesitated with his hand on the knob; perhaps his earlier visitors' orders had changed and they'd come back to finish what they'd started. "Who is it?"

"Special delivery."

It was a woman's voice. He opened the door to reveal a husky blonde in the pale blue uniform of the United States Postal Service. She held her electronic device in one hand and carried a square package under her other arm, slightly smaller than a pizza box but twice as thick. He scratched his signature on the device's screen with the stylus she handed him and accepted the package. He recognized the handwriting on the address. The quality of Craig Hunter's script had deteriorated since the last time a fan had asked him for his autograph.

Valentino's own hands were unsteady when he closed the door and tore the paper off the package. The black metal box was stenciled "Property of Universal Studios" in white. He fumbled with the buckles that secured the woven cloth straps and found two aluminum film cans inside.

By all rights the material should have been handled with surgical gloves, but he was too excited to go back upstairs and search for his supply among the confusion left by the burglars. He prised open one of the cans and, pulling the sleeve of his sweatshirt over one hand, unwound enough of the film to study it against the light.

For old silver-nitrate stock it was in remarkably good condition, neither brittle nor sticky to the touch. The storage vault must have been climate-controlled. When a few feet in he recognized Bela Lugosi's face, he wound it all back and returned it to its can. Icy tentacles slithered up his spine. He'd stared into the eyes of a dead man, and they had stared back with an evil glitter of comprehension.

III

THE AIR IS FILLED
WITH MONSTERS

18

"**IT'S ALIVE! IT'S** alive!"

"Henry—in the name of God!"

"Oh—in the name of God. Now I know what it feels like to *be* God!"

The screening room was light years removed from the sleek Deco comfort of the chamber where those lines had first been heard on film eighty years before. Valentino and Jason Stickley sat side by side in cramped elbow desks in the darkened Film Department classroom while Kyle Broadhead operated an extravagantly expensive air-cooled projector designed to process celluloid and silver nitrate, a combination as potentially explosive as nitro and glycerin, particularly when exposed to the heat of an incandescent bulb such as the one that threw the images onto the pull-down screen in front of the chalkboard.

That line about God, sufficiently volatile in itself to have been censored from the theatrical release for decades, sounded tame in the monotonous cadence of the anonymous studio employee reading it from Robert Florey's script. Dr. Frankenstein had not been cast officially until James Whale took Florey's place behind the megaphone, bringing Colin Clive with him from England. The test had been staged to audition Edward Van Sloan as Waldman, Henry Frankenstein's mentor, and Bela Lugosi as his creation from spare parts scrounged from cemeteries, charnel houses, and executioners' scaffolds. Young Stickley, Valentino knew, would appreciate the last, equating it with his own forays into junkyards and whatnot shops to pimp up his Victorian costumes for Steampunk events. In any case, the intern had earned his invitation to the screening by providing physical and moral support during Valentino's visit to The Grotto.

Today, Jason wore ordinary blue jeans raveling at the knees and a white T-shirt that exposed the piston rods or whatever they were tattooed inside his arms and what resembled a camshaft up his spine, visible through the thin porous cotton. School was in session, and the frock coat and remodeled top hat were inappropriate to the occasion.

Lugosi's close-up a few minutes into the second reel—the one Valentino had happened to unspool first at The Oracle—was arresting, but only for the hypnotic quality of his eyes, forever associated with his signature role as Dracula. His makeup was atrocious. Whatever foundation he'd applied to replicate the glazed appearance of a figure molded from clay gave his face a slimy sheen, as of a stage actor who had used cold cream to cleanse away greasepaint after a performance, and his oversize page-boy wig made him look like a small boy dressed up as Prince Valiant or, worse, Buster Brown. Although he could well understand Junior Laemmle's hilarious reaction to the absurd image, Valentino was saddened by it. But then he had the advantage of knowing the long string of humiliations that would follow the actor for the next quarter century.

The sentimentalist in him wished Florey's command to burn the reels had been carried out, rather than pile one more indignity on Lugosi in his grave. But the archivist in him knew they represented a chapter of Hollywood history that must be preserved.

"Lights, please," Broadhead said.

Jason sprang to his feet and palmed up the switches beside the door, flickering the ceiling fluorescents into life.

"What did you think, young man?" The professor's tone belonged to one of his infrequent lectures. "Your generation's perspective is occasionally of value and invariably amusing."

"It was interesting."

"Only historically. A Depression audience would have laughed it out of the theater. When I ask an honest question I expect the answer to be equally straightforward. Flattery never taught me anything, aside from the miracle of my birth, and I was already aware of that."

"Well, the acting was kind of crummy."

"It was worse than that, but the fellow in the lab coat probably painted sets and Van Sloan was a money player, holding his stuff in reserve for when it counted. Lugosi was the picture in their frame. What, I repeat, did you think?"

"I thought he was bogus."

"Precisely. You and your peers have done the language an enormous service by returning that word to the vocabulary. Transparent fakery is the only unpardonable sin in an industry built on bunk."

"I meant he was bad."

"I know. But if you use a term wrong often enough, the law of averages guarantees that eventually it will describe the situation."

"Don't bully the boy," Valentino said. "He's right. Lugosi was fake *and* bad. His leaving the production was the best thing that could have happened to it. Karloff might have gone on playing hoods and religious fanatics until his contract ran out, and *Frankenstein* would be one more forgotten failure from the Golden Age."

"It's a shame the crazy Hungarian didn't live long enough to walk out on *The English Patient.*"

Valentino asked him just what he had against that film that hundreds of critics hadn't.

"Call me old-fashioned, but I preferred *Casablanca* when the hero gave up his lady love for the cause of freedom rather than the other way around." Broadhead pierced his lips with the stem of his pipe, but he was too aware of the properties of the material spinning off the take-up reel to stuff the bowl with tobacco and light it.

"So is it ours now?" Jason asked.

Valentino said, "Technically it still belongs to Universal. The old studio system would never have surrendered rights to an individual."

Broadhead said, "We'd be better off dealing with Grundage and his goons."

"In this case, I think we'd encounter less resistance from the current stockholders than we would from him. We'd have to prove his father came by it illegally, and even then an experienced attorney like Horace Lysander would make a case for rightful ownership based on eighty years of continuous possession."

"Sort of how we've still got Manhattan."

Broadhead smiled. "I told you you'd like this child. His term papers were no more accurate than the common lot, but original thinking prevailed."

Valentino rose and crossed the room to the wall-mounted telephone. "I need to make an appointment with Smith Old-field in Legal."

"Don't discuss details over the wire. Racketeers tap phones just like the FBI, and next time Frick and Frack won't be satisfied with just chipping a tooth."

Smith Oldfield was a native New Englander who dressed like an English country gentleman in an Ealing film. His moss-colored Harris tweed was acceptably shabby, as if it had been broken in by a manservant, and his gray knitted four-in-hand matched his temples. As far as Valentino knew, he'd never set foot in a courtroom; that called for skills in oratory and theater that his soft speech and quiet mannerisms did not reflect, and in any case he prided himself on the kind of homework and gentle negotiating that made it unnecessary to enter into an open forum. He wore eyeglasses with heavy black rims, but instead of looking naked and vulnerable when he removed them, his pale blue eyes resembled Toledo steel unsheathed from the scabbard.

"The situation is similar to a permanent easement," he said, folding a pair of well-kept hands on the leather top of a desk bare of paperwork. It wasn't that he hadn't any, only that he preferred to spare his visitors the sordid spectacle of the law in actual practice. At cocktail parties, when a dry gin martini had loosened his tongue, he compared it to sausage manufacture. "Common law is a contrary creature, prognostically speaking," he told Valentino. "The decision varies from judge to judge, and some judges contradict their own precedents. Further, there is the question of how the film came into your hands. If your late friend removed it without authorization from a storage unit leased in Grundage's name, Grundage can obtain a warrant and reclaim it."

"His father may have stolen it himself. Do two wrongs make a right?"

"Not in the statutes, in so many words. But in this situation only one tenth of the law argues against it. Frankly, I wouldn't take those odds to court."

Valentino, who knew Oldfield for a cautious man but not a timid one, felt his heart sink. He'd hoped for one of those judicial miracles the lawyer had delivered in the past.

"There is another question to consider." Now the glasses came off, exposing the twin blades of his eyes. "That is the fact that the police may seize the film as evidence in a homicide and two assaults."

"One, if I decide not to press charges in my case. Mr. Oldfield, this is a privileged communication, is it not?"

"Of course. Nothing discussed in this office leaves it without the client's consent."

Valentino leaned forward and folded his arms on his edge of the desk. "The police don't know I have the film. If it's taken and kept under the conditions usually reserved for evidence, for the amount of time usually required to secure an arrest and a conviction, its integrity will be compromised beyond repair."

"Forty years is the record, and that was a civil suit over property. Your concern is understandable."

"Thank you."

"I didn't say it was supportable in a court of law. As an officer of the court, I cannot advise you to withhold information or material evidence from the authorities except when it touches upon your Fifth Amendment rights, which the film does not."

"I have no choice. I'm committed to my profession by ethics

and behavior, just as you are to yours. My client is the UCLA
Film Preservation program. The only difference is I'm not pro-
tected by law. Strictly speaking, sir, *who* has those two reels
won't affect the investigation one way or the other. If someone's
arrested and the prosecution needs it to make its case, I can
print it on safety stock and surrender the original, but that takes
time. Sergeant Gill and Detective Yellowfern aren't patient men."

"I'd advise you against it. That would constitute the assump-
tion of legal possession. You could be tried as an accessory after
the fact, the fact being grand theft."

"I was afraid you'd say something like that."

Oldfield smiled thinly and put his glasses back on. "No one
ever likes to hear what a lawyer has to say. You're not going to
take my advice, are you?"

"About not making a new print, yes. I've been known to
bend the law, but the only time I actually broke it I paid a fine
and got two points on my driver's license." Valentino shook his
head. "I can't negotiate with Grundage as long as there's any
question about how I came by that film, and I can't stand by
while it's mistreated by the system. I thought I could, for once,
but that was before I actually had it. I should have known myself better than that."

"You must not take what I'm about to say as any kind of advice, legal or personal. If you do and it comes out, I'll deny I said
it. I'm nearing retirement age and have no intention of ending
my career with disbarment."

"As you said, nothing leaves this office." He felt a surge of
hope.

"What you need is a devious mind. It so happens we have
one of those under contract to this university."

Hope ran out of him like air from a punctured balloon. "I'd
really be grateful if you didn't say the name."

"Very well. I happen to know that he plays miniature golf at a place called Bob-o-Links in the Valley about this time once a week. It should be an excellent place to carry on a conversation you wouldn't want the administration overhearing." The attorney got up and extended his hand. "Good luck."

Valentino took it. "I'll need more than luck this time around."

"I wasn't referring to your dilemma. I meant good luck shooting against him. He cheats."

19

BOB-O-LINKS SPORTED AN electric sign over the gate depicting a cartoon bird with a putter-shaped head dipping and raising its beak like one of those perpetual-motion office toys executives use to mesmerize visitors. Valentino bought his admission, rented a canary yellow putter and a bucket of balls, and joined Henry Anklemire at the third hole. The little assistant director of Information Services wore a green sweater too tight for his rotundity, electric-blue knickers, orange argyles, and a purple tam-o-shanter with a pompon on top, an outfit that guaranteed him a job if the management ever tired of the bird on the sign.

The park, which was on the National Register of Historic Places, had a show-business theme that hadn't been updated since its founding in the 1950s. Howdy Doody's puppet mouth opened and closed, alternately accepting and rejecting balls rolled its way, a bear crouching in front of Davy Crockett's cabin cuffed at them as they approached the door, and painted plywood cutouts directing the players between obstacles looked like Troy Donahue and a host of others who had flashed in their pans too briefly and too long ago for even Valentino to connect them to their names. A chip shot that landed between Jayne Mansfield's breasts was worth fifty points.

Anklemire, chomping a black cigar that smelled like burning tires, spent a full minute phantom-putting before he knocked his ball through ten feet of zigzag tin pipe and between Jiminy Cricket's spats. "Ha! Take that, you little cock-a-roach." He shifted his cigar to the opposite corner of his mouth and grinned around it, twirling his putter like a baton. "Hey, there, Professor. Care to take a whack?" The PR flack thought everyone outside his department was faculty.

He took a half-hearted swipe at a rented ball and missed the pipe. "I'm no athlete. Not even the miniature kind."

"Probably means you're good in the sack. How's tricks? Find the *Casablanca* director's cut, Bogie and Bergman fly off business class and leave her hubby, the stiff, to the Nazis?"

"Something like that." He gave him an abridged version of recent events.

"Horror stuff, huh? Swell. Lookit the box office all them teenage vampires are doing. Personally, actors that live on Gummie Bears and Clearasil make me heave, but I ain't exactly the demographic. What you do, you stick yours on the extra disc. It don't matter if nobody ever watches it; you still get a hunk of the action on the bloodsucker flick."

"But it isn't about vampires."

"No biggie. You say on the box Lugosi's the star of the greatest vampire picture ever made. You say they shot it on the *Dracula* set?"

"Yes. All the original cobwebs were still in place."

"Bingo! The screen's greatest vampire returns to the vampire's castle. Vampire, vampire, vampire, how many times can you say it before it gets old? Never, that's how many! Oh, you can't make this stuff up."

"You just did."

"I thought this job was gonna be dull. You're a press agent's dream: Tiger Woods, only without all the fooling around." He took a swipe at Clarabell the Clown's nose, missed, and marked it on his scorecard as a success. Anklemire was the only person Valentino had ever met who cheated at miniature golf, and he was playing himself. "Brother, I love this sport: fresh air, exercise, and you don't go broke on caddies and equipment."

"You're sticking the cart in front of the horse. You can't promote the film until we have it free and clear."

"Gangsters are just businessmen with flashier broads. Cut a deal."

"The police want it, too, and it won't cost them a cent, just the half hour it takes to swear out a warrant."

"Well, then, you know what you got to do."

"Turn it over?"

"Cripes, no! My old man taught me you never give up nothing for free gratis, except to B'nai B'rith. You got to go out and nail the murderer."

Valentino, whose swing had begun, missed Clarabelle by yards, striking Roy Rogers' horse Trigger two holes away in a spot that would deny the world a Trigger, Jr.

"I'll give you that one," Anklemire said, writing on the card. "Yowtch."

"I'm supposed to beat the entire San Diego Police Department to the punch?"

"You already done it with Beverly Hills and the LAPD. All them boys down by the border know how to do is break up cockfights."

"That's vaguely racist."

The little man carefully removed his tam and scratched his scalp through a toupee formerly owned by Kevin Spacey. "I'm a sleazebag, Professor. It's why I'm so good at my job, just like you're good at yours. Everything we got to do to do it ain't in the description. Come on; you know you want to." He uncovered his dentures in a too-perfect grin. Although still well short of middle age, the career ad man had worn himself out from both ends and semi-retired from the high-pressure world of Madison Avenue to his present position with cases of pyorrhea and hemorrhoids severe enough to attract the attention of a medical journal. He'd accepted a more meager salary in return for a superior health plan.

"Why is it everyone I know seems to think I enjoy playing Charlie Chan? Just once I'd like to make a discovery of genuine historical value that doesn't involve a corpse."

"I wouldn't knock it. I don't know a man in my line of work that wouldn't commit a little murder to get a mention in *two* sections of the *L.A. Times*." Anklemire tugged his hat back on, rolled a ball down a plastic trough between the turning vanes of a dwarf windmill, and got a mechanical Liberace to come out and take a bow.

The Black Sleep: *appropriate title.*

It is a role one could walk through in his pyjamas, a deaf-mute performing errands that at most studios would bill him only in the closing credits, if at all; United Artists—bless the second string—has pledged to treat him better, but still he will follow John Carradine, Lon Chaney, Jr., and even Sally Whoever, a nobody, which given UA's standing is almost as bad. Chaney is drunk most of the time, and horses around on the set. Casmir—such is the name of Bela's own character—has lived to see both Carradine and Chaney poach the role he created, making a mockery of it in House of Dracula *and* Son of Dracula, *and now, twenty-five years after he turned his back on* Frankenstein *because the part was silent, he is forced to accept another without a single line. His pleas to be granted the power of speech if not hearing have brought half-hearted assurances from the director, but a promise without conviction isn't worthy of the name; this much, at least, he has learned about English, infuriatingly elusive language that it is. On the Hungarian stage he mastered Shakespeare in translation, but in America he can scarcely order a hamburger.*

Not that he could keep one down if it were served to him. His stay in the sanitarium has flushed the morphine from his system and deadened the urge to return to it, but it has left him with no appetite and a system that can barely tolerate weak tea and pale toast. When Basil Rathbone and the others queue up at a catering table laden with sweetmeats, roasts, and heavy cream, the scent of the rich food alone is enough to drive him to his dressing room, which he shares with Akim Tamiroff. The first swig from the bottle settles his stomach. The rest will prepare him for the next take.

The production will not wrap for a week, and already it is quaintly out of date. Giant grasshoppers are the monsters of the moment, the heroes men in lab coats, characters who in his prime were the villains. To a man these players are as bland as his tea and toast, offering none of the quirks and bits of stage business he brought to the mad Dr. Mirakle in Murders in the Rue Morgue, *the feature to which he and Florey fled from* Frankenstein.

Frankenstein, always Frankenstein, *ever and again until the end. What is Karloff doing these days?* The Ed Sullivan Show *on Sunday, reading selections from Poe. Another property poached.*

He glimpses his face in the mirror above the tiny sink, the dead gray hair falling over his temple, folds of skin hanging beneath his chin like the rotted drapes in Castle Dracula. He raises the bottle, gumming a grin at the reflection. "Good evening," he says, in the rich baritone he can still muster when the cough is not rattling his lungs. "Thank you, but I never drink—wine." And pours whiskey down his throat.

The daydream ended when the movie did and the menu popped back up onscreen. Valentino turned off the player and the laser projector, returning the auditorium to shadow. Lugosi had been wrong about his last role but one. (*Plan 9 from Outer Space* would not appear until three years after his death.) Small-budget studio that it was then, United Artists had breathed new life into the horror genre, reviving the faltering careers of classic stars like Rathbone and Carradine and providing viewers with a respite from the thunderous science fiction programmers of the Atomic Age, with their elephantine insects and heavy-handed apocalyptic themes. The ailing actor's turn as the mute Casmir was moving and tragically sympathetic, reminiscent of both the visual poetry of the silent cinema and Boris Karloff's performance in *Frankenstein*. It had been the last brilliant spurt of flame among the embers.

Valentino smiled sadly in the darkness of the projection booth. Ironically, Karloff had argued *against* giving the Monster the ability to speak in *Bride of Frankenstein*, insisting that it would destroy audience empathy, and had pleaded to strike all his lines from the script; surely a unique request in an ego-driven profession. He, too, had been overridden, but like Lugosi, he had been wrong. While his rival's valedictory effort had been overlooked, Karloff's semi-articulate artificial man was met with huge success in theaters and among critics. ("The Monster Talks!" advertisements proclaimed, echoing the success of "Garbo Speaks!") From start to finish, the two European artists had mirrored each other's career in reverse images, meteors whose trajectories had crossed moving in opposite directions. What a strange and arbitrary country was Hollywood.

It was questionable whether Bela Lugosi had seen his last onscreen appearance in life. *The Black Sleep* premiered in June 1956, and he died in August. Karloff, so the legend went, paid his colleague the ultimate compliment at his visitation, where he lay in state in one of the cloaks he had worn as Count Dracula: "You wouldn't be fooling us, would you, Bela?"

Lugosi, most probably, would not have accepted the remark in the spirit in which it was intended. Dry Anglo-Saxon wit was lost on demonstrative Hungarians. In any case, a quarter-century in the West Coast meat-grinder had bled him of whatever sense of humor he had brought to it.

The land line rang. Without switching on a light, he read the caller ID in the glow of the LED, and felt a cold hand on the back of his neck, as from the grave: After two years Lorna Hunter hadn't gotten around to having Craig's name removed from the number.

"Val, I'm sorry to disturb you. Are you busy?"

He hesitated. Her words were slurred. Had he lost one alcoholic friend only to replace him with another? "No. Are you all right?"

"Actually, I'm not. Can you come over?"

"What's wrong?"

"Please? I haven't spoken to another living soul in person in days. I really have to see you."

He calculated the driving time by the standards of homebound L.A. traffic. What he really needed was a calendar. "I'll be there in an hour."

Ice cubes tinkled against glass on her end. "Try to make it sooner, okay?"

He managed to shave five minutes off his original estimate. A truck driver and the chauffeur of a white stretch limo were two people he no sooner wished to meet again on foot than Pudge Pollard and Dickey Wirtz.

He'd barely touched the doorbell when the door opened and she fell against him. He had to put his arms around her to steady himself. He smelled gin—no tonic—and he was uncomfortably aware that she wore nothing beneath a yellow silk kimono that reached barely to her thighs. The warmth of her was overpowering. "Thank God," she said. "Thank God. I was afraid you'd decided not to come." She raised her face as if for a kiss.

He took her chin between thumb and forefinger and forced it away as gently as possible, which wasn't too gently; he was alarmed. Her makeup was streaked, and for a terrible moment he thought she was bruised. Had she had a visit similar to his? He asked again if she was all right.

The roughness of his handling seemed to bring her out of whatever fog she was in. She shuddered in his arms and straightened, pushing herself away. A hand went to her hair, smoothing it back from where it had fallen about her face. There were no marks, except for bluish circles beneath her eyes. She nodded. "I didn't mean to scare you. It's just that I need a friend."

"Has something happened?"

"No. The phone keeps ringing, that's all. They don't leave messages. I guess they've given up on my ever calling them back. They're getting less persistent. Craig isn't that big of a story. They're more interested in who killed Michael Jackson's giraffes."

He was surprised reporters were still calling at all. Hunter's name seemed to have slipped clear off the air. But he didn't say that. "Where do you keep the coffee? I'm sorry to be blunt, but you stink at drinking."

"I'm getting better with practice."

They went into the living room with his arm around her waist. It was impossible to avoid close contact in that position and he tried to keep his mind off the heat coming from her skin. He deposited her gently on the sofa, looking anywhere but at her legs as she crossed them, and went to the kitchen without asking directions again to the coffee. At the arch he stopped, went back, and moved a half-full bottle and a smeared glass out of her reach.

"That won't stop me," she said. "I ran the Malibu Marathon."

"I'm not going to confiscate it. I don't work for the Women's Christian Temperance Union. But it would be a big help if you gave it a rest. I think the ratio of cure to cause is four cups of Maxwell House to an ounce of Gordon's, and I don't know how much you have on hand."

"This is the last of it. Craig pretty much cleaned out the bar when he left."

"How much coffee is what I meant."

"Craig was the coffee drinker. You might find some still in the pantry. It's probably stale."

"It's the caffeine that counts. You'll just have to put up with the taste. Amateur drinkers shouldn't be left on their own."

He found an unopened jar of Folger's instant and a teakettle and filled it with water. While he waited for it to boil he went back out to join her and found her sprawled to one side on the sofa with her kimono gaping, showing more cleavage than he found comfortable. She was snoring softly. He arranged her into a less awkward reclining position and covered her with a decorative shawl he drew off the arm of a chair.

Sleep was an even better restorative than coffee. He returned to the kitchen, took the kettle off the burner, and turned off the stove. Before he let himself out, he'd empty the gin bottle into the sink. It would make him feel like Eliot Ness, but a person unaccustomed to alcohol was less likely to go out for a refill once the supply was gone.

"I find a man in the kitchen sexy."

At the sound of Lorna's voice he turned and saw her supporting herself against the side of the arch. The sash of her kimono was untied, exposing the entire front of her person. She was smiling lopsidedly.

"How about it?" she asked. "Is this anything like you pictured?"

"Lorna, we're friends."

"We could be friends with benefits."

"I can't. There's someone in my life."

"Where is she?"

"Seattle."

"Last time I looked, Seattle was a loooong way away."

He approached her. She pushed herself upright, swaying as she spread her arms. He jerked her kimono shut, tied the sash, encircled her waist again, more tightly this time, and bundled her back to the sofa in the living room. He let go and with a push of his hip dropped her onto the cushions. She went, "Oof!" and glared up at him with an angry flush.

"I don't expect you to thank me," he said, panting a little from the exertion (and—he was honest with himself—desire). "I just don't want you hating us both tomorrow."

She put her face in her hands and sobbed.

He didn't dare try to comfort her. In the present state of affairs he wasn't sure if loyalty to Harriet and respect for Lorna were enough to withstand temptation a second time. He said he'd call her in the morning and left.

He was halfway home before he remembered the bottle still standing on the coffee table. To turn back was dangerous. She was a grown woman, as she'd proven beyond a doubt. He couldn't be there to help the Craig and Lorna Hunters of the world every hour of the day and night.

It was late when he'd gathered the ruins of his sofa bed into something approaching comfort and fell into a deep sleep. He dreamt not of movies or actors, but disturbingly erotic images of Harriet and Lorna and himself. He had a vague sensation they were being watched. At first the voyeur seemed to be Henry Anklemire, got up in his cartoonish golfing togs, cheering them on with a putter in one hand, but then his features blurred and were replaced by Craig's, observing them sadly and solemnly and silent as a tomb.

Valentino sat up straight, soaked with sweat and feeling a terrible sense of naked shame. It was as if he'd betrayed three people at once, one of them deceased.

He had no idea how long his telephone had been ringing before he was aware of it. He read the ID and groaned. It was Lorna again. He considered unplugging it, but the last time he'd ignored a late-night call, tragedy had followed.

He picked up. "Lorna, I—"

"You bounce back pretty fast." A male voice, flat as asphalt but much harder. "I must be losing my edge."

The perspiration coating his body turned to ice. "Pollard."

"This boy's got connections," the thug said away from the mouthpiece. "I bet he knows your name, too."

Dickey Wirtz wheezed something Valentino didn't catch.

Pollard came back on. "I got somebody here wants to talk to you."

There was a pause, then another voice spoke, sober now and shaking. "Val?"

"Lorna?" He gripped the receiver hard.

She started to say something, but was cut off. Pollard said, "You seen enough crime pictures to know how this works. The film for the woman. No police."

"How do you know I've got the film?"

He wanted to take the words back as soon as they left his mouth. The flat voice chuckled.

"I do now. Don't bother coming to Tarzana, 'cause we'll be gone by the time you get here. You got one hour. Here's the address."

Valentino fumbled on the light and reached for a pencil, then stopped. He knew the place nearly as well as The Oracle.

20

POLLARD HAD SAID no police. He hadn't said come alone.

Valentino thought first of Kyle Broadhead, then rejected the idea. For all his mental energy, the professor was advanced in years and even less of a match for a pair of professional bone-breakers than he. If something happened to him, Fanta would never forgive Valentino, and he would never forgive himself.

Harriet would insist he go to the law, an institution to which she belonged, but however careful the police were not to be spotted, he couldn't risk bringing them in with Lorna in the clutches of such as Pollard and Wirtz.

Well, he'd brought luck the first time.

Jason Stickley answered his cell on the second ring. He sounded fresh despite the hour. He listened to the request, then said, "Sure."

"You need to think about it longer. This could be dangerous."

"As dangerous as the last time?"

"More. These characters don't care about the consequences

of their actions. They killed Craig Hunter, they beat me up, and they almost killed Teddie Goodman. I don't feel right about asking you at all. If they find out I didn't come alone, there's no telling what they'll do, except it will be unpleasant. But I need someone to know where I am in case they don't intend for Lorna and me to come out."

"Are you going to give them the film?"

"I don't have any choice. It's her life if I don't."

"There's plenty of scrap film in the UCLA library. One reel looks like all the rest."

"I can't take the chance they won't identify what's on it. I knew just by holding it up to the light. They'd probably kill us both on the spot."

The intern was silent for a moment. Valentino heard throbbing, industrial-style music in the background. "I'm in."

"Only if you agree not even to come into the same block unless I signal you otherwise. We'll rig up something in case they take away my cell."

"Okay. You know the place you dropped me off for a minute last time?"

He remembered the yellow-brick factory building more than a century old. "Yes."

"You can pick me up there. It's on the way."

"I'll be there in ten minutes." Valentino hung up.

"Be *where* in ten minutes?"

He jumped a foot. Harriet had a key to the front door and had climbed the flight of steps noiselessly to the projection booth. She wore the loose-fitting jeans and unstructured jacket she always flew in and carried her travel bag strapped over one shoulder. She looked exhausted but beautiful in the short ash-blond hair that complimented the classic shape of her head, and suspicious in the extreme.

"My gosh, you scared me," he said. "When did you get in?"

"Half an hour ago. Be *where* in ten minutes," she repeated. "It's after midnight."

"Why didn't you call me to pick you up?"

"I started to give you my flight information this morning. After we were cut off I tried you here and at the office. Finally I decided to throw myself at the mercy of an L.A. taxi. I've had more pleasant experiences dissecting corpses three weeks old. I asked you a question."

"I can't tell you. There isn't time."

"Tell me in the car." She dropped her bag.

"Harriet, please trust me. I wouldn't leave you in the dark if the situation weren't crucial."

"Crucial in your case usually means murder. Has this anything to do with Craig Hunter?"

He should have known she'd bring herself up to date on all recent murders. She knew Craig was an acquaintance. "Yes."

"Who were you talking to?"

"Jason."

"Your intern? Just what are you getting that boy into?"

"*Please,* Harriet!"

"I'm going with you or I'm calling the police."

"You can't do that. They'll kill Lorna."

"Lorna Hunter? Who will?"

He gave up then. He'd lost three minutes already. "I'll bring the car around."

"First tell me where you think you're going."

"Where you just came from. LAX."

She watched him gather up the two cans of film. "I might have known this would have something to do with some movie no one but you cares about."

"If I thought I was the only one, I'd never have let myself get

into this. But there are some things more important than movies. Human life, for one."

"I'm glad to hear you say it. So what is it this time, lost footage from the Zapruder film, or the Second Coming? The image
of Christ on an overexposed frame?"

"*Frankenstein.*" He mumbled it, sliding the cans into his di-
lapidated briefcase.

"Excuse me?"

"The test reels for the 1931 *Frankenstein,* starring Bela Lugosi."

"Boris Karloff starred in *Frankenstein.* I've heard that from
you a thousand times if I've heard it once. Val, how hard have
you been working?" She sounded concerned for him for the
first time that night.

"I'll explain later."

"LAX," she said.

"Yes."

"Well, that should give us time for you to fill me in."

He leased space in a garage around the corner. Harriet was
waiting on the sidewalk in front of the theater as he approached. He let up on the accelerator, then as she stepped
forward he pushed down, gaining speed. In the rearview mirror Valentino saw the love of his life with her mouth open in a
furious *O,* groping inside her handbag for her cell. He was a
good deal more worried about the conversation they'd have
later than whatever information she was giving her employers
at police headquarters. The airport had been the first place
he'd thought of when she'd asked his destination. It had been
freshest in his mind.

Light glowed in the high gridded windows of the defunct buzz-saw blade factory. Even from the street he could hear the music from inside, reminiscent of the din that had accompanied its productive years. Either it was just the Halloween season or Steampunks were the party-throwingest creatures in a region notorious for its late-night blowouts.

At the top of the concrete steps worn hollow by the tread of many work boots, Valentino banged on the door. The edge of his fist was aching before someone heard it above the noise on the other side. A young woman—she might not have been more than a girl under metallic makeup that made her resemble a distaff Tin Man from *The Wizard of Oz*—opened up and beckoned him in with a finger encased in a black kid glove. Evidently his description had preceded him. He hoped it wasn't too unflattering.

The floor shook beneath the bass notes of a band playing a switched-on version of the Anvil Chorus. The bulbs of a chandelier rigged up from a tractor tire suspended by tow chains from the twenty-foot ceiling strobed, bathing musicians and dancers in shifting hues; highlighting, then plunging in shadow figures in top hats and bowlers, picture brims and Bobbie helmets, bedecked with gears and pulley attachments and wedding veils fashioned from steel mesh. A massive flywheel twelve feet in diameter decorated a naked brick wall with a full-length coronation portrait of the young Queen Victoria mounted in the center in a jointed pipe frame. The great piece of machinery must have weighed more than a ton and had to have been brought in with a forklift truck at the least. The moment he formed that conclusion, he spotted the truck itself, hitched incongruously to a brace of life-size papier-mâché horses complete with blinders.

Gripping the newcomer's hand in a palm studded with hob-nails, Tin Woman led him serpentine fashion through the press of bodies to a sparsely populated area behind the band-stand, with exposed plumbing on more brick and lingering odors of scorched metal and lubricating grease. He wondered if the smells were that persistent after so many years or if they'd been sprayed from a can just before the guests arrived.

As visitor and escort neared their terminus, the music changed abruptly: Electric guitars and amplifiers were replaced with the sweet strains of violins and the low mellow murmur of a cello. The dancers ceased gyrating and began to waltz, deco-rously and at arm's length. Valentino had spent so much of his rest time lately in dreams that if it weren't for the urgency of his errand he'd have suspected the entire affair was the distorted fancy of an overworked mind and a hyperactive imagination.

Jason Stickley broke out of a small group to greet him. The boy wore his high silk hat accessorized from the scrapyard, frock coat, padlock and chain. "How do you feel about reinforce-ments?" He turned a palm toward the group—young men all, so far as Valentino could determine behind the metalwork, stiff collars, machinists' goggles, waistcoats, and gentlemen's head-gear circa 1890, with a hefty helping of H. G. Wells's *The Time Machine*. Shy grins and gestures of welcome came with clank-ing accompaniment.

The archivist seized Jason's arm and turned him aside. "I didn't give you permission to tell anyone."

"You didn't say I couldn't." The intern sounded hurt.

"I'd be less conspicuous driving a wagon loaded with pots and pans."

"Oh, we'll dump the paraphernalia. We're not stupid."

"You're all barely old enough to vote. I can't be responsible for putting you in jeopardy. I'll go alone."

"Too late, Mr. Valentino. I know where you're going, remember. Anyway, we're old enough to join the army and fight a war."

"I start basic training next month," said one of the others who'd overheard.

"I figure this makes me older." Another smacked his palm with a heavy brass knob fixed to a stout walking stick.

"I can't fit you all in my car." He realized the weakness of the argument even as he raised it.

"Pat's got his dad's Hummer," Jason said. "We can all fit in it with room to spare."

"Me, too." Tin Woman's valley girl accent sounded like the real thing.

"No women." This came in chorus from the group of young men.

She stuck out a tongue that looked blood-red against silver skin. "That Victorian male chauvinist B.S. won't work even here. See, I'm armed." A hobnailed hand dove into her lace décolletage and came up with a steel whistle on a chain around her neck. She blew it. The shrill sound slashed across the chamber music, turning heads their way briefly from the dance floor.

"We're going whether you say yes or no," Jason said. "We're not freaks. When someone's in trouble, we help."

Valentino took his fingers out of his ears. "Just don't blow that thing unless you absolutely have to. If these guys hear a police whistle, they'll shoot first and ask questions never."

"So we're all in?" Jason's grin was almost too broad for his narrow face.

"God help me, but I can't fight the mob and all of you at the same time."

"Way to go, Joy Stick!" said the boy with the bludgeon.

"Joy Stick?"

The intern flushed. "Jason Stickley, you know? We all have nicknames."

"I'm Link."

"Wilde Thing. With an *e*."

"Pat Pend."

"I'm Whiz. Short for Whistler's Daughter." The girl raised her whistle to her lips again. Valentino's hand shot out and grasped it. She colored under the undercoat and dropped it back between her breasts.

He looked at his strap watch. They had less than twenty minutes to go fifty blocks. "You have to follow all my orders to the letter. If you don't agree, I'll call the cops right now and rat you all out as underage guests at a party where alcohol is served." He showed them his cell.

"There's no—" someone started.

"He knows about the keg from before," Jason interrupted. "He's hip for an old dude."

"'Hip'?" Link, the youth in basic training, furrowed his brow under a deerstalker cap with a brass steam pressure gauge cemented to the crown.

"Properly informed." Whiz's upper-class Brit clashed with her Moon Zappa.

Valentino let out the sigh of a ninety-year-old man. "Let's get this show on the road."

The partyers divested themselves of chains, bells, and everything else likely to make noise and climbed into the boxy vehicle parked not far from the compact. Valentino leaned his head through the open window on the passenger's side and asked Jason if he had his phone. Joy Stick showed him his punked-up cell.

"I'll call you just before I go in and leave it on. That way you'll hear what's going on inside. What's your number?"

"I don't know if I have that many minutes."

"I'll pay for the extra."

"I didn't mean that." His tone was plaintive. "It's prepaid. It cuts off when my time runs out."

Whiz, sprawled across three laps in the backseat, said, "This is why we like Victoriana."

"Here." Pat Pend, behind the wheel, excavated an unadorned model from a waistcoat pocket and handed it to Jason. He gave the number to Valentino, who punched it into the memory.

"If things turn sour, call the police," he said.

"What if they take away your phone?" asked Jason.

"Wait fifteen minutes, *then* call the police."

"Fifteen minutes is a long time."

"It's just right if everything goes smoothly. Any less is risky. It wouldn't be smart to startle them with sirens just when we're making the exchange."

"There wouldn't have to be sirens. We outnumber these guys three to one."

Valentino pushed his face close to the boy's. "Do *not* go in, understand? No matter what. These men are killers. They're what the police are for. When things go wrong, nobody calls the Steampunks."

"*You* did."

A chorus of agreement came from the other seats.

And I pray I don't regret it. Aloud he said, "You know where this place is in case we get separated?"

Jason's teeth glistened in the light from a streetlamp. "I'd be one lousy film student if I didn't."

Valentino decided, if he survived the night, to ask his department head to appoint this boy—this young man—to a salaried position. Anyone who could make him smile under those circumstances was worth keeping around.

21

THE HOLLYWOOD WAX Museum was one of Valentino's favorite haunts, a place to go and revisit the giants of his Movie Channel youth in 3-D—the real thing, without a cumbersome pair of glasses coming in between. The white stucco building with its electric marquee-type sign was an ancient institution by local standards: Its oldest figures from the silent age had modeled for the sculptors in person. When the season sagged beneath ponderous special effects and actors with crow's-feet playing horny high school students, the archivist would bring a sack lunch and dine with Francis X. Bushman, Blanche Sweet, and Rin Tin Tin.

But at that hour, with the sign switched off and Hollywood Boulevard as deserted as any street ever got in a major metropolitan area (he'd heard stories of coyotes slinking down from the hills and prowling the Walk of Fame), the museum appeared anything but friendly, a mortuary reflecting the smog-muted starlight from its pale front. A box that had once held a Magic Chef electric range slouched on the corner, providing sleeping quarters for one or more of the L.A. homeless, modern-day Bedouins who folded their tents and stole away come the dawn. Whatever they witnessed during the night vanished with them.

The Hummer had turned off a block short of the address, as arranged, and Valentino had his choice of parking spaces. He pulled up directly in front of the arched entrance so he and Lorna could make their escape as quickly as possible. Or so he prayed.

He remembered to call Pat Pend's number, and after a quick exchange with Jason, left the line open and slid the phone into the slash pocket of his Windbreaker. Despite the delays he'd reached his destination with four minutes to spare, thanks to the thinness of the traffic. Gripping the wheel in both hands, he took a deep breath, held it a moment, and expelled it with a rush. Then he tipped up the door handle and got out.

The front door opened without resistance. He shook his head. Security personnel the world over were underpaid. He hoped that whatever amount Grundage had slipped the person responsible was worth the loss of his job if it got back to his superiors.

No alarm had gone off when he pulled at the door, and when he stepped inside, the motion sensors mounted high on the walls regarded him without interest. They would have been disarmed, most likely by the same person who'd left the door unlocked. Surveillance cameras attached to the ceiling had ceased their relentless oscillation, their red lights dark.

A shudder racked his shoulders. A wax museum is an eerie enough place by daylight, but at night, with the bare minimum of lights left on to discourage intruders, this one may as well have been excavated from the dust of centuries, and he the first man to enter it, and to lay eyes upon freshly interred remnants from the age of superstition and black magic. The deserted ticket counter, the garlands of theater ropes arranged to control visitor traffic during peak periods, the racks of free brochures promoting other local tourist attractions, all took on a grim aspect when shadows skulked about the extremities. A bright banner strung high overhead across the lobby advertising the current featured exhibit in honor of the Halloween season (HIGH STAKES: THE VAMPIRE IN FILM FROM *NOSFERATU* THROUGH *TWILIGHT*) writhed like a venomous serpent in the air stirred by his entrance.

Valentino had never enjoyed being frightened, even in fun. It was one thing to be scared out of one's wits in a crowded theater, where the experience was shared, quite another to walk home down an empty street or climb a dark flight of stairs alone and with one's imagination filled with grisly images. He had never seen a horror movie made since the original 1968 *Night of the Living Dead* more than once, and after his first experience with *The Exorcist*, he had sworn off every chiller that followed. He'd never seen anything in the Wes Craven canon or that of any of his imitators and, based on what he'd witnessed in trailers, doubted that he was any poorer for the decision. He preferred to snuggle up with Henry Hull's werewolf of London, Frankenstein's Monster from Karloff through Glenn Strange, and anyone who played Count Dracula until Hammer Films got carried away and started buying its Max Factor blood by the barrel. In those earlier films the hero always won, defeating the mad scientist and winning the heart of the heroine, and the ghoul thoroughly destroyed, at least until the cameras began rolling on the sequel. But even these pleasant memories became sinister when only the sound of his own breathing and the beating of his heart were present.

He'd thought to bring along a flashlight, which became es-

sential as he passed along the first public corridor beyond sight
of the front windows and saw only pitch blackness at the end.
He switched it on and poked the beam about. The faces of
long-dead movie stars seemed to stir in the unsteady shaft,
their expressions to change from earnest to malevolent as
shadows crawled. Ghosts disturbed in the middle of the night
were never friendly.

Although he hadn't been told where to go in the building,
he didn't wander, nor did he call for guidance. For one thing,
he was afraid his throat wouldn't work, as happened in bad
dreams when he tried to cry out; for another, he didn't want to
take the chance of being overheard by some strolling insomniac outside and prompting a call to the police. Too late, he
thought of the unlocked door and the possibility of an officer
on his rounds discovering it and going in to investigate, but no
power on earth could persuade him to retrace his steps. He
couldn't afford to squander whatever courage he had left turning back around and re-entering that corridor.

It struck him odd that a law-abiding citizen should spend as
much time worrying about the police as a common felon engaged in his work. Was it a kind of madness? The hoarders' obsession that he alone could be trusted to protect something of
value from destruction? Or had he spent too many thousands of
hours in artificially darkened rooms watching melodramatic
characters conducting themselves as no sane person would in
the real world? Both explanations indicated an unsound mind.

He did not wander. He knew where the meeting place was.

The way led him past Indiana Jones and Mr. Chips, *How
Green Was My Valley* and *Star Wars*. Rhett Butler and Scarlett
O'Hara fled the burning of Atlanta (with the bulbs in the elec-
tric flames switched off), *Easy Riders'* Dennis Hopper and Peter
Fonda bent over their choppers, James Dean looked sullen,

Marlene Dietrich straddled a wooden chair in black lingerie and top hat. The figures were exquisite likenesses rendered in minute and lifelike detail, unlike the bland-faced mannequins one saw in roadside attractions got up in iconic costumes to suggest the originals; here, Garbo's silken lashes appeared poised to flutter, Bogart's scarred lip to curl away from his often-imitated snarl, Mel Gibson's brow to wrinkle and his head to twitch. The artisans responsible had been brought in from all over the world, and if their commissions were reflected in the admission price, they were well worth it. As a matter of fact, Valentino found $8.95 more than reasonable for an experience that would last far longer than most movies that cost ten dollars to see and took ten minutes to forget. The place was a permanent fixture in a landscape constantly in flux, like Grauman's Chinese Theater and the two-story-tall wooden letters sprawled across the hills that had given the community its name, along with a culture and an attitude that for better or worse was known throughout the globe.

He came around Johnny Weissmuller in his loincloth wrestling a giant gorilla and descended the broad flight of steps that led to the Chamber of Horrors.

Here all the lights were on. The place was below street level and there were no windows to betray activity inside. He snapped off the flashlight and slid it into the briefcase containing the two reels of film in their cans.

"It's alive! Alive! Alive!"

The maniacal cry echoed around the block-and-plaster walls, startling Valentino, who nearly dropped the case. Belatedly he recognized the voice of Colin Clive from the *Frankenstein* soundtrack. The fragment was followed a moment later by a bestial howl, then the somber voice of Maria Ouspenskaya in her Slavic gypsy accent: "Even a man who is pure in heart, and

says his prayers by night, may become a wolf when the wolf-
bane blooms and the autumn moon is bright." Then came brash
Robert Armstrong: "It wasn't the planes. It was beauty killed
the beast."

Someone knew he was there. Whoever it was had activated
the sound system that piped memorable lines from classic horror movies into the chamber. Claude Rains had just begun his
curtain speech about meddling in things man should leave
alone when he was cut off. A flat, nasty chuckle reached the
newcomer's ears as if the man responsible was standing next to
him. Pudge Pollard laughed the way he spoke.

He was aware suddenly of movement among the figures in a
tableau he'd just passed, a stirring in the corner of his eye and
a rustle of clothing. He turned that way, and his blood slid to
his heels as Boris Karloff shrugged loose of his rotted wrap-
pings and stepped from his sarcophagus. It was the set of the
tomb from the opening scene of *The Mummy*, the 1932 original, and Im-ho-tep was coming to life after three thousand
years just as he had in the film.

It was an illusion, caused by frayed nerves and the atmospheric lighting. The man was emerging from behind the cof-
fin, not from inside, and he wore a contemporary sportcoat a
size too large for him, presumably to conceal his gun when it
was in its holster. It was in his hand, and although Valentino
had never seen the man before and didn't recognize his sunken
cheeks and prison pallor, he knew the moment he spoke that
he was Dickey Wirtz, Pollard's wheezy-voiced confederate.

"Gave you the willies, huh? Same stunt I used to scare the
pants off my ninety-year-old grandmother."

Wirtz stepped down from the platform. "You're the movie
nut. You know what's next."

Valentino set the briefcase on the floor and stood with his

arms out from his sides while the man patted him down with one hand, holding the gun pointed at him but out of easy reach. The hand went inside his slash pocket and came out with the cell phone. Wirtz saw it was turned on with the line open, frowned, and put it to his ear. "Hello?"

Valentino read on his face the moment Jason hung up. There was no mistaking that voice for the archivist's. The sickly pale face grew dark. The hand holding the gun swept up so quickly Valentino had no time to brace himself. A white light burst in the side of his head. He stumbled, but caught his balance. Something warm and wet trickled down from his temple. The jagged gunsight had broken the skin.

"Pudge said no cops!"

The flat voice called out. In that echoing place there was no telling from which direction it came. "What?"

"He's bugged!"

"Wired?"

"Cell." He told him the rest.

A vile curse, without inflection. "Shoo him down here."

Valentino turned back down the corridor without waiting to be ordered. He stiffened for another blow, but it didn't come. Instead he heard a wheezy grunt. The small effort of stooping to pick up the briefcase would tax that damaged throat and his respiratory function. Something prodded Valentino's kidney— Wirtz's favorite spot for persuasion, it seemed—and he started forward with the man's feet scraping the floor behind.

They passed the scene of *Alien*'s bloody birth, George Romero's zombies, the shower scene from *Psycho*. Now he heard snatches of conversation, too low to follow, punctuated at unpredictable intervals by hissing pops like short bursts of steam escaping a leaky valve. After a few more yards a bored mechanical voice, vaguely female, said, "Seven-fourteen, what's

your twenty?" Another pop. Then: "Sherman and Sepulveda."
A male voice, just as mechanical.

The police band. Valentino felt a fear he had never known
watching the movies that had inspired the exhibits. He hadn't
once thought the killers might have brought along a scanner.
They would know the police were on their way long before
rescue arrived.

He stopped. They had entered a series of tableaus devoted
to the horror films of Roger Corman. Figures—he couldn't tell
how many—stood in the shadow of the wall enclosing *The
Masque of the Red Death*. The fact that they were not on a platform told him they weren't made of wax.

Something moved in the shadow and Pudge Pollard came
out into the light, gripping a handgun similar to his partner's.
In his other hand he held the handle of a portable radio receiver, which was silent now between transmissions. Even L.A.
had its quiet nights.

"Dumb move, pal," Pollard said. "Amateur's mistake. Who'd
you call?"

He saw no advantage in lying. "A friend. We have fifteen
minutes before he calls the police."

"We'll know when he does." Pollard set the scanner on the
edge of the platform. "Okay, Dickey. Check out the case."

Wirtz moved back into his line of sight, stuck his gun into
his underarm holster, and rummaged around inside the briefcase until he brought out one of the flat cans. He held it out to
Pollard, who took it but barely glanced at it. "Okay, guy," said
the flat voice. "You know what to look for."

The shadow shifted again and J. Arthur Greenwood came
forward. Valentino froze, as motionless as Vincent Price in his
scarlet robe. The aged collector looked distinctly uncomfortable among cinematic displays that did not belong to him.

22

THE RETIRED PUBLISHER of *Horrorwood* wore a mohair suit tailored to his burly frame and a Tyrolean hat perched at an angle whose gaiety did not extend to his expression. His black-tinted hair and pencil moustache looked even more artificial against the gray of his face. He looked nervous, and not at all as a connoisseur of fantasy memorabilia should look when he was within arm's reach of the gem of any modern collection.

Valentino found his voice at last. "*You?*"

Greenwood shook his head, and went on shaking it as if he suffered from palsy. It moved like the safety plug on a pressure cooker coming to full steam.

Pollard chuckled again. "Get real, pal. He almost wet himself when we dropped in on him. He's just here to get a look at the goods." He extended the can to Greenwood without taking his eyes or his gun off the archivist.

"One moment, please." The octogenarian's head stopped shaking. He tucked his cane under one arm, drew a pair of surgical gloves from one of the flap pockets of his coat, and wriggled his fingers into them.

Wirtz snorted. "Pansy."

Greenwood paid him no attention. His nerves appeared to have settled as he went through the familiar process of authentication. When he had the can in hand he fumbled with the seam, but got it open finally and removed the reel from inside. He set the can on the floor, puffing as he straightened, unspooled two feet of film, and held it up so the overhead light shone through the frames. His breathing quickened; Valentino knew that sensation. At length he rerolled the film and nodded.

"Okay. Let's have the other, Dickey."

A new voice came from the shadows. "That won't be necessary. I know a bit about these people. They'd rather forego an item than break up a set. Thank you, Mr. Greenwood."

The collector hesitated in the midst of returning the reel to its container. "You won't forget our agreement."

"You'll be the sole bidder. Just remember your part of it."

"Of course, although it's a shame I can't show it off."

"After the grand jury's no longer in session and things settle down, you may show it to whomever you like."

"I hope I live that long."

"You won't if you don't hold up your end."

Distractedly, Valentino watched Greenwood return the can to Pollard, who had to tug a little to free it from his hand, and walk up the corridor toward the entrance, his cane and handmade shoes tapping the floor hastily (undoubtedly it was the only time he'd moved that fast away from an acquisition). The voice in shadow was maddeningly familiar, but the archivist had met so many new people in the course of this affair he failed to place it in the crowd. Mike Grundage? No, and that astonished him. If he'd come here knowing nothing else, he'd been sure of whom he was coming to meet.

The scanner crackled. Time stood still, but it was a routine report of a minor accident. Incredibly, it seemed, only a fraction of the fifteen minutes had elapsed.

"I wish you could follow orders as well as you follow a trail," said the voice. "Still, we're almost finished here." As he spoke, he came out into the light. Horace Lysander, Mike Grundage's attorney, had dressed for the occasion, in a dark suit over a midnight-blue shirt with tie to match.

Valentino's breath caught. Then he nodded. "It makes sense. You knew Craig Hunter had stolen the film, and that I was the only likely person he'd entrust it to for safekeeping. That's what he called me about the night he was killed, to tell me to expect it. He knew Grundage wouldn't touch him as long as the film was somewhere his gorillas couldn't lay hands on it."

"He was always safe from Mike. My clients aren't such dumb clucks they'd risk being charged with murder in the middle of a racketeering investigation. Hunter thought he was meeting with Mike, to get him to bid against Greenwood for something that already belonged to his family. That's what I wanted him to think, when he called me from his ex-wife's home. I didn't hang up on him; but you've guessed that by now."

Another transmission came over the air: a two-man team of officers breaking for lunch.

"Are you saying Grundage knows nothing about tonight?"

"He knows almost nothing, period. He directed me to handle Hunter as I saw fit. I suppose he meant legally, but I sent Pollard and Wirtz to meet Hunter at the Grotto instead. He must have spotted them for what they were while they were waiting for the crowd to thin out, and that's when he called you."

"You admit you hired these goons to beat Craig to death and break his arms so you could pin it on your client."

"Elizabeth Grundage was my client long before Mike was. She still is. I'd do anything to protect her privacy and spare her the kind of attention that comes with dredging up her late husband's dirty dealings."

"How would framing her son for murder manage that?"

"She's had very little to do with him for years. Without that film as evidence, the press will never connect her with the case." A bitter smile passed across his well-fed countenance. "I'm afraid I underestimated Hunter when I advised Elizabeth against doing business with him. He sealed his own fate when he went so far as to steal the film. I had no choice but to bring in the professionals."

"Why didn't you have my arms broken at the Oracle?"

"You needed them to carry the reels. I borrowed these fellows from Mike, not that he's aware of it. He never got them off a murder charge in open court. Isn't that right, Pudge?"

"Sure thing, boss."

Valentino understood then. "So it's true love, you and Elizabeth Grundage."

"More like respect. I wish it were more, but she's made it clear she values our friendship too much to jeopardize it with a romantic relationship." His smile turned sad. "One takes what one can get."

"Including, no doubt, a cut of the action when Greenwood buys the film."

"Don't be foolish. I'm one of the highest-paid lawyers in private practice. My beach house in Malibu cost more than those reels will ever bring at auction. I only wanted them to keep from surfacing and causing Elizabeth unnecessary embarrassment.

My second mistake was having your apartment searched before they came into your possession. I guessed that much afterwards, and confirmed it when Pollard called you tonight and you let slip that you had them."

"They didn't just search my apartment. They caught a colleague of mine doing the same thing and threw her downstairs."

"That was unfortunate, but she shouldn't have put herself in that position. In any case, I made up for that miscalculation when I used the film to enlist Greenwood's cooperation. In addition to authenticating it, he arranged this venue through his connections with the owners. They're under the impression he's hosting a private party, and we can make our exchange undisturbed. That, at least, was the plan."

As if it were timed, a call came onto the scanner from the bored-sounding female dispatcher. "All units in the vicinity, proceed to sixty-seven-sixty-seven Hollywood Boulevard. Possible hostage situation."

The archivist knew the address as well as his own. He was standing in the middle of it.

"I'm afraid that's your exit cue, Mr. Valentino." Lysander jerked his chin at Pollard and Wirtz, who spread their feet in target stance, Wirtz retrieving his weapon from his holster.

"Wait! What have you done with Lorna?"

"One moment, gentlemen." The attorney turned and walked a few feet to the nearest wall. Something clicked and a series of fluorescent lights that had been left off flickered into life, illuminating another exhibit.

Valentino recognized the dungeon set from *The Pit and the Pendulum,* another of Corman's garish tributes to the works of Edgar Allan Poe. The painters and carpenters were every bit as talented as the craftsmen who shaped the wax figures. The walls looked realistically of ancient stone, streaked with white mold, and a drop of ruby-colored blood on the razor-sharp axe suspended above the victim's pallet appeared to tremble on the verge of falling. But in place of a lifeless effigy, Lorna Hunter lay spreadeagle, bound with leather straps and gagged with duct tape. Apart from that she was naked. Her eyes were wide open and rolling with terror.

"There wasn't time for her to dress," Lysander said. "Her kimono came off in the struggle."

"Let her go. She has nothing to do with this."

"Hardly nothing. She brought you here. The blade is plywood, I'm sorry to say. Ordinary bullets will have to do."

"This isn't necessary. Teddie Goodman has a chance. You can plead that down to simple assault. Craig Hunter was a has-been, who'd have drunk himself to death sooner or later, or died of an overdose. You of all people know what a smart lawyer can do with motives like love and loyalty. Two cold-blooded murders on top of his would put you in prison for life or worse."

"Why me? A pair of corpses with arms broken above the elbows points squarely at Mike Grundage. He had Hunter killed for welshing on his gambling debts, and his ex-wife and best friend for playing Dick Tracy. Those missing reels were never reported. You didn't, or they'd be in police custody. Without them as evidence, Elizabeth's name need never appear."

"You don't have time to kill us both and get away!" He strained his ears hard for the sound of sirens.

Lysander shook his head. "Greenwood's role was serendipitous. He shared a secret known only to himself and the owners of the museum, a hidden escape route only yards away from this spot. It leads through the storm drains, a feature built into the structure in case a major earthquake sealed all the other exits. But it's useless if I waste any more time delivering my summation to the jury."

Pollard and Wirtz thumbed back the hammers of their pistols.

At the opposite end of the corridor, something crashed, and pieces of it rattled on the polished linoleum of the floor, sounding as hollow as plastic pipe. One of them came tumbling their way down the middle of the corridor: Lon Chaney, Sr.'s grinning skeletal head from the original 1925 *Phantom of the Opera*. Dickey Wirtz pivoted that way and fired. The head flew into a hundred pieces.

The echo of the report rang off the walls and deadened Valentino's hearing. He, too, had turned in the direction of the disturbance, and saw a ragtag army charging his way in eerie silence, dressed anything but uniform in high silk hats, stiff bowlers, tailcoats, riding boots, and one ivory-lace evening dress with the train slung over one tattooed arm, exposing a pair of galloping legs in laddered hose; the person wearing it raised something shiny to her lips, and then a screeching whistle shattered his deafness.

"They have guns!" he shouted, lunging and bumping up Pudge Pollard's arm just as he jerked the trigger. Another shot clapped his ears shut and a shower of plaster came down between them. Then something grazed his ribs and he was sure Wirtz had shot him, but then he saw a brass-knobbed walking stick he'd seen before go bouncing down the corridor and spotted the wheezy-voiced thug gripping the elbow of his gun arm, his lips forming curses that were lost in the aftermath of Pollard's blast: The stick's owner had hurled it at Wirtz, disarming him when it connected. It had then glanced off Valentino.

But rescue was still steps away. Valentino looked around frantically for Wirtz's gun. He saw it on the floor and dived for it, but just then the white light burst in the same spot in his head where he'd been hit before, a split second before he identified the heel of Pollard's shoe coming his way. The blow left him conscious, but unable to react physically as the man, evaluating his targets, spurned him and swung his gun around toward Lorna, who was struggling helplessly with her bonds on the exhibit platform.

A shadow intervened, albeit one with substance; Jason Stickley, charging past Valentino, slashing right and left with his top hat at Pollard's head and upper body, laying open his face and scalp with the toothy brass and steel gears attached to the crown and sending the pistol flying.

Valentino wheeled toward Wirtz, but saw things were in hand there as well, with two steampunks pinioning his arms and Whistler's Daughter blasting her whistle sadistically in his face. Valentino's ears popped again. He heard the sirens at last and Horace Lysander's footsteps slapping the floor, no doubt in the direction of the secret escape route.

IV

HARNESS THE
LIGHTNING

23

"I WONDER ABOUT us," Harriet said. "I do."

Valentino sat absolutely still on the edge of the examining table, feeling only the slight tug as the resident stitched up the gash in his temple. The local anesthetic had kicked in. But he'd have felt numb regardless.

The doctor looked ten years his junior. Sometime during that endless night he seemed to have passed the point where physicians and police officers had surrendered the role of elder statesmen.

"I don't suppose it would do any good to say I'm sorry," he said.

"That's not the magic word your mother told you it is." Harriet was gazing at an anatomical chart on the wall opposite her, not at Valentino. It wouldn't be the surgical operation she found difficult to watch; she'd attended more autopsies and visited more crime scenes than he'd ever heard about. "It implies you won't do it again, but that's not the truth, is it?"

They were in the emergency unit at Cedars Sinai Hospital

(formerly Cedars of Lebanon, although longtime Angelinos still called it by its original name). She was wearing the same rumpled traveling clothes she'd worn on the flight from Seattle, not looking rumpled at all inside them; just chillingly resolute. Incredibly, the calendar date was still the same as when she'd arrived.

"Believe it or not, I've learned my lesson. From now on, I'll do my job and let the police do theirs."

"We've had this conversation before. You've gotten so accustomed to withholding information to get what you're after, your first instinct in answer to every question is to lie. You can't build anything on that, especially a relationship."

"I knew if I told you what I was doing, you'd try to talk me out of it. I should have gone ahead and let you."

"Why? No one could talk you out of doing anything that involved salvaging some hunk of celluloid nobody but a few people cared about."

"Is that what you think of my work?"

"Don't you dare turn this back on me!"

The fire in the retort struck him speechless.

With a show of being oblivious, the doctor tied off the thread and snipped the end with a pair of surgical scissors. "Now we'll just apply a patch. Some nights it's like working in a tire repair shop."

"I didn't want you to worry," Valentino said.

"How's that working out so far?"

"All's well that ends well. I'm the only one who got hurt, and it's just a scratch. Craig's killers are in custody, and the man who hired them soon will be. A prominent lawyer like Horace Lysander can't run or hide long."

"Teddie Goodman got hurt. She's hooked to a machine down

the hall. Lorna Hunter's upstairs, under sedation. Are those just scratches?"

"No one could have predicted what happened."

"That's just another way of saying you went off half-cocked."

"All set." The doctor finished bandaging the wound and gathered up his things.

Harriet thanked him before Valentino could. "Sorry we tangled you up in our domestic dispute."

"I finished my internship just last month. I'm looking forward to having the time to fight with my girlfriend, assuming I ever have one." He smiled at the patient. "There are two men waiting for you outside. They're with the police." He left.

"I admit I didn't handle things well." The archivist stood and pulled his sweatshirt over his head. "No one knew anything at the start. Gill and Yellowfern were working the theory that Mike Grundage was behind the whole thing. Lysander's obsession with Grundage's stepmother made him deranged. You've investigated psycho killings. There's no telling what a man will do when he's lost his mind."

"I know. I've been keeping company with one."

"I mean it, Harriet. No more amateur sleuthing for me."

"The only way you could keep that promise is to quit your job. It's *all* sleuthing. Are you prepared to give up what you do for my sake?"

"Are you?"

She looked at him finally. "We'll talk about it later, after someone bails you out—again." She smiled at his reaction, maliciously and without warmth. "Yes, I know about that. I've spoken to Fanta."

"Don't blame her. I led her to believe I'd keep you informed."

"I know who to blame."

He shook his head. "If it's any consolation, I screwed up all down the line. The police have the film now, and they'll keep it under the worst conditions through the trial and the appeals process. That can take years. I brought about the one thing I was trying to prevent."

"Not to mention putting a bunch of kids at risk."

"That was their decision. I specifically told them to sit still and wait for the police."

"Leading, of course, by example."

He nodded. "Okay, I deserved that."

"Would you rather they'd followed orders?"

"No. If they hadn't charged in, Lorna and I would be dead, and an innocent man charged with our murders as well as Craig's."

"If you consider Grundage an innocent man. I've seen his handiwork. He casts a wide loop, but you never find any of his DNA on the scene. Locking him up for something he had nothing to do with would be poetic justice."

"I doubt you believe that."

"I would, if I didn't think leaving another murderer running around loose was sloppy police work."

"I'm sorry I lied, and that's sincere. With everything that's happened, it's the thing I'm most sorry about. Is it too late for us?"

"We'll talk about it later, I said."

"I think you know the answer. Tell me now, or I won't be in any shape to face what's coming."

She was silent for a moment.

"Under normal circumstances I'd say, yes, it's too late. But it so happens I'm guilty of the same thing."

He watched her, watching him. He didn't want to ask the question, but he couldn't bear not knowing the answer.

"What did you lie about?"

"Remember when I told you I was up late attending a panel at the convention?"

He didn't respond. His body temperature slipped a couple of degrees.

"Well, I wasn't. I was at Jeff's house."

"Jeff?" At that moment the name meant nothing. It was as if the anesthetic had spread to his brain.

"Jeff Talbot. The antiques dealer who used to work for the FBI." She glanced down at her watch. "My shift starts in two hours. I have to go home and freshen up. And you have an appointment with the San Diego PD." She went out, leaving him standing there.

An orderly conducted the three men to a vacant private room and left them alone. There was only one chair, but it was superfluous, because no one sat in it. The bed looked inviting—as inviting as any hospital bed ever managed to look—but the archivist knew instinctively that if he so much as sat down all his defenses would dissolve, and he was in dangerous company to let that happen.

Sergeant Gill, for his part, looked as fresh and youthful as always, despite the pre-dawn hour and the probable fact that he, too, had not slept in many hours. People in law enforcement appeared to observe different sleep patterns from the rest of humanity. He had his neat notebook in hand. "Back to scratch, Valentino. We'll tell you where we came in."

"Funny. Like they used to say in theaters." But Detective John Yellowfern showed no sign of amusement. His Indian-penny features looked haggard, more likely on account of weariness with others of his species than ordinary fatigue. Day or night, he looked as if he could cause milk to curdle at a glance.

So Valentino went back to scratch.

Back to that first call from Craig Hunter, Lorna's anxious summons following his disappearance, the books he'd left behind, the conversations with Lysander and Grundage and J. Arthur Greenwood, and continuing uninterrupted until the point where the two plainclothesmen from San Diego arrived at the wax museum in response to a courtesy call from the LAPD. He left out Lorna's inebriated advances the night before, from the same motives that had compelled him to cloak her nudity with his Windbreaker before he freed her from the straps. Telling the rest from start to finish was like watching a movie he'd once liked and couldn't remember why. He wasn't the same person he'd been the first time around.

Yellowfern broke the silence that followed. "Forget about who killed Hunter, Columbo. Tell us when you found time to eat."

"One mystery at a time, Detective." Gill was staring at what he'd written as if he couldn't figure out how it got there. "They always say don't call the police. It'd be nice if square citizens had as much faith in us as crooks do. Well, your story about what went down at the museum hasn't changed since you told it the first time; that's refreshing. Also it checks with what we got from the freaks."

"They're not freaks." It came out automatically.

"Have it your way. At least they hollered cop before they bulled in. Greenwood's in custody. If his lawyer's any good he'll tell him to give us what we need. Old guy, rich, my guess is he'll never see the inside of San Quentin. I doubt he knew what Lysander had in mind after he left. We've got an APB out on that shyster. The way he likes to talk, he just might filibuster himself onto Death Row."

"Not if Grundage gets to him first," Yellowfern said, no disapproval in his tone.

"He'll have to do it without Pollard and Wirtz. Without Lysander to stand up for them, there's a chance they'll tell us their hat size."

"They can beat the needle if they throw in Grundage. They didn't learn to bust arms in medical school. Anyway, there's plenty where they came from. Let's put Valentino in with Pudge and Dickey. They can talk about movies they've seen."

"Not this time. We got our witnesses, we got our evidence, and we'll get our man soon enough, feet first or no. Don't think you did us any favors," Gill told Valentino. "We didn't run up the best conviction record in the department by holding hands with amateur detectives. We're giving you a pass because your little stunt put two of the worst button men in the state of California in the bag. I won't put that at risk by busting you a second time and handing the defense the opportunity of impeaching your testimony on the stand."

"We've got Hunter's widow for that; no sense giving her grief over lying to us at the start. I never get tired of putting the cuffs on this guy."

"All bad cop, all the time. Give it a rest."

The detective jerked as if he'd been slapped. "Jeez, Ern; in front of *him*?"

"Squawk to the skipper. Just because I spend more time with you than my wife and kids doesn't mean I have to like it." Gill's face changed. "Forget I said anything, okay? It's the overtime talking."

"It should keep its mouth shut." But Yellowfern appeared mollified, or as close as he ever got to it.

"Go home, Valentino, before I change my mind. Get your head clear before you make your formal statement."

He hesitated. "I know I'm not in a position to ask for anything."

"We're keeping the film. That's what you wanted, right?"

"Personally, I never want to see it again, but I have a responsibility to UCLA and posterity. All I'm requesting is that your people consult with experts on how it should be stored. It's the reason I got into this mess."

"I'll pass it along. I wouldn't hold my breath. We get chewed out by the board of commissioners every time we order fresh coffee filters." The sergeant slapped shut the notebook and put it away. "Let's go, Serpico. I'll let you run the siren."

Yellowfern paused on his way out, looking at Valentino. "This picture you stuck your neck out for: Is it even any good?"

"Not very."

"So how come all the fuss?"

"Why are you a policeman?"

"Free burial." He left.

The nurse at the floor station was a strikingly beautiful woman with the longest lashes Valentino had ever seen outside a movie set. He wondered if she'd come to L.A. hoping to break into show business and had settled for medicine instead. She checked her records and told him Mrs. Hunter's doctor had left instructions for the patient not to be disturbed. He asked what her condition was.

"Are you family?"

"Friend."

"I'm sorry. We can't give out that information except to relatives."

"I have another—friend—in intensive care. Are visitors allowed?"

"Not in ICU, family excepted."

He thanked her and used the pay phone in the lobby to call a cab. His cell was in police custody along with Pudge Pollard. When the taxi came, he changed his mind about picking up his car at the wax museum and gave the driver the address of The Oracle instead. He got the dreads just thinking about all those still cold figures. He dragged himself up the stairs to the projection booth and was unconscious the moment he fell into the ruins of his bed, many fathoms below the level at which he dreamed. It was an unexpected lucky break.

24

DURING THE NEXT few days he had only a few fleeting telephone conversations with Harriet Johansen. He told himself not to read anything personal into it: There had been a vicious gang fight in East L.A. the night after the wax museum incident and every CSI team in the county including hers had been called in to sort through the bodies and evidence. Their exchanges had been too brief to interpret anything beyond essentials.

He'd slept around the clock, changed his dressing, swallowed three ibuprofen to dull the throbbing in his head, took another cab to where he'd left his car, which had three overtime parking tickets but miraculously had not been towed, and wolfed down a McDonald's breakfast on his way to the university. The radio news was mostly concerned with the gang fight and there were no fresh details in the Hunter murder case and kidnapping. Horace Lysander was still being sought by police as a person of interest. Valentino's name did not appear. Every investigation withheld some piece of information, and he was grateful that this time he was it. If the press ever tumbled to how often he found himself ensnarled in homicide, he'd never be able to go about his business without dragging along an army of paparazzi. The Fourth Estate had fallen to their level for good and all.

Ruth, of course, was in the loop. Very little had happened locally since the Manson murders that the Film Preservation Department secretary didn't know about before anyone else. From inside her doughnut-shaped fortress she peered up at the bandage on his temple. "I thought rubber hoses didn't leave marks."

"I'm not quite the desperate character you think I am. Are there any messages?"

"On your desk. You can't miss them, although you might miss the desk under all that paper. If you showed up for work a little more often, you wouldn't have to catch up."

"Do you think I only work when I'm in the office?"

"I'm sure I don't know what I think. The mystery to me is why they ever converted this place from a power plant."

He spent the morning touching base. An early Fellini film was his for the taking if he agreed to fly the owner and his mistress from Florence to the U.S. and arrange visas at UCLA's expense. (He heard from this person roughly once every six weeks, and invariably from his wife a few days later, canceling the offer.) The family of a retired studio executive currently in a nursing home in Oxnard threatened to sue the university for copyright infringement because their uncle/father/third cousin claimed ownership of a Mr. Moto film missing from December 1941 until last year. (He filed it with similar communications for Smith Oldfield to read and evaluate in Legal.) Mark David Turkus had called three times through an assistant, leaving only messages for Valentino to call back. (Clearly, the entertainment magnate had read between the lines of the adventure in the wax museum and wanted to shower the archivist in gold in return for betraying his employers and delivering the *Frankenstein* test to Supernova International. He crumpled this sheet savagely and launched it at his wastebasket.) His contact in San Francisco reported that the lead on *London After Midnight* had fizzled out. (No regrets. He'd had his fill of horror films for a while.) There was a routine request from Accounting to clear up discrepancies on his expense sheets, a probably drunken question about movie trivia placed from a nearby fraternity house, with a six-pack riding on the answer, and a wrong number from a woman interested in storm windows.

He checked his e-mails and found them all to be more or less the same thing. He deleted them at a stroke. At such times he understood Ruth's curiosity about the worth of the film preservation program.

Jason Stickley knocked and opened the door wide enough to stick his narrow head through. "Mr. Valentino, are you busy?"

"Never too busy for you. Come in."

Genuinely glad to see the young man, he got up and shook his hand. "I didn't get the chance to thank you and the rest for what you did. You saved two lives at the risk of your own."

Jason flushed slightly. He wore ordinary campus attire: baggy cargo pants, scuffed sneakers, and a plaid long-sleeve shirt that concealed his tattoos over a Bruins T-shirt. "I was afraid you'd be mad at me for not staying put like you said."

"Don't tell your professors I said it, but some orders are meant to be disobeyed."

"The gang's pretty jazzed about the whole thing. Whiz says you can blow her whistle anytime. Um, that means—"

"I think I can figure it out. Tell her thanks, but I'm spoken for." He had no idea if that was still true. "Listen, I'm recommending you for a job with the department, a paying gig. Not just from gratitude for what you did. You're too valuable to waste as an unpaid intern."

"Thanks. I really mean that. People your age look at guys like me and make up their minds against me right away, but you never did. But I can't take the job."

"If you're worried about your classes, we can make the hours flexible."

"It's not that. I'm transferring to MIT at the end of the term. I'm majoring in engineering. Big surprise, huh?" How his grin managed to extend beyond the margins of his face was a mystery best left to experts; which Valentino firmly intended to solve in the future.

"Congratulations. It's a fine school. Are you sure you can afford the tuition?"

"Yeah. My dad gets a nice royalty from the U.S. Navy. He designed the hatch hinges they use on nuclear submarines. Tinkering with things sort of runs in the family."

"I'll be sorry to lose you, and that's a fact. Does this mean no more steampunk parties?"

"No, sir. We've reserved the factory building for Halloween. That's the reason I stopped by, to give you this." He slid something out of a cargo pocket and handed it to Valentino.

It was a formal invitation, lettered in elegant Victorian copperplate on linen stock. The florid language entreated him to bring a guest.

"I'll be there, although I'm not sure if I'll be accompanied. The person I have in mind is pretty busy."

"I can help you with your costume."

"Actually, I think I can manage. Professor Broadhead has a friend in the Universal wardrobe department who can fix me up."

"Just so long as it follows the theme." Another cargo pocket delivered a ruled sheet folded into a square, which Valentino accepted and opened.

He looked up. "A list of movie titles?"

"Steampunk films. The police kept Pat, Whiz, and the rest of us waiting at the wax museum before they talked to us. We put it together to pass the time."

"*The League of Extraordinary Gentlemen?*"

"Totally."

"*Wild Wild West, Van Helsing*—these are all relatively recent. Some of them—" He stopped himself, not wanting to offend his young friend.

"I know. Some of them we watch with the sound turned down. The look's the thing. The art direction. They're not all bad, and some of them have been around for a while. Turn it over."

He did so. "*Twenty Thousand Leagues Under the Sea* is steampunk?"

"Think about it. The *Nautilus?* All those exposed pipes and spinning turbines, that cool iris window? That one was my suggestion."

"I see all the classic *Frankenstein*s are here. I never dreamed the movement went back that far."

"It didn't have a name then. Like I said, machines are different now: no moving parts you can see. A computer's about as interesting to watch in operation as a toaster oven, but any little kid can look at a belt spinning around a pulley and figure out what's going on. When's the last time you saw an ordinary person tinkering on his car with the hood up? The smallest thing goes wrong, they have to do a diagnostic at the dealership. No one can tell the difference between a good circuit board and a bad one just by sight. I'm not saying we want to bring back cholera and child labor, just—"

"A sense of being in control."

Jason beamed, surprised. "Yeah!"

"We can all use some of that." Valentino thanked him. They shook hands again.

After the intern left, Kyle Broadhead called.

"I was planning to bake you a cake with a file in it," he said, "but it's just as well they sprang you. You've seen what I can do to a kitchen."

"Thanks for the thought. How are the wedding plans coming along?" Change of subject.

"Fanta just called to report some new disaster or other. I confess I wasn't listening. I've been a widower so long I thought I'd lost that particular nonskill. I'm relieved to learn I still possess it. It's more useful in married life than you know."

"I'll take your word for it."

Something in his tone must have alerted the professor. "Do I detect trouble in paradise?"

"You can probably guess its source, unless you've stopped listening to your fiancée altogether. Harriet pumped her for information."

"Fanta lacks guile. There are those who consider it a virtue."

"I'm not blaming her. If I weren't up to my hips in guile through this whole business, we'd all be better off."

"Self-loathing. Charming. I'm a bit put out with you myself. How can you take on the mob and not include me in the fun?"

"I didn't exactly take on the mob. Anyway, I'd never have heard the end of it if you were to pick up a stray bullet, from Fanta *or* Harriet."

"Better I do that than blow an artery working at the computer or, worse, pass into my dotage. Frankly, the prospect of being bathed by your wife on a regular basis is far more attractive the first time around. I'm placing my reservation for a seat in your next escapade."

"There won't be any more escapades, Kyle. I'm hanging up the deerstalker and assuming the life of the academic I was born to be."

"You're not cut out for it. The faculty intrigues would slash you to ribbons. You're much safer among gangsters and psychopathic attorneys."

"You're joking. I'm not."

There was a brief silence on Broadhead's end. "Was it that bad?"

"It was too close. The world isn't a Saturday afternoon serial. You don't get out in the nick of time every week. Sooner or later the law of averages catches up with you and the cavalry comes too late. I'm not planning to stick around until that happens."

"Well, we'll discuss it over lunch. Fanta's meeting me at the Brass Gimbal, and I need your presence as a buffer when she starts in on exploding floral arrangements and vengeful bridesmaids in pomegranate and pink."

"I'd like that, if we can agree on some subject apart from homicide and abduction."

"I suppose there's always politics. In which case I may get lucky and choke to death on a mouthful of Green Screen veggie burger."

Valentino ate the Best Boy Bok Choy while his mentor studied the list of films Jason Stickley had provided. "Atrocious penmanship," muttered Broadhead. "They're not teaching it in grammar school these days. An entire generation can communicate only with its thumbs."

"He'd agree with you. It's at the heart of his philosophy."

"*Brazil*, uh-huh. *Metropolis*; well, sure. *Westworld*, the *Terminator* franchise. *Blade Runner*. *Sky Captain and the World of Tomorrow*. So far it's 'Gidget Goes to Dystopia.'"

"Read on. These kids are aficionados, not activists. They're not sci-fi geeks either. You won't catch them at a *Star Trek* convention or playing *Dungeons and Dragons*. *Modern Times* is on the list. *Breakheart Pass, Hell's Angels, Shall We Dance*—"

"Doesn't say whether it's the Japanese version or the one starring Richard Gere."

"I'm sure it's neither. Fred Astaire, tripping the light fantastic in the engine room of a luxury liner. See, there's a theme: pistons and patent-leather shoes. It runs through every genre: comedy, musical, science fiction, western, romance." He pointed at a title. "When's the last time you saw Douglas Sirk lumped in with Otto Preminger?"

"I sort of hoped I never would." Broadhead folded the sheet. "May I borrow this?"

Valentino was surprised. "Sure. I didn't think you'd be that interested. Does this mean you're not ready to pull the plug on everyone under thirty?"

"The jury's still out, and I'm not excluding everyone between thirty and fifty. But our callow Mr. Joy Stick may have given me a hook for my wretched opus. This is the first film movement to transcend category since *noir*. Assuming, that is, it isn't a flash in the pan."

"I doubt it. It represents a cultural backlash against technology on the order of the Luddite revolution."

"Let's leave the hyperbole to the book section of the *Hollywood Reporter*, shall we? If it still has one. I had high hopes, too, for the young man who predicted the eight-track tape would

change the face of music. I even offered to contribute an introduction to his thesis, which retired with him to an ashram in
Yucca Valley."

"You had another protégé before me?"

"I had several. Intellectuals are not monogamous by nature."
Broadhead put away the list, lifted the bun off his burger, and
peeled away a layer of soggy arugula, revealing another under-
neath. He sighed and replaced the bun. "Right now I'd trade
my tenure for a sparerib."

"Don't be healthy on my account." Fanta, materializing out
of nowhere, plunked herself into the vacant chair at the table
and flagged down a passing waitress. "I'll have a zombie."

The young woman frowned. "We don't have a full bar."

"In that case, bring me something to eat that would burn
the hide off a rhinoceros."

"I can suggest the Hot Set. Jalapenos deep-fried in bacon fat
with habanara sauce, onion rings on the side."

"With a pint of stout, dark as the abyss."

Broadhead looked up. "Does it come with a living will?"

When the waitress left, he said, "My sweet, how was your
morning?"

Fanta shot him a look that would fell a Brahma. She looked
uncommonly beautiful, with her color high against the black of
her hair, shimmering like raw film stock to her shoulders. Her
eyes glittered with red pinpoints that might or might not have
been reflected from her turtleneck sweater. "You know, Kyle,
sometimes you're long on humor and short on sense. Do I look
in the mood to banter?"

"Based on prima facie evidence, I would answer in the negative."

"Legal Latin only works in court documents. I am, to use a
hard-working old Anglo-Saxon word, pissed. The Elks Hall can-

celed our reservation for the wedding reception. The registrar, a quaint old gentleman of a hundred and eighty, stirred himself after six weeks to look at the books and discovered that you haven't paid dues since the week Ronald Reagan was inaugurated."

"I overlooked it in my grief. I am, as you well know, apolitical, but I've never forgiven the man *Hellcats of the Navy*."

Valentino said, "I thought it was *Bedtime for Bonzo* you objected to."

"Not at all. I thought it a pleasantly mindless romp. I voted for his costar when he ran against Jerry Brown for governor. The chimp, it pains me to report, lost in the runoff."

"The Elks was *your* idea," she said. "How is it one of the most brilliant minds of our time, to quote you, managed to go decades without writing out a monthly check and fail to reflect upon the fact that he was no longer a member?"

"Nevertheless I did. However, this is the land of wide open spaces. There must be a substitute."

"Not within six months either side of our wedding date. If we change it, the chapel I booked won't be available for another year."

"Why does the word Vegas come to mind?"

She thrust her face within inches of Broadhead's. "A dog can marry a Rockette in Vegas. My parents were united in St. Cecily's. Their marriage has lasted twenty-six years, which may not be longer than your subscription to *Living With Flatulence*, but it's more than a lifetime to me. They're flying in from Luxembourg to attend, and if they witness their only daughter dancing with her bridegroom to 'Danke Schoen' piped in from the lounge, the international incident that's bound to follow will result in a war that will look like a garden party next to the one I'll wage with you. *Fix this!*"

Broadhead paled a full shade; something Valentino suspected had not happened since the Yugoslavian military tribunal or whatever it was had sentenced him to prison for espionage. He appeared at a loss for words for the first time in human memory.

The archivist shifted uncomfortably in his seat, causing something to crackle in the hip pocket of his jeans. He slid out the invitation Jason Stickley had given him and looked at it.

"I have a suggestion," he said, "if neither of you objects to bare brick."

25

"IT HAS POTENTIAL," Fanta said. "Flowers, streamers, Chinese lanterns—"

"Dynamite, a wrecking ball," Broadhead added.

"I'd keep my opinions to myself, old bear. When someone throws you a rope, you don't chew through it. However did you find this place, Jason?"

The intern stood nervously twirling the ring of mammoth keys around his finger. Fanta's presence had a way, Valentino noted, of upsetting the equilibrium of most males past the age of puberty. "Um, one of our people has an uncle in real estate. His firm represents a family that's owned it since it was built. They say half the old-growth redwoods in California were cut up by blades manufactured here."

"Inspiring." Broadhead, incorrigible by nature, stuffed his pipe.

Some steampunks were at work decorating the huge factory room for the Halloween party. Chains with orange and black paper links festooned the portrait of Victoria centered on the gigantic flywheel and a pair of young men Valentino hadn't met stood on stepladders at opposite ends of the room, stringing a flexible steel cable with brass lamps with lenses of red glass suspended from it, scrounged from defunct railroads. A young woman who may or may not have been Whistler's Daughter— scruffy jeans with appliqué flowers and a man's shirt whose cuffs extended past her arms made an excellent disguise, with her hair twisted into a ponytail—walked about carrying a bucket and dipping into it with leather work gloves on her hands, sprinkling steel shavings about the floor.

"You don't suppose they'll sell it before spring?" Fanta asked Jason.

"No way. This whole neighborhood is soaked with diesel oil and lead byproducts clear down to bedrock. Ten oil sheikhs pooling their resources couldn't afford to clean it up to suit the EPA."

"I can't think of a better blessing for starting our life together. Ask your friend's uncle to book it for June sixth."

Broadhead said, "Are you sure, my dear? It's the first place we've looked at."

"The first *you've* looked at. The closest thing to acceptable I found on the Net has a crack house on either side. Instead of those little disposable cameras on the tables, we'd have to set out Saturday Night Specials so our guests can shoot their way out of the neighborhood."

"I'm sure that before June we can find a pawnshop that will give us a good price on them."

She fished a checkbook and pen from her shoulderbag. "What's the deposit?"

"We got it for forty."

Valentino touched her arm just as she began writing. "Let me get it. I've been racking my brains for a suitable wedding gift. So far all I've come up with is his and her boxing gloves. This will be a start."

Her smile was dazzling. She put away the checkbook. "Thanks, Val. Isn't that nice of him, Kyle?"

"There's always a friend willing to help walk a man off the plank." But Broadhead lit his tobacco contentedly. Realization that he'd dodged a relationship bullet had sunk through finally to his educator's brain.

"Come to the party," Jason told the couple. "You can see it in full blowout mode."

"That's very kind of you, but I just sent my iron tuxedo to the dealership for an undercoat."

She transferred her smile to the young man. "Thanks. We're flying to Neufchâteau next week."

"We are?" The professor took the pipe from his mouth.

"It was going to be a surprise, but I don't want Jason to think we're blowing him off. Mom and Dad want to meet you. They're treating us to a holiday as an engagement present."

"Must we fly?"

"I'll have the flight attendants ply you with Scotch as soon as we board."

"I'll have to talk to the department head. A man with my responsibilities can't go jet-setting off to Luxembourg on a moment's notice."

"I've already spoken to him. He says it'll be a hardship, but the university can probably manage to survive by using the assistant who's been teaching your classes all year."

"An exaggeration. I've logged one hundred minutes this semester alone." As his future bride wandered off with Jason for the grand tour, Broadhead seized Valentino's arm and turned him away. "You have to get me out of this. Surely someone in Vancouver or someplace has footage of Byrd at the Pole and you need to bring along a contemporary of the explorer's to authenticate it."

"You're not that old."

"I'm old enough to have taught Fanta's father how to tie a shoelace, but it isn't him I'm worried about. Her mother tells grand dukes what to do. I can't bully her the way I can a room full of post-adolescent undergrads."

"Everyone has to meet his mother-in-law sooner or later."

"But not on her turf!"

"I'm sorry, Kyle. I've given up lying."

"Fine time to pick to adhere to the higher principles." He looked about him, puffing thick clouds from his pipe. "I wonder if this place is as combustible as it appears."

The great Wurlitzer pipe organ was playing when Valentino opened the door to The Oracle, an etude of some kind. The virile bass notes hummed through the channels and made the floor buzz under his feet. He looked a question at a painter on his stepladder applying primer to a cherub prior to gilding. The man answered with a shrug. A man was not king of his castle as long as it was under construction and anyone could wander in and out.

Lorna Hunter sat at the keyboard in the orchestra pit, her long slender fingers gliding up and down the scale. She had her hair tied behind her neck and wore a tailored suit that slyly hinted at rather than disguised what lay beneath. Valentino hoped someday to put that image behind him. It wasn't how one was supposed to picture a friend.

When she finished with a little flourish, he applauded. Her shoulders tensed and she looked back over one, then smiled. "I hope you don't mind. I'm out of practice. I've decided to go back to work."

"Acting?" He hadn't read *Variety* lately. He wondered if there was a casting call out for the role of a musician.

"God, no! The fishbowl situation's gotten unbearable since I last set foot on a soundstage. I used to give music lessons to support myself while I was waiting for my big break. I don't need the money, but there isn't much future in being an idle former celebrity. It's hard on the liver, among other things. Every day a busload of showbiz hopefuls comes into town. Some of them have talent, but can't afford the instruction they need to excel. Call me a cut-rate Svengali."

"That's as unflattering as it is untrue. I think it's a wonderful idea. Are you all right? I stopped by the hospital, but they said you'd checked yourself out against the advice of staff."

"I'm tougher than I was last week. There wasn't a thing wrong with me that a little wardrobe couldn't cure. I made quite a spectacle of myself, didn't I?" She colored slightly.

"That wasn't your fault."

"I meant before. I'm sorry, Val. I had an awful few days, and this town's dripping in sex. Have I lost a friend?"

"Never."

She rolled the cover down over the keys and stroked the mahogany. "It's a beautiful instrument. Wonderful tone."

"It should be. I had to borrow against my life insurance to pay for the restoration."

"You won't regret it. I couldn't resist playing. I came to return this." She got up, retrieving a fold of blue cloth from the top of the organ, and came his way, holding it out. It was his Windbreaker. "That was a gallant thing to do. I didn't think you could surpass yourself that night, but you did. Not that I appreciated the first time. I thought I was losing my charms."

"You're a beautiful woman. As for your charms, you couldn't cover them with a polar coat." He took the jacket.

A vertical line broke the smooth expanse of her forehead. "Will they get that man?"

"I'm sure of it. The police are more efficient than you think. It took me a while to learn that lesson, but it's taken root."

"Poor Craig. I'd have helped him out if I thought he was that desperate for money."

"It wasn't money he was after. He wanted to be successful again, and you can't give a man success. He went about getting it for himself the wrong way. The booze and drugs destroyed his judgment. He wasn't Craig at the end. Not our Craig."

"I wonder if he ever was. Actors, you know?" She smiled sadly.

He knew, but he couldn't tell her without giving away the fact he'd suspected her himself. When you scraped away the sex, the town was built of canvas and balsa and you couldn't trust it. "Would you like a tour?" he asked. "I'm afraid it isn't much to look at just now."

"Another time. I'm expecting my first student at three." She put a palm to the side of her face. "I've got stage fright, can you believe it? First time in years."

"You'll do great. Promise me you'll keep the date open for The Oracle's grand reopening. I wouldn't want anyone else on the keyboard."

"When is it?"

"In about ten years, assuming the unions cooperate."

"I think I'm available." She went up on her toes and kissed his cheek. She smelled of some delicate scent; no alcohol this time. "I hope that that someone in your life appreciates what she has."

He escorted her out without acknowledging what she'd said.

Theodosia Burr Goodman was sitting up in bed, wearing a silver lamé jacket trimmed with feathers over her hospital gown, a twentieth-century update of a Roaring Twenties design. The bandages swathing her head looked like a turban, adding to the effect. She looked more piratical than usual with a gauze patch covering a fractured eye socket. She drew on a plastic straw in a plastic cup and set it down on the table beside the bed. Valentino swore he smelled bourbon.

"Most people protect their homes with an alarm system or a Rottweiler," she said. "Leave it to a movie sap like you to hire a couple of mugs from Warner Brothers."

"They weren't working for me. You know that. What did you think you'd find rummaging through my apartment?"

"Are you wearing a wire?"

He couldn't help noticing that her blood-pressure monitor didn't register anything out of the ordinary while she was asking such a volatile question. She was no longer hooked up to any other machines. Cedars had moved her out of ICU into a private room, establishing a recovery record of some kind. An enormous bouquet with Mark David Turkus' card attached stood by the window. There were no other flowers and no one had autographed the cast on her left arm or on her right leg in traction. Had the woman no friends?

"Teddie, I've already told the police I won't file charges."

"Don't do me any favors. My lawyer says I've got a good case against you for reckless endangerment."

"You were committing burglary!"

"I was doing my job. If you didn't wimp out over a little felony now and then, you'd be the best in the business instead of a distant second. To answer your question, I wasn't sure just what I was after until I found those books on Karloff and Lugosi scattered around and read the underlined sections. I keep a shopping list in my head. I had a pretty good idea you'd snared the *Frankenstein* test, or were hot on its trail. I'd've found something to go on if Dumb and Dumber hadn't come along and checked me down the stairs. Are those things even up to code?"

"I can show you the receipt for what it cost me to bring them into compliance. I'm sorry you were hurt, for what that's worth. No film justifies that."

"If you believe that, you're even more of a loser than I thought. So who has the reels?"

"The San Diego Police Department."

"Idiot! By the time they let go of it there won't be enough left to start a good fire."

He changed the subject. "Can I get you anything?"

"I'd put in my order, but you'd just lose it." She closed her one visible eye. It looked much smaller without shadow and mascara, and her face paler than usual without blusher. "Mark sees to it I've got everything I need. Sweet of him, considering he offered you my job."

"How did you find out about that?"

"I've got people, even in the West Hollywood station of the LAPD. So why didn't you take him up on it?"

"I'm not that low."

"Loser."

He told her he'd be back to visit her later and put his hand on the door handle.

"Valentino."

He turned back. The eye was open, watching him.

"Don't go thinking you did a good deed," she said. "The first time you dropped the ball, Mark would've dumped you like toxic waste and hired me back with a raise and a big fat bonus. You know it, and *that's* why you turned him down."

He felt himself grinning. "Once again, Teddie, you've figured me out before I did."

"You better hustle while you can. I'll be back running rings around you as soon as I get my crutches."

26

HE READ OVER the transcript of the statement he'd made before a video camera and signed it. Sergeant Gill took the pages and slid Valentino's cell phone across the desk, which belonged to a lieutenant with the Armed Robbery division. "You'll need to charge it."

"Thank you."

"Don't include me in that." John Yellowfern leaned in a corner with his hands in his pockets. "I wanted to crack it open, get all the messages, and run down all the incoming and outgoing numbers."

"Except somebody was using the time machine and you couldn't go back and kill James Madison before he wrote the Bill of Rights. No probable cause, Detective."

"Go ahead and bleed. Just don't expect me to mop up."

Valentino asked if there was any news on Horace Lysander.

Yellowfern looked at his partner and shook his head, but Gill shrugged. "What's the diff? Press conference is in twenty

minutes. This morning a late-model Mercedes washed up at
Long Beach. It's registered to Lysander."

"How long has he been on foot, do you think?"

"Not long," Yellowfern said. "He was curled up in the trunk
with a slug in his head and both arms broken above the elbows. Didn't I say there were plenty more where Pollard and
Wirtz came from?"

Valentino shuddered. "Are you questioning Mike Grundage?"

Gill's smile was bland. "Just as soon as he steps off the plane
from Vegas. Those executive types are never around when it
starts raining dead lawyers."

"What about Pollard and Wirtz?"

"Shoes are made to drop." Yellowfern looked smug, in a
sour-lemon way. "Dickey sang and rolled over on Pudge when
Lysander's body showed, in return for murder two. Pudge isn't
taking it well. I say we throw 'em in the same cell and save a
buck, but it'll turn out the same either way."

"So that's the end of it."

"It is for us," Gill said. "We'll help the locals any way we can,
of course, but it's just paperwork. We're headed home today."

"High time, too. The air here should come with a warning
label from the Surgeon General."

Valentino started to ask a question, then remembered his
resolution. He apologized again for the trouble he'd caused and
took himself out.

He barely had the phone plugged into the dashboard char-
ger when it rang.

"Mr. Valentino, my name is Philip Pastern. I'm represent-
ing Mrs. Elizabeth Grundage in the, er, absence of Horace
Lysander." It was a neutral sort of voice, neither young nor old.
This episode seemed to be top-heavy with attorneys.

"He's a bit more than just absent."

"I'm aware of that. I didn't realize the police had gone public with the information. At present I'm engaged in obtaining the release of personal property belonging to my client that is no longer evidence in a criminal case."

That was the question he'd almost asked Gill and Yellowfern. "I don't know why you called me, Mr. Pastern. My employers have no legal claim on the item."

"I'm glad to hear you say it, since if it had been offered to you, the transaction would not have stood up in court. However, as I'm sure you'll understand, Mrs. Grundage has no interest in retaining ownership of something that has nothing but sordid associations. By neither word nor deed did she ever encourage the late Mr. Lysander's—delusions—nor ask him to undertake any unlawful action on her behalf. She is desirous of relinquishing ownership of the item, in return for acceptable compensation and provided no public mention is made of her part in the exchange. I cannot overstress the importance of that last demand. Her name must never appear, or the negotiations will be terminated with prejudice."

Valentino sat back in the driver's seat. The fact that he'd followed every word of this oration was evidence enough that he'd been spending too much time in the company of lawyers. "You have my assurance the university I work for is just as earnest as your client about avoiding negative publicity." Henry Anklemire, he did not add, would be the exception: The little flack would cry murder from the roof of the administration building for the free advertising he'd get from the media. But he needn't know about the business until it was too late for him to interfere.

The archivist gave Philip Pastern the number of Smith Oldfield's office, and when their conversation concluded left a message with Oldfield's voice mail to expect the call.

He felt the old thump of anticipation, like a motor kicking on in his chest. Then he leaned forward and started the car. Just because the thrill was still there didn't mean he was fanatic enough to repeat the mistakes of the past.

He parked the car in his reserved space in the garage and walked to The Oracle, passing a van alongside the curb. Someone shouted his name, and he turned to see Harriet Johansen leaning out the window on the passenger's side. The vehicle bore the markings of the Los Angeles Police Department. It was a coroner's van. As he approached it, Harriet turned her head and said something to the man behind the wheel, who got out and walked away down the street. Valentino recognized him as one of her colleagues he'd seen in the break room at headquarters.

"How's your head?" Harriet asked.

He reached up and pulled loose the bandage. "I just realized it stopped hurting. I guess I can take the stitches out anytime."

"Let a professional do it." She opened the door and stepped down. She was wearing her working smock, from a pocket of which she drew a vinyl case and removed a pair of surgical shears. In a moment the thread was snipped through and cast away. She frowned at the result. "It's just a little scar. When the hair grows back in, no one will notice it."

"That's okay. I don't need it to remind me to mind my own business and let the police mind theirs."

"Actions speak louder than words. Or rather, the lack of them." She leaned back against the side of the van with her hands in her smock pockets. "How have you been?"

"In a word? Miserable. These past few days I've felt farther apart from you than when you were in Seattle."

"It wasn't all you, you know. Would you like a detailed description of what's been keeping me busy? I've been up to my elbows in—"

"Work," he said, before she could get graphic. "I do know. But I also know I've failed to keep up my end of this relationship."

"It isn't just the meddling and the lying. There are trust issues."

He said nothing. He'd feared this conversation almost as much as never having another one with her again.

"If I were going to cheat on you, Val, I could do it here in town just as easily as if I were two thousand miles away."

"If?" He seized on the word as if it were a piece of floating driftwood.

"You have female friends—that Lorna, for instance—but I would never suspect you of fooling around with any of them without proof."

In that moment he came as close as he knew he ever would to telling her what had happened just before the night at the wax museum. His regard for Lorna stopped him. In any case, something told him this wasn't about her, or any other of his woman friends.

"I'm not entirely innocent," she went on; and his heart plummeted. "You got so upset every time I mentioned him, I lied about attending a convention panel instead of telling you Jeff invited me to his home and I accepted. Then when I found out everything you'd been up to without telling me, I let you think there was something going on between us. I wanted to punish you.

"That wasn't the way to go about it. At least when you lied, it was to keep me from worrying, dumb as that was, ignorant as it was of what relationships are all about. Lying with the express intention of causing pain is worse. Val, I'm sorry."

"I'm not sure I understand," he said, "but I have an idea I'm going to be very glad we had this talk."

"I hope so, because as messed up as we are, what we have is healthier than anything I've ever had outside my family. I sort of left out that Jeff's wife was there. Sheila's a world-class chef, and a gracious hostess. What with the food and the conversation and the tour of their beautiful Queen Anne house, the time got away from me and it was almost dawn when I left."

"Thank God. Thank God. Although—"

She smiled. "I know. You'd have forgiven me. I'm not so sure I would forgive you under the same circumstances; but it's the differences between us that makes what we have worth fighting to keep."

"So we're okay?" He was almost afraid to ask the question.

"I have a sneaking suspicion we're going to be better than that in a minute. Would you like to see the reason I took Jeff up on his invitation?"

"Did you bring back a covered dish?"

She laughed, pushed herself away from the van, and walked to the back, practically skipping. There she flung open the rear doors and stepped away so he could see inside.

It was a sunny day, no smog alerts in effect, and his eyes had to adjust to the dimness. At first he thought he was staring at a propped-up corpse, no unusual cargo for the vehicle. Then he realized it was a twin of the vintage Bell & Howell projector in The Oracle, mounted on a sturdy stand.

"Jeff bought it when an old theater in Yakima was condemned to make room for a city parking lot," she said. "He told me he had it when I told him what you do and about the theater you're restoring, and about how you needed two projectors to show old three-D films. None of his regular customers were interested; it was just taking up space in his basement. I offered to trade him even up for the sideboard my grandfather brought with him when he came here from Sweden. He took me up on it, sight unseen. Am I a good horse trader or what?"

"You love that sideboard," he said.

"Nobody loves a piece of furniture, Val. Love is for people—and parakeets and such."

"You and Jeff talked about me?"

"*I* talked. I think part of why he gave me such a good deal was to shut me up."

He started to take her in his arms. Her partner came trotting up waving a cell phone. "We need to unload. We got a dismemberment in Inglewood, maybe two."

"Go help them sort out the arms and legs," Valentino said.

"You smooth talker, you." She kissed him hard.

"Are you sure we're up for this party?" he asked. "Our track record in costume occasions isn't so good."

"You know you never turn down an invitation to a Halloween blast. Anyway, we can't disappoint Jason. We'll probably be the only fossils in attendance." Harriet came out of the bedroom of her apartment, adjusting her wig, which was as tall as Martha Simpson's hair but jet-black, with silver lightning streaks running up the sides. Between it and her high heels, concealed beneath the hem of a long white gown cinched at the waist and padded in the shoulders, she stood nearly as tall as Valentino in his built-up boots and flat rubber headpiece, an exact replica of the one Jack Pierce had designed for Boris Karloff and the host of other actors who'd inherited the role of the Monster; Kyle Broadhead and his contacts at Universal had come through in spades. What was a steampunk party without Frankenstein's creation and his bride?

"You're looking particularly hideous this evening," he told her.

"How sweet. When they made you they didn't just break the mold. They left plenty of it on you." They hooked arms.

The roof of Valentino's compact was too low to accommodate her skyscraper hair, so she'd borrowed the coroner's van, which he thought a poetic touch.

On the way to the buzz-saw blade factory, Harriet watched a pair of youngsters dressed as Harry Potter and Lady Gaga carrying bright paper sacks along the sidewalk. "I can't understand why he asked us to come so early. The trick-or-treaters are barely out."

"Apparently it's a surprise. He said it was something only you and I would fully appreciate."

"I hope it's not some sort of prank." She turned the corner. "This isn't the way I usually go. Are you sure you're not lost?"

"Shortcut. Every few months a homeless person takes a flyer off a roof or gets crushed in a Dumpster or comes out on the losing end of a fight with boxcutters in that neighborhood. I'm pretty sure we carried a frozen carcass out of that address a couple of winters back. The trick is not to break anything off on the way through the door."

"I'll make you a deal: Cut the CSI shop talk for one night and I'll try to throttle back on movie trivia."

"Bet you crack first."

"Our usual wager?"

"Yep."

"Either way I win."

Jason Stickley was pacing back and forth in front of the

building when they pulled up, looking like the Mad Hatter in his high hat and flapping coattails. His nervous energy always reminded Valentino of someone, possibly himself.

"Thanks for coming," said the intern when they stepped out. "I was afraid some of the others might trickle in ahead of you and get in the way. Wow!" He was staring at Harriet. "No offense, Mr. Valentino; you look great. But—wow!"

She beamed. "You're too kind. Just sing out when I get too close to a power line."

Jason scampered up the steps ahead of them (Valentino providing support as Harriet lifted her skirts to climb them in her spikes) and turned one of his keys in the lock. It made a grating noise and he tugged open the door on shrieking hinges.

"How'd you manage that?" Valentino asked.

"I replaced the brass fittings with rusty iron ones I found in a bin in a junk shop. Then the caretaker came along and oiled them and I had to do it all over again." He waved them in ahead of him.

A great deal had been done with the room since Valentino had visited it with Broadhead and Fanta. Someone with an expert knowledge of anatomy and metallurgy (a collaboration?) had welded full-size human skeletons of steel and aluminum and set them about the room in various poses and attitudes, and naked lightbulbs that might have come directly from Thomas Edison's workshop hung from cords of irregular length, dazzling the eye and sparkling off the carpet of metal shavings on the floor. An old-fashioned cast-iron stove served as a refreshment table, with a coal-scuttle centerpiece filled with bloodred punch and surrounded by upended lugnuts the size of fists, salvaged from the great wheel of some obsolete steam-powered device to perform sociable duty as cups. Everywhere, candles blazed in silver and pewter holders, and in honor of the evening the papier-mâché horses hitched to the forklift truck wore gilded masks decorated with ostrich plumes.

However, Valentino's eye was drawn past all these things to a number of infernal machines set up at intervals around the walls, as familiar to his memory as they were unknown to his personal experience: Roentgen rays, Tesla coils, gadgets whose names he didn't know, studded with knobs and dials and row upon row of switches, feral and scientific at the same time, poised to crackle and hum and glow and hurl sparks willy-nilly, all for the dramatic purpose of directing current through an inanimate humanoid thing assembled from grisly spare parts found in crypts and mortuaries and suspended from gallowses and bringing life to something that had never lived. He'd witnessed the scene hundreds of times, beginning with a fuzzy image on a worn-out picture tube, and it had never failed to excite him.

"They're all working replicas of the equipment Kenneth Strickfadden designed for all the Frankenstein films," Jason said, his voice quivering with emotion. "Wilde Thing—you met him the other night, his real name's Kevin—he built it all from scratch. He's working his way to a physics degree as an electrician. I was sure you'd appreciate it."

Harriet clutched Valentino's arm tight. He scarcely noticed.

"Does it work?"

"Does it work!" Jason swept away the cloth covering a huge knife-switch with a varnished wooden handle attached to an electrical box on the wall. "Would you care to do the honors?"

"Careful, Val." But Harriet let go of him, patting his arm on the way.

Valentino grasped the switch and threw it.

ACKNOWLEDGMENTS

I wish to thank my wife, author Deborah Morgan, for Dumpster-diving the Internet for updated information on my outdated sources (any errors are mine), and for suggesting the perfect title for this book. I'm also extremely grateful to her for allowing me to borrow Jeff Talbot and his wife, Sheila, from Deborah's Antiques Lovers mystery series, published by Berkley Books and available on audio from Books in Motion.

In addition, I wish to credit the late great Forrest J. Ackerman, founder and publisher of *Famous Monsters of Filmland,* and all the personnel behind TV's *Shocker Theater* for conducting Boris Karloff, Bela Lugosi, and Lon Chaney, Jr., into my childhood home. (Yes, that was me watching *Frankenstein,* sitting up in bed with Pepi, my Chihuahua-terrier, curled up safe and warm in my lap.)

CLOSING CREDITS

A good cast is worth repeating.
> —Universal Pictures, 1930s

The following sources were crucial in the writing of *Alive!*:

BIBLIOGRAPHY

1. Biographies

Bojarski, Richard, and Kenneth Beale. *The Films of Boris Karloff*. Secaucus, NJ: The Citadel Press, 1974.

Citadel, the gold standard for filmographies subdivided by individual stars and directors, continues its reputation with this lively biography of Hollywood's greatest bogeyman (and an actor whose skills are greatly underrated [1945's *The Body Snatcher* makes a sterling case for the defense]) and meticulous chronicle of his appearances on stage and television, as well as on the big screen. The man made 137 films—fifty-four of them before *Frankenstein* made his name a creepy household word—from 1919 through 1971 (two years after his death!), but as he noted himself, he will always be known as the tragic, inarticulate, misunderstood creation of reckless science and black magic whose flattened head and shambling, stiff-legged walk is familiar to every culture on earth.

Bojarski, Richard. *The Films of Bela Lugosi*. Secaucus, NJ: The Citadel Press, 1980.

Lugosi—the only authentic Transylvanian ever to play Count Dracula on screen, and the man whose interpretation will always be associated with the role—suffered through a career that was in every way the mirror image of Karloff's. The same typecasting that assured his British rival a steady income and a comfortable old age kept him in poverty and helped to bring on the drug addiction that ruined his health and shortened his life. This fine study of his contribution to stage and screen justifiably tips the balance away from humiliation (*Glen or Glenda?*, et al) toward the sporadic but memorable highlights (thousands of live theatrical performances as Dracula under his own direction, to rave reviews before standing-room-only audiences, two Oscar-worthy turns as Ygor, twisted in mind as well as body, but strangely sympathetic, and a brief but resounding role in *Ninotchka*, in which he managed to steal the scene from Garbo, in a rare foray into romantic comedy). This is a tragic but compellingly readable cautionary tale for anyone who considers himself too successful to fail.

Curtis, James. *James Whale: A New World of Gods and Monsters*. Boston: Faber & Faber, 1998.

The Frankenstein series is rife with genius gone horribly wrong. Whale, the brilliant director of *Journey's End* on stage, the original *Showboat* on screen, and the first two talkies in the unstoppable Mary Shelley franchise, was flamboyantly gay at a time when homosexuality was still regarded as "the love of which we dare not speak" (Oscar Wilde), but it was his per-

sonal arrogance, insupportable by a string of box-office disas-
ters, that led to his undoing in Hollywood. His 1957 death by
apparent suicide in the swimming pool of his Pacific Palisades
home, and the mysterious circumstances surrounding it, oc-
cupy much of *Gods and Monsters* (1998; see under Tributes),
a film based on Christopher Bram's novel *Father of Frankenstein*. Bram's research and Curtis's appear to be in close agreement.

Gifford, Dennis. *Karloff: The Man, the Monster, the Movies.*
New York: Curtis Books, 1973.

This was the first Karloff biography to appear after his
death, and it holds up remarkably well in a climate that generally produces gushy panegyrics in the afterglow of a life
recently vacated, then character-assassinating "tell-alls" by
hatchet-throwers freed from the restrictions of civil suits. Karloff's East Indian ancestry is the only revelation that might
have damaged his career in a time of relative intolerance, but
since no shame attaches to it now, its absence from Gifford's
book is hardly a detraction. Much of it (as its title reflects) is
filmography, but the background and personality of its subject
comes through, and the details of the Frankenstein films—in
particular makeup wizard Jack Pierce's deeply researched and
painstaking efforts to "create" the Monster we know and love
(Whale's claim to the design is specious)—were of inestimable
value to *Alive!*

2. Original Shooting Scripts
Riley, Philip J., ed. (Although Riley claimed only "Production
Background" credit for *Dracula*, his acknowledgment as editor
of all the *Frankenstein* titles in the series justifies extending
this liberty across the board. Gregory William Mank, author of

It's Alive!, covered background in all the Frankenstein books.) Absecon, NJ: MagicImage Film Books.

This series, lusciously bound in 8½-by-11-inch glossy paper with reproductions of the original posters on the covers, includes the original shooting scripts of classic Universal horror films presented in facsimile (typescripts with contemporary annotations in hand), copious production histories, photos taken on and off the sets, publicity material, personal memoirs by surviving principals, and/or essays by noted film scholars. They represent unique primary sources, with perspectives on the evolution from page to screen. (The differences are even more illuminating than the similarities.)

Each title is presented in chronological order of release to theaters.

Dracula. (1931) Preface by Carla Laemmle, "Uncle Carl's" niece and Carl, Jr.'s cousin. Published 1990.

Frankenstein. (1931) Foreword by Forrest J. Ackerman, legendary publisher of the seminal *Famous Monsters of Filmland* (for more on which see Film Studies). Published 1989.

The Bride of Frankenstein. (1935) Introduction by Valerie Hobson, who inherited the role of Elizabeth from Mae Clarke in the first film. (As such, she is the actual bride of the title; Elsa Lanchester, in addition to playing Mary Shelley in the prologue, is merely the romantic interest of Frankenstein's nameless Monster.) Published 1989.

The Son of Frankenstein (50th Anniversary Edition). (1939) Oddly, this golden commemorative contains no personal material or scholarly retrospective, although Mank's meticulous production history alone is worth the cover price. Published 1989.

The Ghost of Frankenstein. (1942) Introduction by Ralph Bellamy, who took time out early in an incredibly long career made up of hundreds of character parts to play the romantic lead. Published 1989.

Frankenstein Meets the Wolf Man. (1943) Foreword by Curt Siodmak, who wrote the screenplay, scripted the original *Wolf Man* (1941), and penned the deathless line "Even a man who is pure in heart . . ." Published 1990.

House of Frankenstein. (1944) Interview with Elena Verdugo, introduction by Peter Coe, both of whom appeared prominently in the film. Published 1991.

House of Dracula. (1945) Introduced by John Carradine, who played Dracula this time around, but didn't live to see his account in bookstores. Published 1993.

Abbott and Costello Meet Frankenstein. (1948) Foreword by Bud Abbott, Jr., Vickie Abbott Wheeler, Chris Costello, and Paddy Costello Humphreys. Published 1990.

3. Film Studies

Ackerman, Forrest J. *Famous Monsters of Filmland*. Philadelphia: Warren Publishing Co.

From the time most baby boomers were toddlers until his death in his nineties in 2008, "Forrie" introduced classic (and not-so-classic) horror, fantasy, and science fiction films to a new generation through his magazine. (He coined the term "sci-fi.") It was noted for its thousands of black-and-white stills, interviews with surviving performers, outrageous puns, and exquisitely rendered cover paintings of iconic monsters from Lon Chaney's Phantom of the Opera to Chucky. In private life he was an omnivorous collector of priceless fantasy memorabilia and a generous contributor to the cause of film restoration and preservation. My own affinity for lost Hollywood began with *FMOF,* and although the character of J. Arthur Greenwood was inspired by Ackerman, I want to make it clear that the *Horrorwood* mogul's venality was an invention (although I flatter myself that he'd forgive me, given his pro-monster sensibilities).

Anobile, Richard J. *James Whale's Frankenstein.* New York: Universe Books, 1974.

As mentioned by Valentino, the Film Classics Library was unique for its frame-by-frame representations of great movies from every genre in book form, giving enthusiasts the opportunity to enjoy their favorites at their leisure, which was the next best thing to screening the features themselves. The studios jealously guarded their work prints (nearly all stills were staged for publicity purposes and not blown up from actual frames, as were these images), making this an important series for the serious student of film. Inevitably, the advent of home video led to the discontinuation of the line; but the FCL is still valuable for quick reference and interpreting passages of dialogue difficult to follow on a soundtrack. Anobile (who in his author's photo looks somewhat like a 1970s porn star) makes the mistake of assuming that the "lost" segment in which the Monster throws little Maria into the pond, causing her to drown, no longer existed—it has since been restored—and appears to be the only critic who is unimpressed with Whale's directorial skills; but his dedication to the project speaks for itself. *Frankenstein* is the gem of a highly collectible set of motion-picture-related literature.

Beck, Calvin Thomas. *Heroes of the Horrors.* New York: Collier Books, 1975.

Beck (also editor of *Castle of Frankenstein,* a dourer but more scholarly alternative to *Famous Monsters of Filmland*) provides valuable capsule biographies of Karloff, the Chaneys, Lugosi, Peter Lorre, and Vincent Price, with rarely seen stills and thoughtful dissertations on the secrets of their art. The checklist of films at the back is particularly useful for quick reference.

Haining, Peter, ed. *The Dracula Scrapbook.* New York: Bramwell House, 1976.

An inveterate compiler (*The Sherlock Holmes Scrapbook,* et al), the late Haining takes this seminal figure in world culture all the way from Bram Stoker's novel through all his incarnations on stage and screen and in comic books and boxes of cereal, with asides on the vampire superstition and disturbing instances of vampirism in real modern life. Through it all lurks the cloaked silhouette of Bela Lugosi, without whom the image would not resonate nearly so much.

Hardy, Phil. *The Encyclopedia of Horror Movies.* New York: Harper & Row, 1986.

There's nothing like a compact encyclopedic reference for down-and-dirty research. The titles are arranged alphabetically, but broken down year by year, which creates the minor annoyance of having to look up a film first in the index to determine the year of its release, *then* looking it up again under that heading; but it's petty to find fault with hard work and dedication.

Hirschhorn, Clive. *The Universal Story.* New York: Crown, 1983.

Crown's folio-size books about the great studios have contributed significantly to the study of movies. This one traces the history of the company that invented Hollywood from 1913 through 1982, with a close chronological narrative and lists of directors, casts, writers, and crews on 2,641 films, with more than 1,200 photos. The passages dealing with the years when Universal dominated the horror field are illuminating and succinct, with no breathless lingering over cherished moments (there isn't space). Hirschhorn (who also wrote *The Warner Brothers Story*) set the bar high from the start.

Mallory, Michael. *Universal Studios Monsters*. New York: Universe Publishing, 2009.

This is a scrumptious (and pricey) volume, paved with glossy black-and-white photos, full-color reproductions of vintage posters, and handy snapshot biographies not only of stars and directors, but of great, often overlooked character actors (Dwight Frye) and technicians (makeup genius Jack Pierce) as well. Lesser entries (*The Mole People, Captive Wild Woman,* the Creature franchise) are not ignored, providing an in-depth examination of the full texture of the genre the studio practically invented. A gorgeous display item for the living room, this, but it's destined also to be a staple.

Mank, Gregory William. *It's Alive! The Classic Cinema Saga of Frankenstein*. La Jolla, CA: Barnes & Co., 1981.

Mank established himself as the go-to guy for the Magic-Image Original Script series and the commentary track on Universal DVDs with this modest-looking coffee-table book. As much as *Famous Monsters of Filmland*, this affectionate look at the Monster's passage from Whale's first direction through *Abbott and Costello Meet Frankenstein* brought new recognition to the great collaborative effort, but also respect, even to the final entry; which considering the depths to which Bud and Lou's reputation had fallen by the 1980s (the '70s were all about the Marx Brothers), was no small accomplishment. The material in the appendix tracing the fates of series personnel benefits both the historian and the novelist with historical pretensions.

Skal, David J. *Hollywood Gothic: The Tangled Web of* Dracula *from Novel to Stage to Screen.* New York: W.W. Norton & Co., 1980.

This became a classic almost instantly, oxymoronic as the phrase sounds. Like Haining's *The Dracula Scrapbook,* it traces the development of the character from novel to stage to screen, but unlike the other it eschews the lore of the vampire itself in order to focus on the Count, with emphasis on the Lugosi interpretation. Other highlights appear, including F.W. Murnau's silent *Nosferatu* (1922) and Werner Herzog's German-language 1979 reinvention of the same title, Christopher Lee's many appearances in the role, and such related material as the cult favorite 1970s Gothic soap opera *Dark Shadows,* but only in comparison to Lugosi's watershed performance. A thorough study of the Broadway production that brought the star to the attention of Hollywood and his later tours with the play is the book's most significant addition to the growing literature on the subject. Absent Tod Browning's plodding direction, the reader is left with the conviction that the film would not have aged as badly as it has had Lugosi been given free rein, unrestricted by industry self-censorship. (See comparisons between the English- and Spanish-language versions of the 1931 film, shot almost simultaneously on the same sets, in the Filmography.)

4. Film Landmarks
Endres, Stacey, and Robert Cushman. *Hollywood at Your Feet: The Story of the World-Famous Chinese Theatre.* Universal City, CA: Pomegranate Press, 1992.

Grauman's Chinese Theater—which apparently has reverted to its original name following a generation under egocentric new management as Mann's—doesn't appear in *Alive!*, but The Oracle is a much scaled-down version of the lavishly ludicrous (but no less fabulous for that) motion picture palace that has hosted every great Tinseltown premiere from 1922 to the present day. No excess was spared in the construction of this delirious Xanadu, which is both temptation and torture to one of Valentino's romantic temperament and limited means. What other attraction in the world offers a diversion to compare with the opportunity of standing in Mary Pickford's footprints in the courtyard at Grauman's? Numerous pictures and anecdotes enliven this page-turner, with an effervescent foreword by Ginger Rogers.

Fodor, Eugene, Stephen Birnbaum, and Robert Fisher, eds. *Fodor's Far West.* New York: David McKay Co., 1974.

The Fodor books are the modern American equivalent of the Baedecker's of Victorian Europe. I consult this (admittedly out-of-date; but obsolescence is the Valentinos central theme) guide frequently, for ideas and addresses, which I depend on my computer-literate wife to update via the Internet. This time it gave me the Hollywood Wax Museum. Its official website confirms it's still at the same stand, doing pretty much what it's done from the beginning: showcasing a Hollywood that never really existed outside a soundstage. Its quirky homepage includes visitors' gripes about the (nominal) cost of admission. You have to believe an advertisement that doesn't blanch at consumer criticism.

Margolies, John, and Emily Gwathmey. *Ticket to Paradise: American Movie Theaters and How We Had Fun.* Boston: Little, Brown, 1991.

Despite the "aw, shucks" subtitle, this handsome coffee-table item offers a breezy but informative history of the American picture palace and many full-color photos of movie venues from across the continent in their heyday, after restoration, and in sad decline. There's a whole section on drive-ins—unique to Western culture—and the occasional visit behind the scenes, including to projection booths and inside orchestra pits. David Naylor's *Great American Movie Theaters* (see Historical under the Bibliography section in *Frames's* Closing Credits) is a handy pocket guide to take along on a field trip to the actual sites, but this is a book to curl up with on the sofa and dream.

FILMOGRAPHY

1. The Classics
Abbott and Costello Meet Frankenstein. Directed by Erle C. Kenton, starring Bud Abbott, Lou Costello, Lon Chaney, Jr., Bela Lugosi, Lenore Aubert, June Randolph, Glenn Strange, and the voice of Vincent Price. Universal, 1948.

It was an audacious gamble to link a pair of has-been funnymen with three major horror icons, themselves in decline, but it paid off, leading to a string of thriller-related sequels (*A&C Meet the Mummy, A&C Meet Dr. Jekyll and Mr. Hyde*; plug in your favorite fiend next), catapulting the vaudeville team back to the top of the box office and jump-starting the careers of Lugosi and Chaney. There was no horror-comedy genre before this. It's staggering to think that this was only the second time Lugosi played Count Dracula on the screen and that he never again assumed the role before a movie camera. Erle C. Kenton gained the distinction of being the only director to helm three Frankenstein films. It's still funny, and having the ghouls play it straight works, too. Special effects gain their foothold on the form when Dracula transforms into a bat in animation (an elaboration on earlier experiments in the Carradine Draculas and a remarkable scene with Carol Borland opposite Lugosi in *Mark of the Vampire,* a 1935 remake of Lon Chaney, Sr.'s silent *London After Midnight*).

Bride of Frankenstein. Directed by James Whale, starring Boris Karloff, Colin Clive, Valerie Hobson, Ernest Thesiger, Elsa Lanchester, and Una O'Connor. Universal, 1935.

Notice the top billing; he was identified by only a question mark in the opening credits the first time around. Four years of acclaim for his performance in the first feature placed his name prominently above the title, simply as "Karloff"; an imperial designation formerly granted only to Garbo, and now shared by music-video superstars Bon Jovi and Cher. (He could only top this honor by being named *in* the main title, which happened in 1949's *Abbott and Costello Meet the Killer, Boris Karloff,* in a textbook example of beating a successful franchise to death.) Whale outdid his earlier triumph in this, one of a handful of sequels to surpass their predecessors. Franz Waxman's haunting, multifaceted score (*Frankenstein* had none) unforgettably punctuates every scene. (Rodgers and Hammerstein would baldly plagiarize the Bride's theme when they wrote "Bali H'ai" for the Broadway musical *South Pacific.*) Whale's bold use of comedy never undermines the thrills, as it might have in lesser hands (although one can do without Una O'Connor's trademark dithering, which nearly sank 1932's Whale-directed *The Invisible Man*), and there never was a mad scientist more convincing than Clive, abetted by Thesiger's Joker-like Dr. Pretorius. Karloff's concerns about giving the Monster the power of speech were unfounded, as his monosyllabic, Tonto-esque gutturals call attention to his loneliness and actually increase audience sympathy. Lanchester lends idiosyncratic bits of business to the nonspeaking She-Monster, and also to Mary Shelley in a prologue that slyly negates everything to follow as a figment of her imagination. *Bride* is one of the most entertaining and experimental films of all time.

Dracula. Directed by Tod Browning, starring Bela Lugosi, David Manners, Helen Chandler, Dwight Frye, and Edward Van Sloan. Universal, 1931.

It drops off abruptly when the locale shifts from Transylvania to London, but that's Browning's fault. He owes his laurels to *Freaks* (1932), but that film depends entirely upon its shock value, still potent eighty years after it was banned in Great Britain. For comparison, check out George Medford's Spanish-language *Dracula,* photographed on the same sets at night (appropriately) after the English-language version wrapped for the day, and see what a gifted artist could do with identical material, albeit with the less diverting Carlos Villar in the title role. Most of the action is stagebound, kept alive by Van Sloan and Frye—who would team up again a few months later in *Frankenstein*—but the latter's Renfield is mesmerizing, unlike just about every other Renfield cast in a part that seems tailor-made for a ham. (A kindly nod to Arte Johnson, who lampooned Frye's lunatic insectivore so effectively opposite George Hamilton's urbane Count in 1979's *Love at First Bite,* especially his creepy laugh.) Lugosi, of course, galvanizes every scene he enters. Unfortunately, Stoker's story calls for the central villain to remain offstage most of the time. There is no other Dracula for many, just as Johnny Weissmuller will always epitomize Tarzan despite the occasional presence of better actors in the loincloth. Bela had the chops. He proved it in *Son of*

Frankenstein and *Ghost of Frankenstein*; but he inhabited the cape (and it inhabited him) more than anyone else before or since. Yes, he was buried in it, at his own request. It's doubtful anyone else will dare claim that privilege.

Frankenstein. Directed by James Whale, starring Colin Clive, Mae Clarke, Edward Van Sloan, John Boles, Dwight Frye, and Boris Karloff. Universal, 1931.

Boles is a stiff, but the poor schnook's role was made meaningless by a decision in post-production to have Clive's Henry Frankenstein survive, depriving best-friend Victor (a mistake in Robert Florey's first draft of the script transposed the Christian names of Mary Shelley's characters) of the opportunity to step in and sweep Clarke off her feet. Most of the rest of the cast compensates. Clive's gaunt, frenzied heretic, Van Sloan's plummy-voiced skeptic, and Frye's hunchbacked helper, which created an archetype as enduring as Karloff's monster (no one but a skilled talent would have thought to ad-lib stooping to pull up his raveled sock in mid-scuttle down a Gothic staircase), provide powerful balance to Clarke's stoic heroine, surely the most patient bride-to-be in history. (She would attain legendary status that same year by taking half a grapefruit in the kisser from James Cagney in *The Public Enemy*.) Karloff's the jewel in the crown. Generations of audiences have identified with his tragic brute, so beautifully drawn despite the painful hindrances of makeup and costume. No one suffered more physical hardship under Whale's inexplicably vindictive direction, and his name, when it finally appeared on the end title, came dead last. He wasn't invited to the premiere.

Frankenstein Meets the Wolf Man. Directed by Roy William Neill, starring Lon Chaney, Jr., Patrick Knowles, Bela Lugosi,

Maria Ouspenskaya, Lionel Atwill, Dennis Hoey, and Dwight Frye. Universal, 1943.

It must have galled Lugosi to don the headpiece Jack Pierce created for Karloff a dozen years after he haughtily turned down the part of the Monster in *Frankenstein,* and to accept third billing behind Patrick Knowles, easily the blandest scientist to succumb to the temptation of reanimating the dead. Because Ygor's brain had been placed in the Monster's skull at the end of *Ghost of Frankenstein* (see below), rendering him blind because of incompatible blood types, it was only natural that his voice should again be heard coming from the brute, and that he play the role as sightless, groping about with arms extended. But his speaking scenes were cut after a disastrous sneak preview, and because they explained his affliction, audiences were perplexed by his stumbling. Chaney added a tragic nuance to the haunted lycanthrope he created in 1941's *The Wolf Man,* with Ouspenskaya repeating her performance in *The Wolf Man* as the old gypsy woman, Maleva. Neill, who also directed the Basil Rathbone Sherlock Holmes series at Universal, brought along Dennis Hoey to represent Scotland Yard yet again, only this time not as Inspector Lestrade. The atmospheric gypsy-violin score from *Ghost of Frankenstein* was recycled for this first no-holds-barred monster a monster smackdown. It's a pale carbon of the first three in the series, but there's nary a dull moment.

Ghost of Frankenstein. Directed by Erle C. Kenton, starring Cedric Hardwicke, Lon Chaney, Jr., Ralph Bellamy, Bela Lugosi, Evelyn Ankers, Lionel Atwill, and Dwight Frye. Universal, 1942.

Chaney comes off as more drunken circus strongman than walking corpse, which may explain why the villagers don't seem nearly as frightened as they should to find him in their midst. If Frankenstein's son (Hardwicke) suffers from his father's derangement, he must be in his depressive phase; he never bothers even to gum the scenery. It's left to Lugosi to deliver the goods in his second run at Ygor, and he does. He owns every scene he enters, and even when it's just his voice coming from Chaney's mouth he manages to steal everything but the lightning rods.

House of Dracula. Directed by Erle C. Kenton, starring Onslow Stevens, Lon Chaney, Jr., John Carradine, Martha O'Driscoll, Jane Adams, Lionel Atwill, and Glenn Strange. Universal, 1945.

House of Frankenstein. Directed by Erle C. Kenton, starring Boris Karloff, J. Carroll Naish, Lon Chaney, Jr., John Carradine, Elena Verdugo, Anne Gwynne, Lionel Atwill, Peter Coe, George Zucco, and Glenn Strange. Universal, 1944.

It's easy to lump these two together because they're the same film, although it's refreshing to see Karloff back, even if it's only as another mad scientist and not the Monster, who fell to Glenn Strange, a former professional wrestler who would go on to glory in TV westerns as Butch Cavendish, the desperado inadvertently responsible for creating the Lone Ranger, and a permanent gig as Sam, the bartender in *Gunsmoke*. Carradine is a wonderfully effective Dracula, who in *H of D* seeks a cure for his vampirism; the screen would not see so regretful a bloodsucker until Francis Ford Coppola's execrable *Bram Stoker's Dracula* in 1992. Both films represent a sort of *Grand Hotel* compilation of box-office champions gathered in one place. Strange, who like Karloff played the Monster three times, claimed to have received pointers from the master about how to handle the part on the set of *H of F*, but he seems to have patterned himself after Lugosi's rickety fiend in *Frankenstein Meets the Wolf Man* instead. But he looks formidable.

Son of Frankenstein. Directed by Rowland V. Lee, starring Basil Rathbone, Bela Lugosi, Lionel Atwill, Josephine Hutchinson, and Donnie Dunagan. Universal, 1939.

Karloff's last time in the getup—which this time includes a fleece vest, presumably supplied by goatherd Lugosi—found him unconscious on the operating table for most of the picture, which persuaded him to bow out before the Monster became absolutely comatose, as he nearly did in the five productions to follow. Rathbone, as Frankenstein's firstborn son, is manic enough for both Clive and little brother Hardwicke (neither of whom appear in this one), especially when playing darts and exchanging verbal barbs with police prefect Atwill and his wooden arm. Toddler Dunagan's adorable, which is his purpose, no doubt gleefully anticipating a fat part in *Grandson of Frankenstein*. Atwill and Rathbone would have run away with the whole thing if Ygor weren't on hand, in a characterization that might have netted Lugosi an Oscar had the Academy taken horror pictures seriously. (Admittedly, the competition was fierce this year, which included *Stagecoach, The Wizard of Oz,* and *Gone with the Wind*.)

2. Tributes
Ed Wood. Directed by Tim Burton, starring Johnny Depp, Martin Landau, Sarah Jessica Parker, Patricia Arquette, Jeffrey Jones, and Bill Murray. Touchstone, 1994.

Runaway entertainment, hilarious and moving by turns, and arguably the best movie about heartless Hollywood after *Sunset Boulevard* (1950). Depp is a giddy force of nature in this biopic as Edward D. Wood, who contrary to popular opinion wasn't the worst director of all time (I nominate Robert Altman, with *Nashville* his *Plan 9 from Outer Space*), but was certainly the most clueless. Martin Landau plays Bela Lugosi in his pathetic extremity, Depp the desperate Orson Welles wannabe who befriends the faded star and makes him the focus of his celluloid atrocities. Murray was never better, Jones surpasses his Austrian emperor in *Amadeus,* and the re-enactments of Wood's canon of schlock are sublimely cheesy. Landau earned an Oscar for his unflinching portrayal; another went to makeup artist Rick Baker for matching him so well to the original that authentic close-up footage of Lugosi in *White Zombie* (1932) is shown undoctored. This gem has done more to resurrect a forgotten icon's reputation than any dozen comebacks.

Gods and Monsters. Directed by Bill Condon, starring Ian McKellen, Brendan Fraser, Lynn Redgrave, Lolita Davidovich, David Dukes, and Kevin J. O'Connor. Lions Gate, 1998.

Condon won an Oscar for adapting Christopher Bram's novel *Father of Frankenstein,* but McKellen and Fraser proved up to the challenge as the haunted James Whale and his naïve confidant; the late Dukes is extremely effective in a critically undervalued performance as Whale's former lover. Elsa Lanchester, Boris Karloff, Colin Clive, and Ernest Thesiger (Clive and Thesiger in flashback) are perfect physical matches in casting, and Redgrave received honors for playing against type as Whale's put-upon Greek chorus of a housekeeper. The usually reliable Leonard Maltin reviewed the movie as "Exceptional (if entirely fictional)," but evidently he was unfamiliar with James Curtis' Whale biography, which appeared about the same time as the film.

(Tip: Next time you host a Halloween party, consider screening *Ed Wood* and *Gods and Monsters* back-to-back with E.

Elias Merhige's *Shadow of the Vampire* (2000), a supernatural take on the filming of F. W. Murnau's 1922 silent *Nosferatu*, with John Malkovich as the brilliant European director and an unrecognizable Willem Dafoe as the sinister Max Schreck.)

Young Frankenstein. Directed by Mel Brooks, starring Gene Wilder, Peter Boyle, Marty Feldman, Teri Garr, Madeline Kahn, Cloris Leachman, and Kenneth Mars. 20th Century Fox, 1974.

Wilder, it's said, sat nearly on Brooks's head to curb his reckless genius and preserve the integrity of Wilder's script. If so, he's to be commended for this spot-on affectionate satire of the first three *Frankensteins* (with a dash of *King Kong* during the theater scene; and don't forget to watch for *Ghost of Frankenstein*'s Ralph Bellamy in the audience). Everyone is wonderful, and it's with great difficulty that one picks out a particular highlight, but that would have to be Brooks and Wilder's hysterical take on the scene in the blind hermit's (Gene Hackman's) hut from *Bride*. Is it just me, or do I hear phantom chuckling from Karloff, Lugosi, Dwight Frye, and company every time I screen it?

(Tip: This one is best enjoyed after watching *Frankenstein*, *Bride of Frankenstein*, and *Son of Frankenstein* in close succession.)

AUTHOR'S NOTES

1. Fun-Ereal Fact

Two films in this sub-genre drew their titles from lines spoken in the first: both *Young Frankenstein* and *House of Frankenstein* from Baron Frankenstein's (Frederick Kerr's) toast in the final scene. Hammer Films's *Curse of Frankenstein* (1957) was inspired by a villager's cry in *Ghost of Frankenstein*.

2. Steams Like Old Times

Steampunk is one of the lighter-hearted youth movements of recent years. Part rebellion against Cyber Age technology, part dress-up, it celebrates the visual contrast of massive moving metal parts glistening with oil with the proper dress, genteel manners, and strict mores of Victorian society. It's a relatively new phenomenon, so there is little to be found upon the subject between covers. Ironically, one must turn to its *bete noir,* the Internet, for further information. (But then, hasn't mankind managed to create its own Frankenstein's Monster in the form of the microchip?)

3. Frankenstein Meets Dracula

Bela Lugosi's test as the Monster in *Frankenstein* is no novelist's invention. It was shot under Robert Florey's direction in June 1931, and was by all accounts terrible, drawing derisive laughter from Carl Laemmle, Jr., when Lugosi's close-up was screened. Although rumored to have been destroyed, it resurfaced (perhaps) thirty years ago in a trade-paper advertisement in Los Angeles, only to vanish once again. In view of the fact that the only poster known to exist promoting Lugosi as the star sold at auction recently for six figures, it's anyone's guess what those two reels would bring.

ABOUT THE AUTHOR

Loren D. Estleman has written more than sixty novels. He has netted four Shamus Awards for detective fiction, five Spur Awards for Western Fiction, and three Western Heritage Awards. The Western Writers of America recently conferred upon Estleman the Owen Wister Award for Lifetime Contribution to Western Literature. *Alive!* is the third Valentino film detective mystery. He lives with his wife, author Deborah Morgan, in Michigan.

Learn more at www.lorenestleman.com.

A brilliant, incisive biographical novel about the iconic American mobster

THE CONFESSIONS OF AL CAPONE

A NOVEL

LOREN D. ESTLEMAN

MULTIPLE AWARD WINNER LOREN D. ESTLEMAN has produced a major biographical novel on Scarface, rigorously researched and deftly nuanced to offer an intimate portrait of the man whose terrible crimes and larger-than-life persona have both fascinated and appalled the world for nearly a century, whose legacy is still widely debated, and whose brutally ambitious career continues to inspire filmmakers and writers to plumb its excesses and its contradictions.

With subtly nuanced portrayals of those in Capone's circle—his underrated wife, Mae Capone; members of the Chicago Outfit, including the deadly Frank Nitti—as well as his nemesis, J. Edgar Hoover; Hoover's secretary, Helen Gandy; and others, *The Confessions of Al Capone* is a major literary achievement.

"REMARKABLE RESEARCH, RICH STORYTELLING, AND A RAPID, RIVETING PACE...HITS WITH THE FORCE OF A BURST FROM A TOMMY GUN."

—RALPH PETERS, *New York Times* bestselling author of *Cain at Gettysburg*

tor-forge.com